PAUL BUCHANAN

VALLEY OF SHADOWS

Legend Press Ltd, 51 Gower Street, London, WC1E 6HJ
info@legendpress.co.uk | www.legendpress.co.uk

Contents © Paul Buchanan 2021
The right of the above author to be identified as the author of this work has
been asserted in accordance with the Copyright, Designs and Patents Act
1988. British Library Cataloguing in Publication Data available.

Print ISBN 978-1-80031-9-394
Ebook ISBN 978-1-80031-9-400
Set in Times. Printing managed by Jellyfish Solutions Ltd
Cover design by Simon Levy | www.simonlevyassociates.co.uk

Paul Buchanan earned a Master of Professional Writing degree from the University of Southern California and an MFA in Fiction Writing from Chapman University. He teaches and writes in the Los Angeles area. The first PI Jim Keegan novel *City of Fallen Angels* was published by Legend Press in 2020.

For Heidi Lup and Lyle Wiedeman,
fellow members of the Order

CHAPTER ONE

KEEGAN PULLED OFF Wilshire into the north parking garage of the Ambassador Hotel. It was a Thursday night, coming on eight o'clock, so there were only a couple of cars in front of him waiting for a valet. That was a good sign, in his opinion; the Cocoanut Grove wouldn't be too crowded. The place had never appealed to Keegan. It was too kitschy—all those fake palms and the gaudy red bunting and the hopeful tourists craning their necks to see who was coming in through the door. It was old Hollywood at its seediest: overwrought, caked with makeup, and ready for its close-up.

But he couldn't avoid tonight's gathering, much as he would have liked to. The party was a send-off. Old Mike Donovan was pulling up stakes and moving out to Arizona. Donovan was one of Keegan's old cronies, so here Keegan was. Sure, he was arriving at the party more than an hour late, but that was his prerogative.

When he got to the front of the line of cars, he put his MG in neutral, pulled up the parking brake, and left it running. He grabbed his herringbone blazer from the passenger seat as the young valet jogged over. Keegan got out of the car, straightened up, and pulled on the jacket. The valet tore off the ticket stub and handed it to Keegan, then he tucked the other half under the windshield wiper.

Keegan slipped the stub into the inside pocket of his jacket. He could hear distant orchestra music carried to him on the cool late-September air. The tune was something sultry and sleepy, a slow-dance number. The valet got in the car and put it in gear.

Keegan rapped on the window. "Hang on," he told the valet. "I forgot something." He went behind the car and popped the trunk. The new putter was angled across the spare tire and the rusty jack. It was a Wilson club; the best one he could find without having to go too far out of his way. Mrs. Dodd, Keegan's secretary, had wanted the gift to look a little more festive, so she'd insisted on tying a red ribbon around the shaft before Keegan left the office that night.

Mrs. Dodd had seemed a little too happy to hear that Keegan was finally spending a night out. She was of the opinion that Keegan would be in a better mood if he had more of a social life. In her unsolicited opinion, it wasn't natural for a man Keegan's age—fifty-four—to stay holed up in his hilltop bungalow every night of the week. It was too remote, too lonely. He needed to get out more, make a few new pals, maybe find himself a girlfriend. Her enthusiasm when he'd told her he was going to Donovan's send-off party had made him wish he'd never told her.

Mrs. Dodd's bow was a little squashed down on one side now—but Donovan wasn't the type for frills. The gift would do nicely. He grabbed the club, slammed the trunk, and headed towards the hotel carrying the putter tucked under one arm.

There had been a time—about a decade ago—when Keegan would have called Donovan a *friend*. Maybe even a *good* friend. For years, Keegan had covered the crime beat for the *Los Angeles Times*. But—long story short—he got fired and had to come up with a new career. He applied for his PI license. A month or so after that, Donovan's pension maxed out at the LAPD, and he retired as vice detective.

The two of them had been little more than acquaintances up until then—the cop and the crime reporter. Donovan, a middling detective at best, had never rated much column space, and Keegan had rarely written about him. But in those uncertain months of fresh unemployment, neither man quite knew what to do with himself. They'd spent a lot of time together: afternoons at the Santa Anita Park racetrack, a couple of fishing trips to Arrowhead, too many nights sipping bourbon at the downtown dives on West Fifth Street. But then things had begun to fall into place. Both of them got their PI licenses. They were working men again, and everything changed.

In those early days, they'd talked about maybe going into business together: D & K Investigations—or K & D—they never got far enough to even agree on a name. The idea of a partnership was chimerical at best. Both men knew, deep down, that whatever camaraderie let them sit on adjacent stools at the Frolic Room bar wasn't nearly enough to make them compatible as business partners. Then there was Donovan's work ethic. At the LAPD, his efforts had always been second-rate, sloppy, full of excuses. He'd never risen through the ranks so far as Narcotics, let alone Robbery-Homicide. No detective worth their salt should still be working vice by the time they retired.

The truth was, Donovan wasn't terribly bright. The only thing that had kept him from getting fired was his good-old-boy demeanor. He was a glad-hander, always ready to pay for a round and to laugh at a joke, no matter how many times he'd heard it before. The man was quick with a slap on the back, but he was painfully slow on the uptake. Everyone around him had covered for him, picked up his slack. A partnership with Keegan would never have worked. Donovan couldn't have been trusted to carry his share of the weight. It wasn't long before they had a falling out anyway—something about a spousal abuse case that came Donovan's way; Keegan couldn't quite remember the details anymore, just the nagging sense that Donovan valued a paycheck over any other moral consideration. At any rate, the two of them had drifted apart.

Keegan had set up his office downtown on Sixth Street, among all the bus routes and foot traffic. Donovan had landed over in Santa Monica, where his well-heeled beachside clientele from the Palisades drove Silver Clouds and Coupe de Villes—*if* they couldn't afford a chauffeur to drive the cars for them. Keegan eked out a living with divorce and insurance fraud and the occasional skip-trace. Donovan got fat doing corporate background checks and finding out whether the banker's daughter's new beau was a gold digger.

KEEGAN WAS ON the concrete walkway to the Cocoanut Grove's entrance now, and the orchestra music inside had shifted to something more upbeat. There was a welcome nip in the evening air, now that summer's bleary heat had loosened its grip. Keegan checked his watch. It was a little after eight, so the party had been going more than an hour now without him. With any luck, he could put in an appearance, bestow his gift on old Donovan, and slip back out when the opportunity arose. When he looked up from his watch, he saw Louis Moore striding out through the Grove's brightly lit archway, headed in his direction. Keegan glanced around, half wishing for somewhere to hide.

Lieutenant Moore. Of course he'd have been invited to Donovan's send-off. He was still the LAPD's golden boy, after all—the black pioneer cop Keegan had so often championed in *The Times* as he rose through the ranks. Moore was as close to a local celebrity as a working cop could hope to get—and tonight he was the last man Keegan wanted to see.

"Jimmy?" Moore called out, grinning. "Is that you?" He picked up his pace.

It was just Keegan's luck. If he'd arrived a few minutes later, the two of them wouldn't have crossed paths. Keegan slowed his stride. He took the golf club out from under his arm and gripped it with one hand. "Lou," he said coolly. He'd managed to avoid the Lieutenant for almost a year now. He would have happily stretched the interlude another decade.

Moore stopped walking when Keegan got close to him, blocking the walkway, so Keegan had to stop too. The two men stood facing one another. Jaunty orchestra music lent the moment an incongruously upbeat soundtrack. The Lieutenant was still tall and lean, but he'd put on a little weight in the months since Keegan had last seen him. His hair was going a little gray at the edges now too. The effects of middle age were finally starting to show.

"Where have you been hiding yourself?" the Lieutenant said, holding out his hand for Keegan to shake. He seemed genuinely glad they'd chanced upon one another, which made Keegan feel at an even greater disadvantage.

"Here and there," Keegan told him. He gave the other man's hand a shake, as quick and perfunctory as he could make it. "But I guess I didn't hide well enough." With his left hand, he swung the golf club up, so he could hold it in front of him with both hands, a kind of barrier between them.

The Lieutenant looked Keegan over. "You're looking well," he said.

"You're looking well fed," Keegan told him.

The Lieutenant grinned amiably and gave his belly a rub. "The wife's way ahead of you," he said. "Got me on a diet. Cottage cheese and canned peaches. It's enough to make a man weep."

Keegan didn't respond. The orchestra inside played on.

The Lieutenant nodded, dug his hands into the pockets of his dress slacks, and jingled some coins there. "Look, Jim," he said, "I know we never got to talk about what happened."

Moore was still looking Keegan in the eye, and Keegan fought the impulse to look away, to brush past the man and be on his way.

"That was one big, unholy mess," Moore said. "But I was

just trying to look out for you. You know that, don't you?" Moore looked past Keegan and then looked him in the eye again. "I feel bad about how it all played out."

It had only been a year, yet the man made it sound like some bygone minor mishap—a chipped tooth, a dented bumper—something ancient and trivial that could be swept under the rug and forgotten. But Keegan couldn't forget. A young woman—her name was Eve—had died because of the two of them. That fact was a raw, guilty wound Keegan still tended.

The Lieutenant watched Keegan intently, reading what he could of him, the high-beam, interrogatory gaze of the professional detective. The man seemed to read something hard and implacable in Keegan's expression. He took a small step backwards and gave Keegan a knowing nod. "The boys are in the back corner," he said, his voice now devoid of emotion. "You can't miss them." He looked down at the golf club Keegan was still holding between them in two fists. "Donovan's going to love the putter."

Keegan nodded. He tried to slip past, but the Lieutenant caught him by the elbow, a grip that felt good-natured but insistent. It was a gesture only a certain kind of man could get away with, someone who knew the scope of his own considerable powers and exactly what they entitled him to. Keegan froze, looking straight ahead and not at the Lieutenant. The Grove's grand entrance stood just a few yards away—the dangling palm fronds, the wide scalloped archway, the gaudy lighting. So close, so far.

"Look, Jimmy," Moore said. His voice was close to Keegan's ear. "The two of us go way back. We need to get past this." He squeezed Keegan's arm. "Give me a call when you're ready. I'll buy you a beer."

Keegan kept his gaze fixed straight ahead. "Sure thing," he said. He made no effort to make the words sound sincere. The Lieutenant let go of his arm, and Keegan strode numbly to the grand entryway and through the door, into all that gaudy light and sound.

DONOVAN'S GROUP WAS just where Moore said they'd be, in the nightclub's farthest corner to the left of the dance floor. The orchestra started up 'Sleepy Lagoon' now, and a few dozen couples, all overdressed for a Thursday night out, headed out on the dance floor. Keegan threaded his way among the close-set tables, through the haze of cigarette smoke. He had to be wary of the silver putter he carried, making sure not to hit anyone's shin. Keegan edged past ringing laughter and bright conversation and the clinking of glassware. He felt awkward and out of place, a funeral director at a wedding.

Donovan's group had pushed together three round tables into an awkward clump to hold all their dirty glasses. There were seven or eight men in all—florid, stubbled faces puffed up by middle age. These were the older cops who'd been on the job when Donovan had aged out of the LAPD. Other than Donovan, Keegan didn't know a single one of them. A couple of the silver-haired ones—near retirement themselves, no doubt—were already sloppy drunk when Keegan borrowed an empty chair from a nearby table and pulled it up to join them.

He leaned the putter against the table's edge where it would be out of the way. He'd wait until the orchestra took a break and make some kind of formal presentation. The other men leaned in close to talk now and again, but it was impossible to hear what anyone was saying over the music. That was fine with Keegan; he was here to make an appearance, clink a glass or two, and wait for the first opportunity to leave.

When Donovan had called Keegan at the office last week to invite him to the party, he'd said he was headed out to some Phoenix suburb. Tempe or Mesa, Keegan couldn't now remember. Keegan had been to Arizona a couple of times on business, and the desert air had seemed so scorched and

13

oxygen-deprived it was barely worth the effort of breathing. Why Donovan would want to leave LA and move there was beyond Keegan's ability to fathom. It couldn't be money. Given Donovan's well-to-do clientele, he had to have quite a bankroll to fall back on.

Keegan caught a passing waitress's eye and waved her over. He asked for a double Jameson with ice. He could nurse that one drink for the next hour or so and be back home before ten. In the morning, at the office, he'd lie to Mrs. Dodd. He'd tell her he'd had a great time and that it was good to get out of the house. Maybe it would get her off his case for a while. Mrs. Dodd was worried about how much time he spent alone, and Keegan didn't like that kind of attention.

Donovan was sitting directly across from Keegan, in a green plaid sports coat with no tie. He seemed to be having a great time, laughing and elbowing the other guys. Donovan, too, had put on a few pounds since Keegan last saw him, and he'd lost a bit more hair. His belly strained at the buttons on his shirt front, and he'd added an ample second chin that made his face look round and cartoonish. His cheeks were flushed with good cheer and whiskey, and he kept ducking this way and that, listening to the others as they spoke into his ear. Old Donovan had always loved a party. He leaned over and made some sly comment to one of the other men when the young waitress brought Keegan his drink. The two of them made no effort to hide the fact that they were eyeing her as she walked away.

Two orchestra numbers later, the bandleader announced a ten-minute break, and the sudden silence that followed unveiled the sound of voices and footfalls and the clatter going on back in the kitchen. This was Keegan's chance. He'd have a few words with Donovan, hand over the gift, slap him on the back, and slip away when the orchestra came back out.

"Jimmy!" Donovan said, a little too loudly now that it was quiet. "I didn't think you'd actually come."

Keegan nodded and wondered if Mrs. Dodd had had a

word with Donovan before she'd put the call through. "Just wanted to make damn sure you were really leaving town," Keegan said. "It'll be a big relief for everyone concerned to get you across state lines." Jokes and insults. That had always been the custom among the cops Keegan knew: affection masked as animosity. Or perhaps it was the other way around.

Donovan let loose with one of his booming trademark laughs, but it devolved into a short fit of coughing, fist to mouth. "Jimmy, Jimmy, Jimmy," he said when he'd caught his breath again. "What am I going to do without you?" His red face was glossy under the overhead lamps. "You missed the L-T, by the way," he said. "He left just before you got here. He was asking about you."

Keegan felt his elbow tingle where the Lieutenant had gripped him. "Well, that's a damn shame," he said. He picked up the putter. Gripping it by the head, he held it out to Donovan across the table. "There's no ocean where you're going," he said, "so a sailboat was out of the question."

Donovan grinned and took the club by the leather grip. "I just put a down payment on a place that's down the street from a golf course!" he said. He stood, with a little effort, stepped back from the table, and made a big show of lining up a putt. Then he set the club down so it was angled across the table amid all the empty glasses and patted the front pocket of his sports coat. He nodded over at the big open double door at the far side of the room. "Let's you and I have a word in private, Jimmy," he said.

A private word with Donovan was the last thing Keegan wanted, but he stood gamely and tugged down the sleeves of his jacket.

"Bring your drink," Donovan told him. He headed toward the side doors, carrying his own half-filled glass.

Keegan picked up his whiskey and followed Donovan across the room, past all the other tables and out the doors. Donovan led him through the big patio and around to the main pool. It was a mild night, but there was enough of a nip in the late-September air that no one was swimming. A few couples sat at the tables back under the palms, making the most of the shadows.

The deck chairs that lined either side of the big pool were all abandoned, and that's where Donovan headed. He chose a quiet stretch between two potted palms and set his drink on a small circular table. With a groan, he settled down into one of the deck chairs and stretched out, full length. "Sit down," he told Keegan, nodding at the adjacent deck chair. "Make yourself at home."

Keegan set his whiskey on the table next to Donovan's glass and sat down in the empty chair. He was relieved to find it was dry—though the cushions did smell faintly of chlorine and cocoa butter.

Donovan smiled and pulled a couple of cigars from inside his jacket. "Been saving these beauties," he said. "Top-shelf Cubans. No longer technically legal, perhaps, but who's going to complain? Got 'em from a client."

Keegan took the cigar he was offered. He slipped off the label and waited his turn with Donovan's punch and Zippo lighter.

Before Keegan lit his cigar, Donovan rolled his own cigar between his fingers and sniffed at the wrapper, like the connoisseur he wasn't. "Fresh from Havana," he said. He used the punch on one end and then handed the tool across to Keegan. "*El Jefe's* own brand." He lit the cigar, coughed a little, and passed the Zippo over.

The worn lighter had an LAPD shield engraved on one side. It was no doubt a gift back when he'd retired from the force. Keegan hadn't been invited to that party. He sparked the flame and puffed until his own cigar was lit. He closed the Zippo and set it on the table between the two chairs, next to their whiskey glasses.

Donovan settled back in his chair and took a long, slow draw on his cigar. He looked up at the few stars that dotted the LA sky. "You and me, Jimmy," he told Keegan wistfully, "we're a dying breed."

Keegan could have pointed out that, breed-wise, they were of vastly different pedigrees; Keegan had never been a cop, just a crime reporter. As for dying, Keegan was nearly fifteen years younger than Donovan. Still, this was a good cigar, now that Keegan was tasting it, and this was old Donovan's send-off, so he'd let the man talk if he wanted to.

"I appreciate the putter," Donovan went on. "But I won't be making it out to the golf course. I'm under strict orders to stay off my feet as much as I can." He held his cigar out in front of him and swept it through the air, indicating the tall swaying palms, the dipping strings of lights, the mild late-summer night. "I tell you, though, buddy," he said, "I'm going to miss all this."

Keegan nodded. "I'm sure Arizona has its good points," he said, though, if pressed, he'd have trouble naming one himself.

Donovan chuckled. Again it trailed off into a rattling cough. He pressed his fist to his sternum. "Tempe may not be hell," he said, a little out of breath, "but it probably shares the same phone exchange."

Keegan smiled and let his head fall back against the deck chair's padding. He looked up at the palm fronds silhouetted against the milky night sky. "So why are you leaving LA, then?" he asked.

Donovan didn't answer right away, and Keegan looked over to find the man looking back at him, unsmiling.

Donovan turned away and regarded the glassy swimming pool philosophically. "It's the damn heart, Jimmy," he said. "It's bad. Doctor thinks the change in climate might give me another year. Two years if I'm lucky." He looked back at Keegan and shrugged. "No more drinking or smoking, either."

Keegan glanced from Donovan's glowing cigar to the glass on the table next to him and raised an eyebrow.

Donovan shrugged again. "One last hurrah," he said. He

picked up his glass and swung it over to clink against Keegan's where it sat on the table by his elbow. "After tonight, I'm leading the life of a Baptist." He leaned back in his chair and stretched out his legs, smiling up at the California sky.

Keegan had forgotten how good-natured and jovial Donovan could be. He *was* good company—just a lousy detective. Sure, they should never have been business partners, but it was a shame they hadn't spent more time together over the years. Now it was too late.

"Hey," Keegan said, affecting an upbeat voice, "it's a good plan, if you ask me. No booze, no tobacco. Who needs them? You'll live longer."

Donovan wheezed another laugh. "It'll only *feel* longer, without the whiskey and cigars," he said. He took another toke on his Cuban. He seemed to roll the smoke around on his tongue, savoring it, before he blew it out again.

The two of them sat a few moments in companionable silence, and then the orchestra started up again inside. They were playing 'Sentimental Journey', which felt apt. Some of the couples hiding in the shadows rose and went back inside to dance.

Keegan settled back in his deck chair. Out here, the music, muted as it was, was smooth and soothing. Strings of white poolside lights dipped between the palm trees and reflected on the pool's surface. The lights undulated, as if swaying in time with the distant clarinets. Keegan picked up his whiskey and took a sip.

"I always liked you, Jimmy," Donovan said, "which is why I'm giving you a parting gift."

Keegan felt a sudden wariness. He thought of the six-dollar putter he'd brought—now abandoned among all the empty glasses and cocktail napkins on the pushed-together tables inside. "A gift for me?" he said. "This is *your* party."

Donovan shook his head and held out a plump, pale hand, palm up. "Just hand over one of your business cards," he said.

Keegan dipped into his jacket pocket and passed a card

over to Donovan. The other man slipped it into his own jacket. "I'm going to pass this along to my new favorite client," he said. "You're going to love the old broad." Donovan picked up his glass and shook it. He looked down into it. It was all melting ice now. Without asking permission, he picked up Keegan's glass and tipped out a half-shot of whiskey into his own glass.

"I've kept the old girl under covers so far," he went on. "But she's a dream, Jimbo. She's old and paranoid and richer than Jesus."

"You mean 'Croesus'?"

"Huh?"

"The saying," Keegan explained. "It's 'Richer than *Croesus*.' I'm pretty sure Jesus was dirt poor."

Donovan took a sip of his stolen whiskey and eyed Keegan drolly—like this was part of their well-worn shtick. "Whatever you say, professor," he said with an eye roll. "I'm just telling you the old lady's rolling in it."

"Duly noted," Keegan said.

"And, get this, Jimmy," Donovan said. "She insists on paying cash for everything, so there won't be a paper trail. She won't even let you write her out a receipt." He grinned over at Keegan. "The IRS don't need to know a thing." He reached over and tapped an inch of ash from his cigar onto the concrete between them. "Ida Fletcher is her name, and she's all yours now, buddy." He gave his jacket a pat to let Keegan know he'd be passing along the business card. "When she calls, pick up," he said. "You won't be sorry."

KEEGAN DROVE PAST the last dark turnoff and kept climbing the incline in low gear. His watch told him it was well after ten. The smoke from Donovan's Cuban cigars still lingered in the folds of his shirt.

From this point on, the paved public road Keegan drove along might as well have been his own personal driveway. No one used this stretch of asphalt but him. His hilltop cottage was the only place it led to. Fifty yards beyond his own carport, the road dead-ended at an old wooden barricade that was studded with reflectors. END OF ROAD, the battered sign read. Lately, the words had begun to ring in Keegan's head like a symbol of something. Maybe Mrs. Dodd was right: a man his age shouldn't let himself be so isolated. It wasn't healthy.

When he pulled up through the last curve, he braked. A scrawny coyote, tail tucked low, stood in the center of the road facing away from him. It had been heading uphill too, but it looked back over its shoulder now, unruffled. Keegan's headlights reflected in its coppery eyes.

Coyotes were common in these hills. Their moon-drunk yipping at night was no more unusual than a cricket's chirp. There were bobcats up here too—even a few mountain lions. Keegan spotted one of the big cats every year or so, slinking back into the oak-dotted ravines in the first light of dawn.

Without any evident alarm, the coyote in Keegan's headlights trotted to the road's edge and disappeared into the brush. Keegan eased his foot off the clutch, his headlight sweeping across the wild sage at the road's edge. Up on the last stretch, his cottage came into view, a few dim lights hunkered down in all that velvety darkness. He was home.

As he came up the porch steps, he could hear Nora, his Welsh Terrier, scratching at the front door's baseboard. She wasn't used to him being out so late, and she'd been cooped up inside since he'd brought her home from work. He turned the key in the lock, pushed the door open, and she was up on him, jumping and whimpering, quivering with excitement to see him. He went inside and closed the door behind them. The dog darted through the dark kitchen, to the back door. Before Keegan let her out, he put some ice in a glass and poured himself a Jameson at the kitchen counter. With the coyote around, he'd have to go outside with the dog.

When he opened the door, Nora rocketed down the back

steps into the garden. She went to her usual corner between two rosemary bushes to do her business. Keegan turned on the back porchlight and took his drink over to the edge of the hillside. The bright city lights sprawled below him. They shimmered—ruby red and diamond white—all the way to the dark abyss of the Pacific.

This cottage had belonged to his family long before the mansions had arrived to fill up the hillsides below. He'd inherited the place—along with the dog—when his mother died. The land was worth a not-so-small fortune these days, but Keegan couldn't bring himself to let go of it just yet. It had been in the family too long, and, at this point, he'd rather have the view than the money.

Directly below his cottage was the old Ormsby place, a rambling lot with a big house, a pool, and a sprawling garden. It had been dark and empty for a year now, a nightly reminder of Keegan's most recent failure. A young woman, Eve Ormsby-Cutler, had briefly lived down there. She'd trusted Keegan, and she'd died because that trust was misplaced. And now her family's big house was dark and empty—a haunted borderland that lay between Keegan and the rest of the living world.

I feel bad about how it all played out, the Lieutenant had told him tonight outside the Cocoanut Grove. The words had rung pathetic and cavalier in Keegan's ears, wholly inadequate to describe the tragedy the two men had brought about. Keegan downed the rest of his whiskey in one gulp and turned his back on the view.

"Come on, girl," he said to the dog.

She sniffed the air one last time and the two of them headed back toward the welcoming porchlight and the lit windows of their little home.

LONG AFTER MIDNIGHT, Keegan was jolted from sleep. He sat up on the bed groggily. The dog was out in the living room again, barking. She'd been doing this for weeks now, every few nights: these bouts of late-night urgent yapping. For reasons Keegan couldn't pinpoint, the poor thing had grown skittish. She bristled and cowered at imagined threats that were entirely invisible to Keegan. Tonight, when he stumbled out to the living room, barefoot and only half awake, Keegan found her standing beside the coffee table, hackles raised, head bent low, growling at the big, empty easy chair. A blanket lay strewn across it. One corner dangled down over the chair's arms. The dog had probably taken that dark, amorphous shape to be an intruder.

Keegan switched on the floor lamp next to the doorway. In the sudden light, the blue blanket leapt out of the darkness to become the harmless thing it was.

"See," Keegan told the dog, "it's just an old blanket. Nothing to it."

The dog stopped growling, but she backed warily away from the chair, hackles still raised. She turned and darted back into the bedroom.

Mrs. Dodd had once informed Keegan that dogs could see ghosts. They had been leaving the office for the day, and Nora, for no earthy reason, had refused to get on the left-hand elevator. "They're more attuned to the spiritual world than we are," Mrs. Dodd had said. She spoke the words with such assurance, such offhand authority, that Keegan hadn't thought to ask why a ghost would need an elevator or which floor it might be riding to. Keegan had just waited there in the hallway until the bell chimed for the other elevator. The doors opened, the dog boarded without complaint, and the three of them rode down to the lobby in silence.

Now, in his well-lit living room, Keegan paused with his fingers on the lamp's switch. He couldn't remember bringing out the blue blanket. It hadn't been cold enough at night to need one. Still, who else could have done it? He went over and picked it up. He folded it and set it on the end of his mother's old settee and looked at the empty easy chair.

One night, not that long ago, Eve had sat in that very spot when she had visited him with a bottle of good wine, stolen from her uncle's cellar. They had laughed and flirted and gotten tipsy together, both of them happily blind to all the anguish that lay just ahead of them. She had kissed him that night, at the doorway of the big empty estate down the hill. Lieutenant Moore might be able to brush off such tragedies, but Keegan wasn't up to it.

When he got back to the bedroom, Nora was curled up at the foot of the mattress, already asleep again. Keegan lay back down on the bed and pulled the covers over himself, but his heart was beating so fast he knew he wouldn't sleep.

CHAPTER TWO

ON WEDNESDAY AFTERNOON, Keegan had the Dodgers game on the radio he kept atop the file cabinets. All told, it had been a stellar season for LA; the Dodgers had finished six games ahead of St. Louis, and now they were facing the Yankees in Game One of the World Series. When the phone in the outer office rang, it was the fifth inning, and the Dodgers had a five-run lead. Keegan wouldn't take the call. Not now. Not in the middle of a game. The old lady could leave another message. He'd call her back in the morning before Game Two.

Since Monday, Mrs. Dodd had jotted down three urgent messages from Ida Fletcher—Donovan's favorite client, the woman who was richer than Jesus. But each time a call had come in, Keegan couldn't bring himself to take it.

"SHE SOUNDS HARMLESS," Mrs. Dodd told him when she was packing up her purse to go home that afternoon. She was leaving an hour early—something about one of her grandkids and a dental appointment. "Who cares if she's a bit crazy?" she said. "All that matters is that her checks clear."

"According to Donovan, she only pays cash," Keegan said.

"That's even better," Mrs. Dodd told him. She stood up

from her desk and looked around to make sure she wasn't forgetting anything. "Have you even looked at the books this month?" she said. "You'll be going into the red just to pay me and keep the lights on." She straightened up and fixed him with one of her looks. "And you *will* be paying me," she said. She lifted her purse off the desk by its strap. "Some old lady's cash is *exactly* what we need. I don't know why you're avoiding her."

She was right, of course: they *did* need the money, and Keegan *had* been avoiding Ida Fletcher's phone calls. "I've just got a feeling the old lady will be more trouble than she's worth," he said. "I'm not very good with crazy people."

"You're not good with people, period," Mrs. Dodd told him, which stung a little, though Keegan had to admit it was fair. Mrs. Dodd took her coat from the rack by the door and pulled it on. "Besides, you need something to keep yourself busy."

"*That* again?" Keegan said.

Mrs. Dodd shook her head wearily, like Keegan was being willfully obtuse. "It's been more than a year since the girl died," she told him. Her words were blunt. She was clearly done tiptoeing around the subject. "It's time to let go and move on." She slung her purse over her shoulder and went to the door. "Get out of the house, boss." She didn't turn to look at him. "Have a drink with somebody. Go see a movie." She put her hand on the doorknob and looked down at Nora, who had trotted after her, wagging her tail.

The dog seemed to think she was going home for the day too.

"Me and a Welsh Terrier," Mrs. Dodd said. "We're your only company." She gave the dog a rueful smile, her hand still on the doorknob. "It isn't fair to us, is it?" she said to the dog, her voice all singsong. "Someone else needs to share the burden."

The worst thing about all Mrs. Dodd's nagging was that Keegan knew she was right. He was spending an unhealthy amount of time on his own. "Maybe I'll go to a baseball game," he told her, though she was out in the hall now, trying to keep the dog from following her out.

"That would be a step in the right direction," she told him. She pushed the dog back inside with her foot. "Go buy yourself a ticket," she said as she pulled the door shut.

A FEW MINUTES later, Keegan fastened the leash on Nora's collar and led her out to the sixth-floor hallway. He was still feeling good from the Dodgers win. He pushed the button to summon the elevator, and the haunted elevator, the one on the left, arrived first. The bell dinged and the doors slid open. He looked down at the dog. She sniffed at the elevator's interior—it was empty, but someone had been smoking a cigar—and then boarded it without objection. Today, the ghost had apparently taken the stairs.

Down on the street, the two of them walked along Sixth and waited at the corner for the light to change. He found an empty bench in Pershing Square near the lawn and let the dog off the leash to chase a few birds before they called it a day and went home.

Here, in the park, the sun still reached the trees' bare upper branches, and they were lacquered golden in the light. It was late afternoon, Keegan's favorite time of day in the city, just before the workday ended and the streets filled with traffic. And it was October, Keegan's favorite month, when the leaves fell and the weather cooled and baseball season wrapped up. He liked the nip in the air and the slow build-up to Halloween. He stretched out his legs and interlaced his fingers behind his head. The dog ran back and forth to him across the grass.

When Nora tired herself out, she came and plopped down beside Keegan's feet, panting, satisfied with her efforts to rid the world of pigeons. Keegan stroked her head and hooked the leash back on her collar.

The two of them headed over to Kipper Lusk's newsstand on the square's easternmost corner. Lusk was an old friend of sorts. He'd once been a small-time operator—nothing serious, just some bookie work and some fencing and some black-market rum brought up from Mexico. He'd been a good source of information all those years when Keegan was covering crime for *The Times*. For a guy who spent his day on a folding chair inside a plywood hut, he'd always had a good handle on what was going on around town.

These days—older, wiser—Lusk was still always looking for an angle, but he limited himself to misdemeanors, nothing likely to put him behind bars. He had a wife and a Pomeranian and a house out in Echo Park, and he probably paid most of his taxes. But if you needed a box of illegal Cuban cigars, he'd have them waiting for you the next morning. If you needed a fake ID, he'd tell you to buy one of the postcards from his rack, then he'd jot a phone number on the back as a kind of bonus. If you wanted World Series tickets, and you were willing to pay—well, he'd be the first guy you'd ask.

At Lusk's newsstand, Keegan waited behind a tall man in a charcoal suit who seemed to be buying a single copy of every local paper. He set them in a pile on Lusk's counter and then dug in his pockets for change.

Lusk sorted through the man's purchases. "A buck eighty," Lusk told him, without enthusiasm.

The man counted out exact change—mostly nickels and dimes—and dumped it on the counter before he took up his stack of newspapers and left without a word. Both Keegan and Lusk watched him walk away.

"You don't see many avid readers these days," Keegan said.

"That's the Chief Deputy DA," Lusk told him. "He likes to check his press. He's got his eye on grander things." He swept the scattered silver coins into his palm and went about sorting them into the till beneath his counter. "You'd have known who he was," Lusk said dourly, "if you ever coughed up a dime and actually bought a newspaper from me every now and again."

Keegan picked a pack of Juicy Fruit gum from Lusk's candy rack and set a nickel on the counter. "With customers like that guy, you should be in a better mood."

Lusk looked at him and shook his head, like Keegan couldn't be expected to understand his plight. "It's a dark time for me, my friend," he said cryptically. "Mirrors have been broken. A pall has descended."

Keegan peeled open the pack of gum and unwrapped a stick. "Your metaphor escapes me," he told Lusk. He put the gum in his mouth and the crumpled wrapper in his pocket.

"That's because it's no metaphor," Lusk said. "I'm talking literal mirrors, which have literally been broken." He jabbed a thumb in the direction of the old box truck he used to haul his goods. It was parked a quarter block down Hill Street, in the shade of a sycamore. "A guy paid me to haul a whole shipment of bathroom mirrors out to a new hotel in Pasadena," he said. "The rope broke, and one of the crates ended up in the Arroyo Seco slow lane under a semi-truck." He shook his head morosely. "Insurance will cover the cost," he said, "but it's the metaphysical fallout I'm worried about. There were twenty mirrors in that crate." He tapped the countertop with one finger. "I'm just trying to figure out if it's seven-years-per-incident or seven-years-per-mirror. Either way, I'm serving serious time."

Keegan barked a laugh and almost swallowed the gum he'd been chewing. "You're kidding, right?" he said, coughing a little. "Tell me you're not serious. Tell me you know that sort of superstition isn't real."

Lusk made a nodding-shrugging gesture that seemed to indicate the jury was still out. "The next day the wife's car battery dies," he said. "Then, last night, a skunk comes in the yard and sprays the dog." He presented his palms to Keegan beseechingly. "You tell me if the bad luck is real," he said. "Superstitions had to start somewhere, right? They weren't made up out of thin air." He shrugged. "So, who knows? Maybe I'm cursed."

Keegan grinned. "Couldn't have happened to a more deserving guy," he said. The gum in his mouth was already beginning to lose its flavor. "Let me tell you why I came by, Kip."

Lusk shot him a surly look. "Yes, please do," he said wryly. "For a minute there, we were almost talking about someone else for a change."

"You wouldn't know where I could get a ticket for a World Series game, do you?"

Lusk's mood seemed to brighten. He sat up straighter on his folding chair. "Games Three, Four, and Six," he said. "They go on sale Wednesday. There's already a line a mile long out at Chavez Ravine."

"And if I don't want to wait in line?"

"Then you'd need to talk to a particular local businessman who will soon have a number of choice seats for sale," Lusk said.

"And where might I find this scalper of yours?"

"You might be talking to him presently," Lusk said. "I got half a dozen kids from up at the high school camping out outside the stadium in shifts. Even bought them a pup tent to keep them happy. If you want a ticket, I'm your man."

Keegan nodded. Kipper Lusk was now a scalper. How had he not seen this coming? "So how much would you be charging for one of those choice seats?"

Lusk looked both ways before he spoke. This, after all, was a crime, and the Chief Deputy DA might still have been in earshot. "Fifty bucks for Saturday's game," Lusk said, "if you're not picky about where you sit. The better seats? Those'll run a little higher."

Keegan recoiled. He'd been guessing twenty bucks—twenty-five at the most. "Now, come on, Kip," he said. "The tickets can't cost you more than ten bucks a piece."

"*Twelve* bucks, I'll have you know," Lusk said. "And you're forgetting my overhead. High school kids don't come cheap. And did I mention the camping equipment?"

Keegan shook his head. "You know scalping is illegal," he said. "You're not supposed to sell a ticket for more than face value."

"And you're not supposed to let your mutt off her leash in the park," Lusk countered. "Yet here we are, two outlaws in broad daylight." Lusk leaned forward a little, and his face was suddenly lit up in the afternoon sun. "Look, Jimmy, there are fifty-six thousand seats in Dodger Stadium," he said. "And every seat's going to be full. Nobody much cares if one of those butts is yours."

He was right, and Keegan knew it. If he didn't pay Lusk's prices, someone else would be happy to. This was the World Series, after all. "Okay, fine," Keegan told Lusk. "Put a ticket aside for me. And make it a good one."

Lusk nodded and sat back in his chair, his face muted in shadow again. "That'll require a ten-dollar deposit," he said.

"What? *Seriously?*"

Lusk shrugged and made a show of straightening out his till. Keegan could take the offer or leave it.

Nora tugged at her leash. An old woman was walking a toy poodle over by the drinking fountain.

"Just a sec," Keegan told the dog. He dug out his wallet and flattened two fives on Lusk's counter.

Lusk folded them and put them in his shirt pocket, keeping them separate from the money in his till. "Always a pleasure doing business," he said. "Swing by Thursday afternoon with the rest of the cash, and there'll be a ticket here with your name on it."

AGAIN, A LITTLE after midnight, the dog started up her barking. She was out in the living room, her claws skittering on the oak flooring. Keegan tried to ignore the noise. He pulled the pillow around his head and tried to will himself back to sleep. But her barking was so strident, so insistent, there was no way he could tune it out. He got up and trudged out to the living room.

Nora stood just where she had all the times before, next to the coffee table, ears pricked, hackles raised. She growled at the big easy chair, inched toward it tentatively, then stopped and growled some more.

Tonight, the big chair was empty. There wasn't even a blanket there to make an ambiguous shadow. Keegan reached over and turned on the corner lamp again. In the sudden light, the dog sat down and whimpered. She eyed the empty chair keenly, cowering a little.

"Nothing there," Keegan told her softly. "Nothing to be afraid of."

The dog stood and edged toward the chair. When she got to it, she jumped up into it, quivering with excitement. She sniffed at the arms and at the seatback, wagging her stubby tail. Whatever scent she found there seemed to please her.

"So, are we done now?" Keegan said. "Think we can call it a night and go back to sleep?"

The dog kept up her excited sniffing, ignoring Keegan completely. She seemed transported by whatever scents the old chair was confiding to her. At least she wasn't barking.

"Well, okay then," Keegan said. "You stay out here if you want. I, for one, am going back to bed."

Keegan reached over and switched off the lamp. In the new darkness, he thought he might have caught a whiff of something too—a subtle hint of perfume in the air, perhaps. It was a scent so slight and delicate it was difficult to know if it was real.

He slouched into the dark bedroom and rolled back onto the waiting bed. He lay on his back looking up at the ceiling, too awake now to hope for sleep.

CHAPTER THREE

THE CHATEAU MARMONT lay off Sunset Boulevard, just west of Laurel Canyon. It was an old, high-end hotel that towered over the palms and eucalyptus trees, looking quaint and coquettish amid all the nightclubs and the liquor stores. Its architecture— at least what could be seen of it from the street—was at odds with the rest of the neighborhood. It might have been a castle from the French Renaissance, uprooted from its vineyards and dropped down here on Sunset Strip among all the billboards and neon. As a hotel, it was mostly famous for its privacy. It was the preferred destination for a well-heeled, illicit tryst or a movie star's mental breakdown. You went to the Ambassador or the Garden of Allah if you wanted to be seen. You came to the Chateau Marmont if you wanted to be invisible.

Keegan parked his car on Sunset, just outside Schwab's drugstore. He got out and waited beside his car, watching for a break in traffic. When he saw his opportunity, he jogged across the Boulevard. He paused on the opposite sidewalk and looked up at the hotel. Not much of it showed above the overgrown hedge, just high white walls, windows, and balconies—a splash of old Europe amid all the sun-bleached stucco.

He found a narrow entryway and ended up in a dimly lit lobby that seemed far too small to belong to a hotel. There was a front desk, a row of muted hanging lamps, and a few battered leather wingback chairs. The room's burgundy carpeting was stained and threadbare, like something you'd see in an old movie house. Most of the light came from a pair of French doors at the room's far end.

The concierge behind the desk wore round spectacles, an old-fashioned white dinner jacket, and a red bow tie. He was tall and stooped. Balding. Middle-aged. The way he bent over the desk as Keegan approached him gave the impression that he might be using it to stay on his feet.

"I'm here to see Ida Fletcher," Keegan said. "She's expecting me."

The man regarded Keegan through his round, smudged lenses. He seemed unimpressed with what he saw. He reached up and adjusted his glasses, wincing as he did. "I'm afraid I can't help you, sir," he said haughtily. The mere act of addressing Keegan seemed to pain him a little. "We don't have a guest by that name."

After Keegan's smoggy drive out here in traffic, the man's smugness struck a nerve. Sure, if the old lady was as paranoid as Donovan said she was, she'd probably left strict orders at the desk not to let anyone in. But she was the one who had begged Keegan to come, and he had traipsed all the way out to the Strip in good faith. He wasn't about to be turned away by some tinpot sycophant, dressed in his grandfather's dinner jacket.

"Look, I talked to her on the phone this morning," Keegan said. "She asked me to meet her here. The Chateau Marmont."

The man straightened up a little and stood with his hands braced on the desk's edge. This small change in posture also seemed to pain him. "I'm afraid I can't help you," he said. He glanced over at the door Keegan had come through. "There is a phone booth across the street," he informed Keegan without looking in his direction. "It's right outside the drugstore, if you need to make a call."

There was also, Keegan could clearly see, a much closer

payphone. It was in a little alcove built into the wall right behind the front desk. The concierge drifted a little to his left, as if to block that phone from Keegan's view.

Keegan moved his jaw from side to side. He'd only agreed to this meeting because Mrs. Dodd had insisted they needed the money. He would have happily ignored the old lady's call again and spent the afternoon behind his desk, listening to Game Two of the World Series. He put his own hand atop the desk and gathered himself up to his full six feet. "Look," he said, glaring squarely at the concierge, "I don't know what your problem—"

Keegan never finished the sentence. He was caught up short by a meaty hand on his shoulder. He turned to find a thick, craggy face smiling at him. The man had all the markings of a Sunset Strip bouncer. He was broad-shouldered and barrel-chested, with olive skin and close-cropped black hair. Though an inch or two shorter than Keegan, he made up for it with muscle mass. Keegan braced himself.

"You must be the new detective," the man said. His grin broadened when he saw Keegan's confusion. The man wore a tight blue polo shirt that seemed to be designed for a much smaller man. "I'm with Mrs. Fletcher," he said. "I'm supposed to bring you on back." He held out a thick hand for Keegan to shake. His grip was leathery and oversized, like someone's well-worn baseball glove. Keegan noted the faded blue tattoos on the extended forearm: an anchor, a hula girl, the stars and stripes. This was a Navy man.

"I'm Jim Keegan."

"Frank Romano," the other man said.

The name fit, Keegan thought. It was no nonsense, plain and blunt and hard enough to break a bone or two.

"I'm supposed to look you over first," Frank said amiably. "Mrs. Fletcher's orders." He made a show of stepping back to give Keegan the once over. "You seem okay to me," he said. He turned, strode to the lobby's far end, and opened the French door.

Keegan glanced back at the concierge, who was now bent over the ledger, pretending to be immersed in something. Keegan shook his head and went through the door Frank Romano was holding open for him.

Outside was a shady arcade walkway that skirted a courtyard garden. The other man led Keegan between two ivy-laced pillars into the sunlight.

Now that Keegan had a better look at him, Frank struck him as more of a boxer than a mere bouncer. He had the agile build; the blunt, slanted nose; the cauliflower ears. Above one of his heavy-lidded eyes, the brow had a notch in it, a bare slit where it had no doubt been quickly stitched between rounds so he could get back in the ring. Brigade Boxing Champ in the Navy, Keegan guessed. The man's bulging triceps suggested he would have packed a good wallop, but—judging by the ears and crooked nose—he was a bit slow with his ducking and weaving.

The courtyard they crossed felt secluded and removed. The cool air was filled with birdsong and the sound of running water. It was as if they were in some high-mountain getaway far removed from the city. The distant hush of traffic passing out on Sunset Boulevard might have been the rush of wind among the pines. Keegan followed Frank the Boxer past a small oval swimming pool to a row of bungalows.

They approached the nearest bungalow. A wrought-iron gate was set into a redbrick wall. The ex-boxer stepped in front of Keegan and blocked his way. "I'm going to need to see some ID before I take you inside," he said. He shrugged and smiled apologetically; these were not his rules. "And your PI license, if you have it with you."

He stood—feet planted wide, blue-inked arms folded across his chest—while Keegan fished out his wallet. These might not be his rules, but he was clearly going to make sure Keegan followed them. "She's picky about this kind of thing," he said amiably. "But who can blame her?"

Keegan handed over the two cards, and Frank the Boxer

looked down at them, one in each hand. He held Keegan's driver's license up so he could match the photo to Keegan's face. He did all this good-naturedly, like the two of them were playing along in some kind of pantomime. "She's a sweetheart once you get to know her," he said. He held the two IDs in the air between them, as if assuring Keegan that he'd take good care of them. "She'll want to see these first," he said.

Keegan nodded.

"This'll only take a minute," the boxer said. He turned and disappeared through the big iron gate, making sure to latch it behind him.

While Keegan waited, he took in his surroundings. The day out on Sunset had been mild, cool for so early in October. Inside the hotel's walls, the atmosphere was a shadowy, damp November—a good five degrees cooler than it had been outside Schwab's. He looked up at the walls of the main hotel, a warren of mismatched windows and odd balconies set into the walls, elegant and shabby in equal measures.

Two men lay on adjoining deck chairs by the pool in shorts and undershirts, making use of a small scrap of sunlight that filtered down through the palms. They wore nearly identical tortoiseshell sunglasses—that Italian brand that was always showing up in Mrs. Dodd's movie-gossip magazines. The men's chairs were pushed closely together. It wasn't something you'd see at any other hotel. Privacy was hard to come by in Hollywood.

The iron gate behind Keegan swung open again, and Frank Romano stood there, taking up most of the gateway with his shoulders. "Right this way, Mr. Keegan," the boxer said. "Sorry for the wait." He gave Keegan back his ID cards. "Or should I call you James?"

"Jimmy or Jim," Keegan said. "Suit yourself. Anything but James."

"Jim, then," Frank the Boxer said. He held the gate and stood to one side so Keegan could pass through. Keegan slipped the cards into his jacket's inner pocket. The other man crossed the patio and rapped twice on the bungalow's door. He swung it open and again stood aside so Keegan could enter.

Inside, the bungalow was dimly lit. Keegan paused in the kitchenette. None of the lamps around the living room were on, and the curtain was drawn across the sliding glass door. The only light came through the frosted windows on either side of the front door. Keegan looked around the shadowy front room.

Despite the top dollar Ida Fletcher must have been paying for a private bungalow, this could have been a blue-collar living room in San Pedro. A battered sofa and armchair were rearranged to face a large console television. The carpet, olive shag, looked worn and in need of a steaming. The living room's one landscape painting hung askew on its nail. The kitchen's furnishings—stove and refrigerator, round kitchen table—looked more Sears than Sotheby's.

A pretty woman who looked to be in her forties sat glumly at the kitchen table smoking a cigarette. Her hair was piled up in a gravity-defying bouffant, and she barely glanced up from her thick Michener paperback when Keegan came in. The air in here smelled of toast and Aqua Net—and there was another scent Keegan couldn't quite place. Was it the tang of marijuana? Keegan raised an eyebrow. Everyone minded their own business at the Chateau Marmont.

Frank the Boxer gestured to the living room sofa, so Keegan went over and took a seat. Frank plopped down at the sofa's far end, exerting a kind of gravitational pull when his weight sank in.

The old woman herself sat in a big easy chair with her back to the sliding glass door. Even with the curtains drawn, the light coming from behind her made it difficult to see her features clearly. She looked small and frail in the big chair. She might have been sixty or ninety from all Keegan could tell, but he could make out a striking widow's peak in her silver hair and a pair of deep-set, knowing eyes.

"So good of you to come, Mr. Keegan," she said. Her voice was spindly but sure. "Sorry about the formalities, but one can't be too careful, can one?"

Keegan nodded. "One cannot," he said.

"You've already met Frank," the woman said, brushing a gaunt hand in the boxer's direction. "I suppose you'd call him my factotum."

Big Frank nodded from the far end of the sofa, still with the air of playing along. Keegan nodded back. Was *factotum* French for bone crusher?

"And that over there is Mildred Zinnia, my companion and personal assistant."

Keegan leaned forward to see past Frank's bulk at the other end of the sofa. The woman in the kitchenette set her paperback face down on the table to mark her place. She nodded to Keegan demurely, her cigarette tucked between two fingers.

"Like the flower," Keegan said. "Your name, I mean."

Mildred Zinnia acknowledged his comment with a silent nod and then picked up her paperback again.

Keegan leaned back on the sofa. An old lady, a bodyguard, and a wallflower; what grand times these three must have.

For the next few minutes, Ida Fletcher explained what she expected of Keegan, and he did his best to look interested. Her voice was clipped and imperious, and, though the lighting made it difficult to see her face, her head bobbed in a way that emphasized that her notions were not to be taken lightly. How had someone as careless and sloppy as Donovan managed to stay in this woman's good graces?

Her monologue continued: Though she currently lived at the Chateau Marmont, she did own a house in Bel Air and another in Newport Beach. She was spare with the details, but certain parties persisted in plotting against her. An extensive cabal of them had been conspiring for years, hence she required the services of a discreet and dependable investigator to ensure her safety.

Keegan had come highly recommended, she assured him. If this job interested him, he would be supplied with a strongbox that was to be kept in his office safe. Keegan's first duty as her employee would be simple but essential: he was to visit her two properties at least once each week to make sure nothing was amiss. The keys to both those houses were in the strongbox and should be kept in Keegan's safe when they were not in use.

Her instructions were well spoken and clear—and deceptively rational. With all her talk about secret machinations and schemes against her, she was no doubt as mentally afflicted as Donovan had promised. But her illness did nothing to cloud her precise and formal diction. She wore her paranoia like a designer gown: with poise and with her chin held high.

It took her about fifteen minutes to outline her expectations for Keegan, and then, abruptly, she was done.

"I expect you to keep my best interests always in mind, Mr. Keegan," she said. "And for that, I will pay you handsomely." She shifted aslant in her chair then, so she was no longer quite facing Keegan. "If you should see Mr. Donovan," she said, "do give him my best."

It took Keegan a beat to realize it, but he was being dismissed.

Frank the Boxer stood, so Keegan did as well. Keegan took a step toward the old woman and held out his hand. "It was nice to have met you," he said, but the old woman glanced at his extended hand and then looked away. Perhaps she was a germaphobe as well. Frank the Boxer laid a consoling hand on Keegan's shoulder and subtly steered him back through the kitchenette to the front door.

Zinnia had left her spot at the kitchen table and stood beside the doorway now. She held a strongbox in front of her with both hands as if making a formal presentation. Like a bashful teen, she didn't seem capable of looking at Keegan as he took the box by the brass handle on top. Her mission accomplished, she slipped back in the direction of the paperback novel that waited for her, face down on the kitchen table.

Frank the Boxer opened the door, and Keegan went out through it, carrying the strongbox by its handle.

Outside in the courtyard, with the gate closed behind them, the big man glanced over his shoulder at the bungalow and then offered Keegan a shrug and a grin, like the two of them were in on a joke.

"She's got her ways," he said, "but she'll grow on you. It takes her a while to warm up to a stranger." He held up a key—presumably it opened the strongbox. "The box goes in the safe," Frank reminded him. "The key stays with you at all times." He grinned again, as if to say he was only the messenger.

Keegan nodded and took the key with his free hand. He slipped it into his trouser pocket. The two of them headed back across the courtyard. In the small lobby, the bow-tied concierge was still behind his desk. He fussed with some papers and ignored them both elaborately.

Frank the Boxer reached inside his trouser pocket and pulled out an envelope, which he held discreetly in the narrow space between them. "This is your retainer," he said. He pressed it into Keegan's free hand, and Keegan slipped it into the inner pocket of his blazer.

OUT ON SUNSET Boulevard, the traffic, the billboards, the shabby strip malls had all persisted during Keegan's respite in the Chateau Marmont. Outside that shadowy oasis, the light seemed implausibly bright, the air acrid with smog. Keegan paused again on the sidewalk, watching for a lull in traffic.

He could see himself reflected in Schwab's big front window across the street, a run-of-the-mill Angeleno, notable only because he was holding a strongbox by the handle. When he saw a lull in traffic, he jogged across the street, pausing in the middle to let a red open-aired sightseeing bus pass by. He unlocked his car on the driver's side, bent to set the strongbox in the passenger seat, and climbed in behind the wheel.

Keegan put the key in the ignition but didn't start the engine. He slipped the envelope from inside his jacket pocket. It was unsealed, the flap tucked in. He took out the cash. It was all in hundred-dollar bills—how many of them, Keegan couldn't guess—but it was enough that he reflexively glanced around at the passersby on the sidewalk and reached back to push down the door's lock.

"Richer than Jesus," he said out loud.

He glanced across the street at the high walls of the Chateau Marmont and then back down at the fan of banknotes in his hands. The old lady was the golden goose old Donovan had promised she would be. Why did the situation only make Keegan feel uneasy?

He put the money back in the envelope and set it on the passenger seat next to the strongbox. He started up the car and pulled out onto Sunset. The last innings of today's World Series game were on the radio—another Dodgers' win. His heart wasn't in it, though. He kept glancing down at the envelope in the seat beside him.

BACK IN THE office, Mrs. Dodd sat behind her desk with her reading glasses perched on the end of her nose. Keegan, who'd been pacing while she counted, watched her lean back in her swivel chair and frown down at the stacks of cash she'd taken from Ida Fletcher's envelope. Five stacks of ten bills, each one a hundred-dollar note. Five thousand dollars was more than Keegan had brought in so far that year, and it was already October. Mrs. Dodd took off her glasses, looking a bit pale, and set them on the desk blotter in front of her.

It made no sense to either of them, this kind of windfall. It was obscene, and there was no record that this money even existed—no voucher, no invoice, no itemized receipt. They'd scrimped throughout the summer, saving pennies here and there, taking whatever piecemeal divorce or insurance cases came their way. More than once in the last few months, Keegan had had to ask Mrs. Dodd to wait a day or two before she cashed her paycheck. Twice he'd been so late to pay the phone bill he'd received the envelope stamped FINAL NOTICE.

Now, suddenly flush, he didn't feel the surge of relief he would have expected. He felt—well, he wasn't sure what he felt. *Apprehensive* was the word that came most readily to mind. None of this felt right. Old Donovan might have been able to turn a blithe blind eye in this situation, but Keegan had too many questions. He looked down at the stacks of cash and then at Mrs. Dodd. "Well?" he said. "What do you think?"

"Would it be too soon to ask for a raise?"

Keegan dug his hands into his pockets and shifted his weight from one foot to the other. "I'm serious," he said. "You think we should keep it?"

Mrs. Dodd looked up at him, eyebrows raised, her forehead a stave of nearly parallel lines. "Why *wouldn't* we?" she asked wryly. "We need money"—she hovered a palm over the stacks of cash on her desk—"and this is what people actually meant when they invented that word."

Keegan sighed. It was hard to put into words the reservations he was feeling. He just had a sense of foreboding, a sense that something wasn't kosher. "You don't think this counts as fleecing an old lady who doesn't know any better?"

Mrs. Dodd shrugged, as if maybe, in some circumstances, swindling the elderly might not be as unsavory as he was making it sound. "You met her," Mrs. Dodd said. "Did she *seem* crazy?"

Maybe that was where the problem lay. The old lady's manner—her precise diction, her imperious demeanor, her exacting directions—undercut what seemed to be a clear case of delusion. But who was to say she didn't have good reason to act paranoid? When you were richer than Croesus and Jesus put together, wouldn't there be plenty of schemers angling for your fortune? Her suspicions might be perfectly rational.

But then again, maybe *Keegan* was rationalizing. Maybe he was trying to shine the best light on something a better man would see as a clear ethical breech. It was a quandary to be sure. He thought of Donovan that night at the Ambassador's pool. *She won't even let you write her out a receipt*, he'd bragged. *The IRS don't need to know a thing.* Donovan had probably never entertained an ethical concern in his life. Shaking down an old lady. Hiding funds from the IRS. That kind of thing was par for Donovan's course.

Keegan again looked down at the cash on Mrs. Dodd's desk. There the dilemma lay, in neat piles, under harsh fluorescent lights. Much as he needed money, there was no way Keegan could ignore all its messy implications. It made his head ache.

But did she *seem* crazy? That had been Mrs. Dodd's question.

"Remember Dottie Gordon?" Keegan said. She'd been a client from a few years back, an old divorcee out in Redondo Beach.

"The one that wanted you to check out her daughter's fiancé?"

"Yeah," Keegan said. "Her. Did I tell you she thought her father-in-law was involved in the Lindbergh Case?"

"Really?"

Keegan nodded. He dug his hands in the pockets of his trousers. "And my own mother used to ward off bad luck with a pinch of salt."

Mrs. Dodd nodded and made a rolling motion with one of her hands, goading Keegan to keep going. She seemed to like this line of reasoning. "I think I see where you're headed with this," she said. "Continue."

Keegan shrugged. "I guess Ida Fletcher didn't seem any more irrational than some other old women I've known." He could, of course, have mentioned Mrs. Dodd herself. She carried a rabbit's foot on her keychain and consulted her horoscope every morning before she'd take the cover off her typewriter. And, of course, there were her theories about ghosts and dogs and elevators. "So maybe 'crazy' is too strong a word."

Mrs. Dodd nodded, like she'd been waiting for him to arrive at the conclusion she'd known all along. "I think you're absolutely right there, boss," she said. "She's a grown adult. She can spend her money how she likes."

Keegan nodded. "It just *feels* wrong," he said.

Mrs. Dodd circled a hand over the desktop again. "For this kind of money, I think we can put up with a little discomfort," she said. "So, what's with the strongbox?"

Until she'd mentioned it, Keegan had more or less forgotten the steel box he'd set on the corner of Mrs. Dodd's desk when he'd first come in through the door. The cash had mesmerized him, and he scolded himself for letting it distract him from the actual job he was hired to do. "We're supposed to put it in the safe," he said. "I'm not sure what's in it."

"Well, let's take a look," Mrs. Dodd said. "Did she give you a key?"

Keegan fished the key from his trouser pocket. He looked down at it in his palm, a thumb-worn brass thing no longer than a paperclip. He wasn't sure about this.

Mrs. Dodd held out her palm. "If this thing is being kept in our office," she said, "we need to know what's inside it."

"I don't know," Keegan said. "What if we don't end up taking the job?"

Mrs. Dodd gave him a look like he was being impossibly contrary. She looked down at the money and back up again. "Looks to me like you've already taken the job," she said. She held out her open hand and waved her fingers impatiently. "Come on, boss. What if it's full of drugs?" she said. "What if there's a human head in there? If it's going to be kept in the office, we need to know what's inside."

"A human head wouldn't fit," Keegan told her.

"It would if you tried hard enough," she corrected him. "Just give me the key already."

She was right, Keegan knew. Money had changed hands. At least until he could talk to Ida Fletcher again, he was in her employ. And Mrs. Dodd was also right about opening the box. This was a PI's office, not a safe deposit vault. If there was anything iffy in the box, he'd be taking the fall if it came to light. He dropped the key into Mrs. Dodd's hand.

She pulled the box in front of her and slipped the key into the lock. She turned it and then glanced up at Keegan, clearly enjoying the drama of the moment. With an odd flourish, she lifted the lid.

A brass key ring with a dozen or so keys on it lay on top of a stack of papers—sheets and receipts and envelopes of various sizes. Mrs. Dodd dug through to the bottom, but all she found was paper. She seemed a little put out that there wasn't a drawstring pouch of emeralds or a cache of Spanish doubloons, but her disappointment was short-lived. She picked up the top envelope and pulled out the document it contained. She put her reading glasses back on and started to skim. After a few seconds, she smiled and turned the pages to face Keegan, marking a certain passage with her index finger.

"Right here, boss," she said. "'...*of sound mind and body...*'" It was a will she was holding. "If the old lady's sane enough for the State of California, she's sane enough for us." Her case closed, she went back to skimming the will, flipping through the pages one by one. She got to the final page, the one with all the formal signatures. "Say," she said, glancing back at the first page, "this thing's brand new."

"What do you mean?"

"August thirtieth," she said, again turning it so he could see. "The ink's barely dry."

Keegan took the will from her and looked it over. It had been drawn up by a Santa Monica law firm and signed as witness by old Donovan himself, in his big, blocky ballpoint cursive.

Keegan flipped back through the pages. He was no lawyer, but it looked like the bulk of Ida Fletcher's estate would go to a nephew by the name of Daniel Church, who lived in Paris.

Smaller shares were parceled out to a few others, including Frank the Boxer and Mildred Zinnia, the old lady's assistant. There was another name that Keegan didn't recognize: Lillian Cole. Donovan, himself, was included at the very end. He'd be getting ten thousand dollars when Ida Fletcher cashed in her chips—enough for a lifetime membership in Tempe's swankiest country club, if he ever wanted to try out his new putter. Keegan again thought of old Donovan, poolside at the Ambassador, cigar in hand, scarlet-faced from all that coughing. All he had to do was manage to outlive the old lady, and he'd get the cash. Keegan wouldn't bet on it, though.

Keegan folded the will and put it back in its envelope and then he and Mrs. Dodd dug through the rest of the box's contents. They opened the envelopes and reported the contents—deeds and leases, stock certificates and tax returns, the pink slips to a Cadillac, a Daimler, and a Jaguar. There was a deed to another house the old girl hadn't mentioned in her instructions, this one in Avalon, over on Catalina Island. It hadn't been put on Keegan's weekly rounds, thank God. The ferry ride out there and back would have taken up most of a day.

When they were done, Mrs. Dodd straightened the envelopes on her desktop and slipped them back in the strongbox. She closed the lid, locked it, and handed Keegan the key.

"Disappointed?" Keegan said.

She shrugged. "A human head would have made a mess of my blotter," she said. "So, what does the old girl want from you?"

"I'm supposed to swing by the two houses every week and report back to her." It wasn't much of a job. He could do it in a few hours. It might even be a pleasant break from the office. He took another guilty look at the stacks of cash that still lay on the desk.

Mrs. Dodd seemed to read his mind. "Look," she said, "humor her for a few weeks, and see how it goes. Give her until Halloween. If it doesn't feel right by the end of the month, you can hand in your resignation."

That seemed a reasonable compromise to Keegan, so he nodded. He started to gather up the stacks of hundred-dollar bills. "Guess we put it all in the safe for now."

Mrs. Dodd plopped her hand down on one of the stacks before he could pick it up. "I don't want you to say you didn't see this," she said, looking Keegan evenly in the eye. She took the top hundred-dollar bill, held it up in front of him, and snapped it between her hands. She folded it neatly in half and slipped it into the pocket of her blouse. She kept her eyes on him, as if daring him to object.

"What's that for?" he asked her.

"Necessities," she said, as if that were any kind of answer.

Keegan decided to let it go. They'd been scrimping and cutting corners for so long, he probably owed her more than that for the pens and the pads of paper and the other office supplies she kept bringing in from her husband's dental practice. He put the rest of the money back in its envelope and set it on top of the strongbox. Four thousand, nine hundred dollars. It was more than he knew what to do with. He'd go by the bank tomorrow at lunch and deposit a few hundred in the checking account. Then he'd spend the afternoon catching up with his bills. For now, it was all going in the office safe.

CHAPTER FOUR

THE NEXT MORNING, around six-thirty, Keegan walked the dog to Kipper Lusk's newsstand before he headed up to the office. The sun hadn't risen above the downtown buildings, so Pershing Square was all blue shadows and silence. There was an October nip in the air, and the mist from the central fountain chilled Keegan's face. He'd checked his wallet before he left home to make sure he had two twenties to pay Kipper Lusk the rest of what he owed for his World Series ticket.

There weren't many people in the park, but the streets around it were filling with cars and buses, everyone arriving, *en masse*, for the workday. Nora, on her leash, tugged him along, following some scent she'd found trailing along the walkway.

Lusk was already inside the newsstand's shack, loading one of the candy racks with Tootsie Rolls from a cardboard box. He glanced up when he saw Keegan approach and offered him a dour nod.

"You got my ticket?" Keegan called.

Lusk glared at him. He set down the box of candy and turned to face Keegan squarely. "If that's meant to be a joke," he said, "it's in poor taste." He moved the Tootsie Roll box somewhere out of sight in his plywood lair.

"Joke?" Keegan said. "Did something happen?"

Lusk looked Keegan over dolefully. "You really should keep better track of world events," he said. He reached out from inside the shack and plucked a copy of the *Los Angeles Times* from the news rack. He turned it over and held it out, pointing to one of the front-page headlines below the fold: SERIES TICKET SALES NEARLY CAUSE RIOT.

Keegan reached out to take the paper, but Lusk held it tight. "You got a dime for me?" he said. "If not, I'll thank you not to smudge the ink." Lusk made a show of flattening out the paper on the countertop and then slid it back into the rack.

"What the hell happened?" Keegan asked.

"Apparently, it was a nightmare," Lusk said. "People been lined up since Monday, and suddenly—at sunup—the parking lot is swarming with new arrivals. They open the whole wall of ticket windows and all hell breaks loose. One of my guys broke his collarbone in the brawl. By the time the boys in blue arrived, every last ticket was gone."

"You didn't get *any*?"

"Not a single seat, my friend," he said. "I'm out fifty bucks on the guys I hired—not counting a doctor's bill for a broken bone, which apparently I've got to pay to keep the peace. And if I want to see a game myself, I have to pay some scalper through the nose." He seemed deeply offended by that idea.

"But, Kip," Keegan said, "you were going to scalp the tickets yourself."

He shrugged, as if that were neither here nor there. He leaned on the counter. "It's the curse," he said. "It's those damn mirrors I broke."

"So, a million Dodgers fans got screwed over because you happened to break some mirrors? That seems a little grandiose."

"Stop," Lusk said. "You're only making me feel worse."

"I'm just saying that this might not be about you, Kip," Keegan said. "Don't get a big head. You seem to think you've got more clout around here than Mayor Yorty."

Lusk shrugged. "Believe what you want, big shot," he said. "I carry a lot of weight in this town."

Nora tugged at her leash. It was cold out, and she wanted to get moving.

Keegan looked down along Fifth Street and then back at Lusk. In that momentary lull, it registered to Keegan how much he'd been looking forward to going to the game. It had been a small good thing to look forward to, a hopeful light on the far horizon. It was only a baseball game, he knew—and he could listen to it on the radio—but the profound disappointment he felt seemed all out of proportion. He looked at Lusk, hunkered there in the shadows of his shack. "What about my deposit?" he said. "I gave you ten bucks."

Lusk shot him a withering look. He shook his head grimly. "Insult to injury," he said. He dug a couple of wilted fives out of his till and slapped them down on the counter. "Go buy yourself something nice," he said. "And don't worry about the little guy out here trying to scrape together a decent living."

"Don't blame me," Keegan said. "*I* didn't break any mirrors."

MRS. DODD WAS already in the office when Keegan got there. There had been no new calls, no messages. It was a Friday, and there was no baseball game, so Keegan thought he might as well make the rounds for Ida Fletcher. It would get him out of the office for a good part of the day. He'd see the ocean. Maybe it would keep him from dwelling on the letdown. And he'd take the dog along for company. She always seemed to enjoy the sea air. He got the ring of keys from the strongbox in the office safe.

Nora rode in the MG's passenger seat with her forepaws up on the dashboard, eager to see where they were headed. They took the Harbor Freeway south to the Coast Highway and then headed down through Seal Beach and Huntington.

They passed all the beachy diners and the surf shops and the age-old waterfront hotels that were slowly falling into ruin.

The salt air was chilly, but it felt good coming in through the dashboard vents. At a stoplight, he reached across the passenger seat and rolled the window down a bit. When the light changed, Nora put her head out into the salty wind. KNX was on the radio—Bob Crane's morning show—but he turned the volume down so low he could barely make out the comforting burble of human voices.

Ida Fletcher's Newport Beach house turned out to be on the landward side of the bay, facing Balboa and the peninsula. The map Keegan used to find it showed a spindly black line, Waverly Lane, running alongside the blue of the bay and quickly dead-ending. What the map didn't show was a gated guardhouse at the top of the lane.

Keegan coasted up to the red-and-white arm angled across the asphalt blocking his way. He cranked down his window. A face in the guardhouse window looked him over from behind a pair of dark sunglasses. The guard slid a window open and leaned out. Though he was clearly just hired security, he wore a full formal uniform shirt, powder blue and flawlessly ironed. A row of medals would not have looked out of place. The man looked to be in his thirties with a lean, tanned face and his blond hair in a crew cut. The tag above the pocket said his name was VOGEL. "Can I help you?" he asked Keegan doubtfully.

At the sound of his voice, Nora hopped over to Keegan's lap to get a look at him. She seemed to approve; her stubby tail wagged furiously, and she tried to scramble up on the car window's sill.

Keegan held the dog back by her collar. "The name's Jim Keegan," he said. "I'm here to look over the Fletcher place. I'm guessing she put me on the list."

The guard found a clipboard and flipped through the pages unhurriedly. "First time?"

"Yeah," Keegan told him. "I just got hired."

The other man looked up from his clipboard. "What happened to Donovan?"

"Retired. Moved out to Phoenix for his health. I'm filling in for now."

The guard nodded. "Good man, that Donovan," he said. "Tell him I said hello."

"Copy that," Keegan said. If he ever talked to Donovan again—which seemed unlikely—there was no chance he'd remember Vogel's greeting.

The guard found the right name on his clipboard. "James P. Keegan?" the guard said.

"The same."

The guard came out of his shack and stood behind Keegan's car, writing down the license plate number. Keegan watched him in the rearview mirror. The man was in no rush. He came around Keegan's side to the open car window. The dog strained at her collar, quivering with excitement. The guard bent down towards her.

"He a puppy?" Vogel wanted to know. "Some kind of Airedale?"

"She's a Welsh Terrier," Keegan said. "This is as big as she'll get."

The guard nodded. "Got a couple of Westies at home," he said. He reached out a hand to pet the dog but then seemed to think better of it. "She friendly?"

"Friendlier than me," Keegan allowed.

The guard grinned and looked at the dog. "It's just your old friend Vogel," he told her. He rubbed the dog's head and then stepped back. "You'll want number 7," he told Keegan. "It's at the very end. The big one." He went back into the shack and raised the boom gate.

WAVERLY LANE WAS so narrow it seemed unlikely that two cars, moving in opposite directions, could hope to pass on it. Despite the sunny day, the lane was deep in shadow. To the left was a steep hillside. The right side was a line of towering, perfectly trimmed privacy hedges, worthy of the Chateau Marmont.

Nora stood with her front paws on the dashboard again, keeping a keen eye on the windshield. As they edged slowly along, they passed an occasional imposing gate. Every now and again, a high dormer or a gable appeared fleetingly above the leafy ramparts. The lane curved right then left, following the contours of the hillside.

It dead-ended at a stately double-swing gate that was about eight feet high. It was all wrought iron with ornate scrollwork and black fang-like finials studding the top edge. It would be hard to imagine a barrier more fortress-like, less welcoming. It had Ida Fletcher written all over it. In the center, holding the two sides of the gate together, was a tight-coiled chain and a brass padlock the size of a grilled cheese sandwich. Someone had hammered a red plastic sign, slightly askew, into the ground beside the gate: NO TRESPASSING. As a message, it struck Keegan as a little redundant.

Keegan put his MG in neutral and set the parking brake. He had to slip out the door sideways to keep the dog from jumping out after him. The wind off the bay rippled Keegan's shirt. The temperature seemed to have plummeted a good ten degrees since he'd left the highway.

He took the old lady's brass key ring from his trouser pocket and looked for one that might fit a padlock. He tried three before he found the one that matched. The lock sprang open with a jolt, and he unwound the chain from around the two wrought-iron spindles. Once it was free, he looked back along the narrow road and thought of Vogel in his guardhouse at the far end. There was no godly reason to lock the gate behind him when he went up to the house. He coiled the chain and set it, with the open lock, on the edge of the asphalt where he wouldn't run over it when he drove back out. He pushed open one side of the gate, just far enough that he could slip the car through.

Keegan got back in the car, put it in gear, and pulled through the gate onto a long drive. The gray gravel popped and shifted under his tires. The dog jumped back up to her lookout position, eager to see what was ahead. The driveway to the house arced between curved hedges that had grown rangy with neglect and the damp sea air. The house at the end of the drive was a broad Cape-Cod-style mansion, all white clapboard and shuttered windows. A row of dormers jutted from the steep slate roof. Keegan could imagine the Kennedy clan playing touch football on the sloping lawn, while old Joe watched from his wheelchair on the porch. Keegan parked the car in a patch of sunlight and got out.

Nora followed him up the front steps to the big wrap-around porch, her claws skittering on the painted wood. Keegan imagined that Ida Fletcher wouldn't want a dog in her house, but really, how would she ever know? The dog was good company. She didn't shed, and she was generally well behaved. There'd be no harm in it.

Again, Keegan had to try a few keys to find the one that fit the front door's deadbolt. There were no other cars down on the gravel drive, and the house was obviously empty. Still, Keegan knocked the door smartly and waited a beat before he turned the knob and pushed it open. "Hello?" he called inside. "Anyone home?" There was, of course, no answer.

The dog followed him inside, sniffing at the baseboards cautiously. The entryway was all white-painted woodwork with crown molding and a quarter-turn stairway leading up to the second-floor landing. A dusty phone sat on a hallway table. The dog stood, testing the air, ears pricked. Keegan tried a light switch next to the door, but nothing happened. Fletcher must have had the electricity shut off, since the house was not in use.

The ways of the wealthy made little sense to Keegan. Here was a woman who'd pay him a small fortune to keep an eye on an empty house, yet she'd save a few pennies by having her assistant call PG&E to cut off the power. He left the front door wide, for the light it shone into the entryway, and went through a broad open threshold into a big front room. There wasn't much furniture. What little there was was sheeted over—a congregation of bulky, misshapen ghosts lurking in the gloom. Keegan lifted the corners of a few sheets: a wingback chair; a Queen Anne end table; a towering mahogany grandfather clock, its pendulum dangling motionless. The white-painted walls were uniformly bare, though they were dotted here and there with nails where paintings or photos must have once hung. It was like someone had purged the place of every image, every memento.

Keegan wandered from room to room. Everything about the place felt leaden and oppressive—the sluggish air, the creak of floorboards, the dust motes swirling in each sliver of light that seeped between the drawn curtains. The deeper he explored, the more a dismal sense of emptiness pervaded the house. All those big, abandoned rooms, devoid of any sign of life, were weirdly unsettling. Even the dog seemed wary. As they made their way through the big kitchen, she trotted so close beside him, her flank kept brushing his leg. "Good girl," he told her, bending to scratch behind her ear. "You're being very brave." His voice, as he spoke, was swallowed up in the house's disquieting hush.

The dog shadowed him closely through a formal dining room. A sheeted table offered seating for ten beneath a cobwebbed chandelier. Keegan inscribed a line in the buffet table's dust veneer with one finger as he passed. Next, he found himself back in the front entryway, though it was darker now. The door he'd left open had blown shut. He hadn't heard it slam.

Keegan started up the stairs, and Nora scurried behind him, her claws clacking up the oakwood runners. At the top of the staircase, he looked down the dark second-floor hallway. The bedroom doors stood open, offering dim patches of what little light came in through the dormer windows. When he started down the passageway, the dog stayed put at the top of the stairs. He went to the first open doorway and looked back at her. She didn't sit. She just stood watching him, head lowered. It was clear she wasn't about to follow.

"Nothing down here to worry about," Keegan told her. "I don't see a single elevator." He slapped his thigh as an invitation to come to him.

The dog barked twice, then sat down and whined. She wouldn't budge from the spot.

Keegan went into the first empty bedroom and saw only the bare essentials—a stripped mattress on a box spring, what looked like a dresser and chair beneath more white sheeting. It might have been a six-dollar motel room in the off season. Again, the walls were bare.

What was Ida Fletcher's worry? There was nothing in this house worth stealing, as far as Keegan could see, and any squatter would have to get past Vogel out there at the gatehouse with his starched shirt and clipboard. This was a fool's errand, and Keegan was being immensely overpaid to play the part of the fool. He didn't like it.

The other bedrooms looked much like the first but with small variations—an empty bookshelf, a gaping steamer trunk, a bare music stand. The biggest bedroom, at the hall's farthest end, had the most impressive view of the bay and a fireplace between the two big windows. It also seemed to be the room most recently used. A few dresses hung limply from the wardrobe's wooden hangers. A desiccated philodendron sat, withered and brittle, in a pot on the window's sill. Two books lay abandoned on the bedside table, topped with a dusty pair of half-rimmed reading glasses. He wondered who the glasses belonged to and whether they were needed—but then a woman as rich as Ida Fletcher might have prescription spectacles enough for every bedside and corner table in every house she owned.

When he came back out to the hallway, Nora was still waiting for him at the far end. He stopped halfway and smiled at her. He slapped his thigh and called her name, but she wouldn't budge. "Come on, girl," he said cheerily. "There's nothing to be frightened of." The dog squirmed in place and barked once sharply, but she wouldn't come to him. He could hear Mrs. Dodd's voice in his head: *They can see ghosts, you know.*

When he reached the landing, Nora turned and scrambled ahead of him, elated to be going back down the stairs. He caught up with her in the foyer, where she was sniffing the crack under the front door and pawing at the baseboard.

"All right, all right," he said. "We're done. We can leave." She slipped out through the door as soon as he'd pulled it wide enough and darted down the porch steps to the lawn. She waited there for him while he sorted through the keys again and then turned the deadbolt behind them.

He left the dog to sniff around the untrimmed lawn and went around to the back of the big house to where the lawn sloped down to a small, sandy cove and a private dock. A sailboat was moored at the dock's far end. It was bare-masted, the sail wrapped in a blue sun cover along the boom.

The dog trotted around the side of the house, following his scent. Keegan called to her and then started along the dock. The decking swayed and shifted beneath his feet, undulating gently on the bay's protected waters. Breeze off the distant ocean pressed Keegan's trousers against his thighs. The boat's christened name was scrolled on the transom in gold paint: *The Seven of Swords*. Keegan paced the dock alongside the craft to get an idea of its size. It must have been more than thirty feet from stem to stern, with teakwood decks and three oval portholes on either side of the cabin. A pair of white rubber fenders, pressed between the hull and the dock, squeaked as the boat rose and fell. The yacht wasn't ostentatious as far as the vessels anchored in Newport went, but it wasn't modest either.

The dog had followed him out as far as the first piling and then she'd stopped and plopped down on the dock to watch him.

When he turned back, the dog ran ahead of him to the lawn and waited for him there. She didn't seem to be enjoying this outing as much as Keegan had thought she would. She seemed skittish to find herself in such an open and unfamiliar place. She was a cottage dog, an office dog, a dog who liked urban parks; here there was too much sky and wind.

She jumped into the car as soon as Keegan opened the door and then scrambled across to her passenger seat, happy to be leaving. Keegan got in and pulled the door closed. He would drop her off at the office with Mrs. Dodd before he headed to Ida Fletcher's house in Bel Air. The poor thing had had adventures enough for one day.

CHAPTER FIVE

THE BEL AIR house also lay beyond an imposing gate. Keegan pulled as far onto the shoulder of Monticello Drive as he could, to get clear of the road. He put his car in neutral, set the brake, and left it idling. He took the ring of keys up to the gate. He found the padlock open, though, which surprised him. It was hanging by its U-shaped shackle. The hasp, too, was unlatched. Ida Fletcher would not be pleased. Any old conspirator passing by on the street could have swung the gate open and slipped inside to plot her downfall. Keegan pushed open the gate, got back in his idling car, and pulled it through.

The house at the end of the cobblestone driveway was broad and imposing, much more the prototypical mansion than the Newport house had been. It was Greek revival, Keegan guessed, all flat surfaces and Doric columns, symmetrical rows of rectilinear windows gazing blankly down on a sloping lawn and a row of evenly spaced cypress trees. A red Jaguar was parked at the foot of the house's broad front steps. Keegan pulled in close to its back bumper and parked.

He got out of his MG and looked in the other car's side window. A man's blue blazer was draped over the passenger seat and a poorly folded map lay scrunched between the windshield and dashboard. There had been quite a few car registrations in the old lady's strongbox—including a Jaguar, Keegan seemed to remember. It probably belonged to her, but what was it doing here? Had she actually ventured out of the Chateau Marmont?

Keegan climbed the front steps to the mansion's paneled doorway. He had the key—it was somewhere on the ring he held—but he rang the doorbell. He stepped back and listened, then stepped up and rang it again. Footsteps approached on the other side, and the deadbolt scraped back. One of the big doors swung back.

A young man—maybe thirty—stood in the opening, a cigarette dangling from his lips. He was handsome—matinee-idol handsome—with fine dark features and a rakish tilt to the head. The clothes he wore—a blue silk shirt and twill slacks—looked expensive but slept in. His shaggy dark brown hair was rakishly unkempt. Perhaps Keegan had wakened him. More likely the tousled look was a carefully arranged effect. He seemed to have a good sense of his own good looks.

"And who might you be?" the young man wanted to know. He spoke in a pleasing baritone, the cigarette bobbing in his lips.

"I might be Jim Keegan," Keegan said. "Am I at the right address? I didn't expect anyone to be home."

The young man stood back and swung the doors wider, as if to invite Keegan in. "I just got in yesterday," he said. "Where *is* everybody?"

Keegan made no move to enter the house. None of this made sense to him. "Is this Ida Fletcher's house?" he asked.

The young man nodded, as if the answer couldn't be more obvious. "Twelve Monticello," he said. "My key still fits the lock. But where the hell did everybody go?"

Keegan still stood, bewildered. "I'm sorry," he said. "But who are you?"

The young man nodded like he'd forgotten his manners. He tugged down his shirt front and stood straighter.

"I'm Danny," the young man said. "Daniel David

Church." He clicked his heels and bowed. "The Prodigal Nephew has returned from distant lands to the bosom of his household." He turned and swept out an arm to take in the whole house behind him. "Though, as I've mentioned, said household is nowhere to be seen." He turned back and held out a hand to Keegan with a formality that seemed both ceremonious and mocking.

Keegan nodded. It was sinking in. This kid was the old lady's nephew, the heir in Ida Fletcher's will. But wasn't he supposed to be living in Paris? Keegan shook Church's hand. The grip was firm, but the skin was soft. This Daniel David Church struck Keegan as a young man in good health who had gone out of his way to avoid anything that might be classified as work.

"I take it no one was expecting me," Church went on. "I had to take a taxi from LAX. Aunt Ida must not be opening her mail. But *mea culpa*. I have, perhaps, not written to the old dear as often as I should." He took the cigarette from his mouth and turned from the door. "Where *is* my sainted auntie, by the way?" Now that he was facing into the house, his voice had taken on an echo.

Keegan stepped into the broad marble entryway and took a quick look around at the sweeping double staircase, the lofty molding, the grand chandelier that dangled over the expanse of pearly tile. Keegan had to admit the place made a dramatic first impression. He looked at the young man, who was walking away from him across the entryway, apparently expecting Keegan to follow. Someday all this would be his. What was it like to know you would be so rich? Nothing would be beyond the kid's grasp with Ida Fletcher's kind of money—cars, starlets, tropical vacations, maybe even a ticket to a World Series game.

Keegan closed the front door and followed Church through an arch and down a vaulted corridor.

"I've never seen the place so empty," the nephew said, his voice reverberating in the tiled hallway. "Did she have one of her little spells and fire everyone in sight?" He turned back to Keegan. "So, when should we expect her to be home?"

"We shouldn't," Keegan said, taking in the row of urns that lined the hallway niches. "She's staying elsewhere."

"*Newport!*" the young man said, turning away again and heading farther along the hallway. "I should have called there first, of course. This is fine sailing weather after all."

Keegan shook his head. "She's elsewhere, elsewhere," he said. He didn't like to admit it, but the house's opulence was a little distracting. "I'm not really at liberty to say."

The nephew entered a broad room that had an enormous claw-footed billiard table at its center. A vast fireplace—one Keegan could have stood in without ducking—took up most of one side of the room. On the farthest wall, tall windows ran floor to ceiling. A pair of French doors offered a glimpse of a formal, perfectly symmetrical back garden. A full bar—all brass and mahogany—was built into the corner, with a row of four stools.

"I don't think she knows you're here," Keegan said, still a little distracted. His voice echoed back at him.

"Well, then *she's* in for a pleasant surprise, is she not?" the nephew said. His bright, dapper voice seemed tailor-made for these cavernous rooms. Church went to the bar and stubbed out his cigarette in a big crystal ashtray. He sat down on one of the stools. "I've been in Paris for a bit. Haven't been home for…" He picked up a powder blue pack of Gauloises cigarettes from the bar, rattled one loose, and put it to his lips. "Heavens," he said, "it's been almost three years." He pulled a sleek silver lighter from his trouser pocket and lit the cigarette. "'I wasted time, and now doth time waste me,'" he quoted, releasing a cloud of smoke along with Shakespeare's borrowed sentiment.

As first impressions went, the kid struck Keegan as shallow and showy, all crown molding, crystal, and polished brass. He was a peacock, a popinjay. He spoke like he belonged in a Cole Porter song. That kind of glib manner might pass for charm, but only among the Bel Air and Newport crowd. Keegan had met his kind before. The kid had no doubt gone to all the first-rate schools and still come away with a third-rate education—The Bard's quotes notwithstanding. He was, Keegan suspected, what happened when a man's only real occupation in life was to bide his time, imbibing in the finer things, until the family fortune finally came his way.

"I really need to talk to Aunt Ida, you know," the kid said. "I've got a business opportunity. I think she'll be thrilled." He took the cigarette from his mouth and spread his hands out on either side of his beaming face—as if he were inviting Keegan to imagine something written in lights on a Broadway marquee. "A bit of old France on Sunset," he announced. "A traditional brasserie in the heart of Los Angeles." He dropped his arms and looked at Keegan expectantly. "You know," he said, "beef bourguignon, steak frites. We'll brew our own *bière de garde*. Someone will be crooning at a grand piano." He nodded, a distant look in his eye, like he was conjuring the whole thing up in his mind. "We'll call it Le Petit Jardin," he said. "A cozy, exclusive nightspot like no other."

"Sorry, but I've never been to France," Keegan said. "I'm just a local PI. Your aunt hired me to keep an eye on things." He reached into his jacket pocket, found one of his business cards, and handed it over.

The kid nodded, looking down at the card. "Well—*James*—could you tell me where I might find the old dear?" he said. "It's just that I need to have a word in her ear at the earliest opportunity."

Keegan had always been happy to answer to *Jimmy* or *Jim* or *Keegan*—even, in Mrs. Dodd's case, *boss*. Nobody called him *James*. The name sounded odd and blunt in his ears, and he didn't like it.

The nephew smoked and watched Keegan, and when Keegan didn't answer, he filled the silence: "Believe me, I understand your reticence," he said. "The old girl can be quite the autocrat—but I assure you, she'll want to see me."

Keegan wasn't sure what to do. Fletcher had made it clear that no one could know where she was staying—but this was her nephew, her heir apparent. Better, Keegan supposed, to play it by the book. "I'm sorry," he said, "I've got strict instructions."

The nephew nodded. He mulled a moment and then seemed to settle on a more conciliatory tack. He glanced down at the card again, as if he'd already forgotten Keegan's name. "Well, *James*, I completely understand," he said. "I suppose it wouldn't be against the rules for you to convey a message, would it?"

Keegan nodded. "I suppose it wouldn't," he allowed. "And what's the message?"

Church reached over and tapped ash into the crystal ashtray. "That her beloved nephew has returned from afar and is eager to embrace her to his bosom," he said. He took a pensive draw on his cigarette and blew the smoke out again. "Or words to that effect," he said.

Keegan nodded. "I'm sure she'll be glad—"

He was cut off when the nephew stood suddenly and walked over to the fireplace, eyes fixed on the blank space above the mantel. "She took down the family portrait," he said. "It's been there since time immemorial." He seemed shocked, even a little distressed.

"Portrait?" Keegan said.

The nephew gestured up at the big blank space. "Uncle Leo, Aunt Ida, and me," he said. "Greta Kempton painted it the year before my uncle died. I was just a pup." He turned back to Keegan. His brow was now creased with something like consternation. "You don't suppose I've fallen out of favor, do you?"

Keegan made a helpless gesture. "Look, I'll see your aunt tomorrow morning," he said. "I'll let her know you're home."

The answer didn't seem to appease Church much. "Are you an educated man, James?" he asked.

Keegan had, in fact, graduated with a degree in literature from USC. That education had been useful when he was a crime reporter for *The Times*—but now, as a private detective, he'd learned it was a fact best kept to himself. "Not so anyone would notice," he said.

Church nodded. "Well," he said, "if you were to make an educated guess, what do you think my current status is with her?" He glanced again at the bare wall above the fireplace. "I might be guilty of having let the alliance lapse a bit. And my aunt—well—she's been known to turn on people."

Here was a man accustomed to greased wheels, Keegan thought—shortcuts to every destination, bailouts from every predicament. How drastically his life would change if Ida Fletcher ever turned against him. Keegan chose his words carefully. "I'm sure she'll be pleased to know you're home safe," he said. "All I can do is pass along your message."

When Keegan got back to the office, it was late in the afternoon, and Mrs. Dodd was pretty much packed up and ready to leave for the day. It was a slow Friday after all.

When he came in, Nora, who had been sleeping under Mrs. Dodd's desk, got up and stretched and went to stand by the hat rack, where her leash was hanging. She seemed to be ready to call it a day too. Keegan didn't even bother to take off his jacket.

"I just met the heir apparent," Keegan said.

"The old lady's nephew?" Mrs. Dodd said. She got her purse out of the file drawer in her desk. "What did you think?"

"I'm not crazy about him," Keegan said. "He seems a little oily. A schemer. I wouldn't trust him."

"Well, you don't really have to," Mrs. Dodd said reasonably. "He's Ida Fletcher's headache, not ours." She took her coat from the rack and pulled it on.

Keegan nodded and took the leash off the rack. The dog wagged her tail and then sat, waiting.

"Wait a minute, boss," Mrs. Dodd said. "Before we call it a day, I got a little something for you." She went back to her desk, picked up a white envelope waiting there, and held it out to him.

Keegan took it from her, apprehensively. "What's this?"

"Relax," she told him. "It won't bite."

The envelope was unsealed but it felt empty. He lifted the flap and found a ticket inside. He pulled it out and looked it over.

"It's a good seat," Mrs. Dodd said. "Pretty close to the action. It's for tomorrow night."

Keegan worked his lips as he tried to comprehend what, exactly, he was holding in his hand: a yellow-and-green ticket to Game Three of the World Series, right here in LA at Dodger Stadium. "Where did you get this?" he said. "How—?"

"Don't worry about it," Mrs. Dodd said, pulling the strap of her purse over her shoulder. "Just go. Get out of the house for once. Have a good time."

Keegan was genuinely moved. He'd been dogged all day with the disappointment he'd felt since he'd left Lusk's newsstand. And here it was in his hand, the thing he'd given up hope of ever seeing. "This is too much."

Mrs. Dodd had never been one for big shows of emotion. She shook her head at him and turned away, like he was being impossibly sentimental. "Just go to the damn game," she told him as she headed out the door, "and for God's sake keep an open mind." She pulled the door shut behind her.

She was gone before it occurred to Keegan to ask her what the hell she meant by that last phrase.

EARLY THE NEXT morning, when Keegan pulled open the Chateau Marmont's lobby door and stepped inside, he saw the same concierge was on duty at the front desk. Apparently, the man worked weekends.

Keegan sighed. He'd been having a good day so far. Hell, he had tickets for a World Series game that afternoon; he was practically elated. There was no reason to let some over-starched lackey bring him down. He fixed a smile on his face and let the door swing shut behind him.

The concierge saw Keegan approach and gripped the desk's edges. He wore the same white jacket as last time, and he had another bow tie cinched high under his chin. The tie was lavender this time.

"I'm here to see Ida Fletcher," Keegan said. "Again."

The concierge looked Keegan over, pretending not to recognize him. "I'm afraid we have no guests by that name," he said. "There's a payphone out on the street if there's a direct number you'd like to call."

Not today. Not with Keegan's good mood. Not with Game Three on the horizon. "Well, here's the thing," Keegan told him. "I don't have time for the runaround. I was here last week, and you know it. The old lady is waiting to see me. Get on the phone and let her know I'm here."

The concierge stared at Keegan, and Keegan stared serenely back at him. It was good to see the man rattled.

"Do you perhaps have a business card?" the man finally asked.

Keegan fished one out of the inner pocket of his jacket and handed it across the desk. The concierge pulled on a pair of reading glasses and squinted down at it. He made a face. "'A private investigator'," he said aloud, with great distaste.

In a place like the Chateau Marmont—a hotel famous for misbehavior and secret trysts—a PI was as malapropos as a Baptist at a brothel. Still, Keegan wasn't about to let it get to him. He smiled at the concierge. "The old lady hired me," Keegan said. "She's expecting me." He leaned a little forward and dropped his voice. "And believe me, buddy, I have zero interest in the seedy goings on in your little flophouse." He leaned back and smiled. "Just do us both a favor and get on the phone."

The man gave his head a wearisome little shake. His disdain was palpable. Still, he turned his back and picked up the house phone on the stand behind him. "Please take a seat," he said, without deigning to glance in Keegan's direction.

Keegan went over and sat on an uncomfortable wooden bench against the room's far wall. He leaned back and kicked his heels out, feeling a little smug. He'd report to the old lady, and the rest of this Saturday would be his own. Don Drysdale was on the mound tonight, and the radio weather report said it would be a perfect seventy degrees at Chavez Ravine when he threw the first pitch. The Dodgers had won the first two games, and Keegan could smell a sweep in the making. Life was sometimes good.

It couldn't have been more than two minutes later when Frank the Boxer strode up outside the French door. He opened the door, leaned in, and waved Keegan over, all smiles. Keegan stood and glanced at the concierge, who immediately busied himself with highly important tasks behind his front desk. Keegan smiled and followed Frank out to the courtyard.

"You'll have to excuse Klaus," Frank told him, nodding back at the lobby's door. "He's supposed to keep the world at bay for everyone in here. It's more or less his job to be a complete ass."

"In that case, I commend him," Keegan allowed. "He's very good at what he does."

It was sunnier in the Chateau's garden courtyard today, and there were more voices in the air, perhaps because it was a Saturday morning. They passed the small oval swimming pool. A young woman sat on the edge with her legs dangling in the water while two young men splashed around her in the water. It looked like some kind of well-heeled mating ritual.

The girl wore a blue one-piece bathing suit with a ruffled plunging neckline and a pair of oversized sunglasses. She sat, leaning to one side with her calves crossed, as if she were posing for a magazine cover. Her glossy brunette hair was shoulder length and shaped in careful waves. Both her hair and her pristine bathing suit suggested that she planned to be seen by the pool, but she had no intention of actually going in. Keegan looked away and then glanced back at her. He knew her from somewhere.

This time, when they got to the bungalow's gate, Frank opened it for Keegan without hesitation. Keegan stepped through and paused outside the bungalow's front door, which stood ajar.

"Go on in," Frank told him brightly. "She knows you now. You're officially one of the gang."

Keegan nodded. He pushed open the door and stuck his head in the dark room. "Mrs. Fletcher?" he said.

"Mr. Keegan." The old lady's voice came from the darkness. "Do come in."

Keegan pushed the door wider and stepped into the dimly lit front room.

Ida Fletcher was sitting on the sofa today, facing the large console television. On the screen, George Raft was talking to an old man in a book-lined library. The old lady barely glanced at Keegan before she turned her attention back to the television.

Frank pushed the door shut behind them and took a seat on the sofa next to Fletcher, which left the armchair for Keegan. He went over and sat in it. It was too soft, and it smelled of hairspray.

Zinnia, the old lady's much younger companion, was in her same spot at the kitchen table, reading a paperback under the hanging lamp. It was a different book, Keegan noted—an Agatha Christie novel this time.

Keegan crossed his legs and cleared his throat, but Frank the Boxer shot him a wry smile and shook his head. He nodded at the television. Apparently, Keegan's report would have to wait until the next commercial break.

Keegan leaned back in the chair and looked around the shabbily furnished room. The chairs and lamps and tables were old and mismatched, though they looked like they had once been expensive. They might have been the offerings at a church-basement rummage sale in Beverly Hills. At the Chateau Marmont, elegance was clearly a secondary concern to privacy.

Again, Keegan thought he could detect the faint whiff of

69

marijuana in the air. He looked from Frank to Zinnia and back again. Cannabis didn't seem like the old lady's kind of vice—and he doubted she'd condone it in the other two. The smell had probably been lingering in the folds of the heavy drapes for weeks before the three of them checked in.

Keegan watched the old lady watch television. The screen lit her gaunt face with a jittery, blue-tinged energy. She might have been a beauty in her youth, Keegan thought—what with her pointed nose, those high cheekbones, and her widow's peak. It would have been her green eyes, though, that turned heads. They still held a calculating, youthful intelligence.

On the television screen, George Raft was riding through the night in a convertible with an actress Keegan couldn't name, and then a Kool-Aid commercial came on the screen, and Ida Fletcher turned her attention to Keegan.

"And what do you have to report, Mr. Keegan?" she said.

Beside her, Frank the Boxer gave Keegan a nod of encouragement. This was his cue. He was on. He just needed to act naturally and never look at the camera.

"I made the rounds," Keegan told the old woman. "The Newport house is fine—locked up tight. It turns out your nephew is staying at the Bel Air place, though. He says he just got into town."

The sly smile faded from Frank's face. Behind him, Zinnia set her paperback down on the kitchen table without bothering to mark her place.

Keegan felt an invisible shift in the dimly lit room, a small tectonic tremor that set everything on edge.

A Slinky jingle started up on the television. It seemed much too loud in the room's sudden silence.

Something had happened, and Keegan had no notion of what it might be. He looked from Frank to the old lady and back again.

"My nephew?" Ida Fletcher said. Her voice sounded thin.

"Danny Church," Keegan told her. "He said he was your nephew. He had keys to the place. So, I thought—"

Zinnia was staring down at the table now, her head tipped

into the oval of light from the overhead lamp. She seemed to be holding very still, listening.

"He seemed surprised to find the house empty," Keegan went on, filling the silence—not sure what to say and what to keep to himself. "He drove a red Jaguar."

"Yes," the old lady said. "That would be my nephew. I wasn't expecting him. I suppose he's just passing through on his way…?" She let the question trail off.

Keegan measured his words before he spoke. "He made it sound like he planned to stay in town a while," Keegan told her. "He wanted to talk to you about some business—"

"Did you tell him where I am?" the old woman asked, cutting him off.

Keegan shook his head. "Of course not," he said. "You said not to tell anyone. I agreed to tell you he wanted to see you, though. I said I'd pass the message on."

Frank leaned forward on the sofa. He glanced from Fletcher to Zinnia and back again, as if hoping for a signal. "The thing is," he said, "the kid's caused a bit of trouble in the past. Things have become a bit strained."

Keegan nodded. The news came as no surprise. Danny Church had struck him as trouble from the get-go. "He told me he wants to open some kind of restaurant here in town," he told Fletcher, guessing it was probably best to get everything out in the open. "He's going to ask you to invest in the venture."

The George Raft movie came back on the television, but Ida Fletcher didn't seem to notice. She bit her lower lip and stared down at the oval rug on the floor between them. Zinnia turned now and watched the other two from the kitchen table.

"Look," Keegan said, "if I did something wrong, I'm happy to go back there and—"

"You did nothing wrong, Mr. Keegan," the old woman told him, still looking down at the rug. "The problem lies entirely with my nephew." She raised her eyes to Keegan. "I'm sorry to put you in the middle of a little family squabble."

She looked at Frank the Boxer then, appealingly, as if he

might offer help—but none seemed forthcoming, so she turned her attention back to Keegan. "Give me a few days to mull the situation over," she told him. She gathered herself straighter, and her old imperious manner seemed to reemerge. "Until then, please stay away from my nephew, Mr. Keegan," she said. "I urge you to have nothing to do with him. Is that understood?"

"Crystal clear," Keegan told her.

She turned her face to the television then, though she didn't seem to be actually watching it. It was another of her signals. Keegan was being dismissed.

Frank cleared his throat. He stood and crossed to the door. He opened it and sunlight flooded in from the little garden.

Keegan rose to his feet. "Well, it was good to see you again, Mrs. Fletcher," he lied. "I'll await your instructions."

The old woman gave no answer, just stared blankly at the television—though the vacant expression on her face hinted that her thoughts were far away from George Raft and the actress Keegan couldn't name.

Keegan stepped past Frank and out into the bungalow's little walled-in garden. The door closed behind him. He'd been expecting Frank to walk him back to the lobby, and he stood flat-footed a few seconds among the ferns and the hanging baskets of lavender, before he opened the gate and headed out into the hotel's courtyard. It was not the meeting he'd expected, but he had a baseball game to go to. He wasn't going to let the old woman and her ne'er-do-well nephew ruin his mood. He headed back towards the lobby.

As Keegan passed, the young woman still sat posing on the pool's edge. The two boys now sat on either side of her with towels draped over their tanned shoulders. Their damp hair was tousled. Keegan watched them as he walked. It was impossible not to. They were just too perfect, all of them. Even the lighting seemed designed for their moment. The girl laughed suddenly at something one of the boys said, and even the sound of her voice rang familiar. She threw back her head in a way that looked practiced, camera savvy.

Keegan was almost to the lobby door when he heard his name called. He turned to find Frank the Boxer chasing him down. Keegan stayed by the French door and let Frank come to him.

"Sorry about all that," Frank said, grinning sheepishly. He was a little out of breath. "It's the nephew. He's always stirring up trouble. Always wanting things. We weren't expecting to see him, that's all."

Keegan nodded.

"The truth of it is," Frank said, "Mrs. Fletcher? Well, she's very impressed with your work so far. In fact—" Rather than finish the sentence he pressed an envelope into Keegan's hands. "Think of this as a bonus," the boxer said. "Just keep the kid at bay a while until you hear from her."

Keegan looked down at the envelope in his hand. It felt as thick as the first one, maybe even a little thicker. The first pile of cash might have passed as a legitimate retainer from a woman too rich to know the value of a dollar. This envelope felt like a bribe.

Frank seemed to sense Keegan's reluctance and backed away a step or two, hands held up in a pantomime of innocence. "Just take it," he said. "She wants you to have it. It's nothing. Really."

Keegan nodded. Sure. Okay. Fine. He had a baseball game to get to. He turned and opened the lobby door.

He passed through the lobby and was back out on the street, digging for the car keys in his pocket, when the realization finally hit him: the girl he'd seen at the pool was Natalie Wood. The idea caught him up short. He'd had a movie-star sighting. Mrs. Dodd would be thrilled.

HE HADN'T PLANNED on going to the office—it was a Saturday, after all—but the second envelope of cash made him wary. He didn't like having that kind of money lying around the house. Best to lock it up in the office safe.

Up on the sixth floor, he slipped the money out of the

envelope and bent counting it out on Mrs. Dodd's desk. It was in different denominations this time, and the bills were facing every which way. There were a good number of fives and tens slipped in among the hundreds. It was like someone had swept together a stash of money in a hurry. He could picture it happening back in the bungalow while he was passing by Natalie Wood and her two young admirers out by the courtyard pool. He could imagine Frank the Boxer stuffing all the cash in the envelope and running after him to hand it off. But why? Keegan hadn't done anything to earn it. The old lady didn't owe him a thing.

Keegan looked down at the stacks of bills. The total was $3,455 this time. Another small fortune for doing nothing. He sighed, feeling even more uneasy with the situation than he had before. He jotted the total on the outside of the envelope with one of Mrs. Dodd's ballpoints and stuffed the money back inside. He was just straightening up when the phone on Mrs. Dodd's desk rang.

Who would be calling the office on a Saturday? He picked up the phone.

"James?" the voice on the other end said. "Is this James?"

Keegan sighed. He recognized the chipper voice, the oily, polished tones. It was old lady's nephew. Of all the people to call him today. Holding the phone to his ear, he went around the desk and sat down in Mrs. Dodd's chair.

Ida Fletcher's orders had been clear: *Have nothing to do with him.* But it was Keegan's own fault. He shouldn't have given the kid his business card.

"Look, Mr. Church," Keegan said into the phone, "I can't really—"

"Oh, *please*, James," the voice interrupted. "Call me Danny. I like to think we're friends."

The very idea made Keegan wince. "*Danny*," he said, not liking the taste of the word as he spoke it, "I can't really talk to you right now. I've got—"

"But you spoke to my auntie, right?" the nephew plowed

on. "You said you'd be seeing the old dear this morning. How did she seem? Did she say anything about me?" The kid's words cascaded out in a worried rush. Keegan thought of the empty spot above the Bel Air mansion's fireplace where the family portrait had once hung. *You don't suppose I've fallen out of favor, do you?*

"I don't want to be rude," Keegan said. "But I have strict—"

"I called the Newport house, but nobody picked up," Church pushed on, his voice insistent. "Maybe she's got a new number. Have you seen the beach house, James? It's like something on the Cape."

Keegan rubbed his temples with his free hand. He could feel a headache coming on. "Yeah, I was just there—"

"So that's where she's hiding!" the kid crowed. "I'll head over in the morning. You have never steered me wrong, James. You've been a good soldier."

"No, Danny, she won't be there—"

"She's going somewhere else?" the kid said. "Well, where else is there, James? Where could she be headed?" There was a thudding on the line, like he was tapping the mouthpiece with a finger while he thought. "So, not Bel Air and not Newport," the nephew prattled on. "I'm a bit at sea, here, James. Where else *is* there?" The kid seemed to think they were playing some sort of telegraph game. *Warm. Warmer. Hot.* If he guessed enough places, Keegan would eventually give away the answer.

"There isn't anything I can do for you," Keegan told him. "I'm not going to tell you where she'll be."

"I'm not sure what you're getting at," the nephew went on, ignoring the actual, literal meaning of Keegan's words.

"That's because I'm not getting at anything, I'm—"

"*Avalon!*" Church burst out, triumphantly. His voice was so loud, Keegan held the phone away from his ear. It was as if he'd come up with the right quiz-show answer, just as the buzzer was about to sound. "Of course!" he prattled on.

"She's heading out to Catalina! I don't suppose you could give me the number out there. I'm sure I've got it written down somewhere, but if she changed the Newport number, maybe the one on Avalon is—"

"Danny, I never said anything about—"

"Right!" Church said, in a tone that was the verbal equivalent of a wink and a nod. "Of course you didn't. Your lips were sealed. I didn't hear it from you, James. Hell, I bet I've still got a key to the place somewhere."

Keegan shook his head. It was all too much. The kid was impossible, so glib and clueless, so infuriatingly self-assured—and now he seemed to think he'd won Keegan over as an ally. But fine. Keegan hadn't told him a thing. The kid could call out to Catalina Island all he wanted, and Keegan would be in the clear.

"Okay," Keegan said. "I guess we're done here."

"Yes, thank you, James," the nephew was saying. "I owe you. Good talking to you, old boy. It's been—"

Keegan hung up the phone before the kid could finish.

THE AFTERNOON TRAFFIC was a nightmare, but that was no surprise—not with fifty-six thousand fans converging on Dodger Stadium from all over Southern California. It took Keegan almost an hour just to get from the freeway to Chavez Ravine, and, once he was there, a good twenty minutes of idling in a smoggy line just to get to a parking space.

But it was all right. He'd expected as much, and he'd allotted himself ample time to get there. He was determined to enjoy himself, the old lady and her nephew notwithstanding. He'd listened to the pregame show on the car radio on the drive over, so he was primed and ready for the game. He locked his car and joined the stream of people creeping along the walkway to the stadium's front gate.

The ticket Mrs. Dodd had given him turned out to be surprisingly good: Box B, Seat 1. It was close to the field, a seat right there on the aisle, with a perfect view of the first baseline. He checked the number on the empty seat's arm against his ticket stub, just to make sure his good fortune was real. It was. He couldn't help but grin. He paused in the sunlit aisle to take off his jacket and drape it over the seatback.

The woman in the seat next to his watched him, smiling. She wore a wide-brimmed straw sun hat and oval sunglasses. Her blouse was Dodger blue.

Keegan gave her a polite nod and took his seat. He looked down at the sunny field, the crisscrossed emerald lawn, the brick-red baselines. The view was perfect—about fifteen rows above the visitors' dugout, almost even with the pitching mound. He could practically call the balls and strikes from where he sat. How had Mrs. Dodd managed it?

The woman next to him leaned in his direction, still facing the field. "You must be Jim," she said.

Keegan turned and stared at her, and, after a second or two, she turned her head to look back at him. She was in her forties, Keegan guessed. A pretty brunette, with bright hazel eyes and a smile that was just a tad crooked. It made her look sly and knowing. She raised her eyebrows.

"Sorry?" Keegan said. "What was that?"

The smile on the woman's face froze and then faltered. She pulled her sunglasses down a little so she could look at him over them. "Jim *Keegan*?" she said. "That's who I'm supposed to be meeting." She looked down at the seat number on the armrest. "Oh God, am I in the wrong seat?"

Keegan stared at her while the truth began to sink in. Mrs. Dodd's obsession about his social life and her sudden generosity. *Just go to the damn game and keep an open mind.* It all made perfect sense now. Damn that meddling woman. A better detective would have seen this coming.

Keegan smiled back at the woman and shook his head. "No," he said, "I'm pretty sure you're in the right seat. And, yes, my name is Jim Keegan."

The woman blushed deeply. "Oh no," she said, flustered.

"Oh God no. You've been blindsided, haven't you?" She covered her mouth with one hand. "This is absolutely mortifying," she said. "I'm going to kill her."

Keegan grinned. "If we're talking about Mrs. Dodd and you need an accomplice," he said, "I'm your man. So, how do you know her?"

"Next-door neighbor," the woman said. "Look, I'm sorry. I thought you knew this was happening. She told me *you* paid for the tickets."

Keegan laughed aloud. He pictured Mrs. Dodd tucking the folded hundred-dollar bill into the pocket of her blouse. *I don't want you to say you didn't see this.* He shook his head again. How had he missed all the signs?

"Yeah," Keegan allowed. "I suppose I did pay for them."

The woman seemed so ruffled, so embarrassed; he couldn't help but feel bad on her behalf. He offered her a consoling smile. "I'm sorry about the set-up," he told the woman. "The two of us have been bamboozled. That Mrs. Dodd can be a real…" He wasn't sure how to finish the sentence—there were too many options—so he just stopped talking.

"'Meddler'? 'Busybody'? 'Yenta'?" the woman offered. She gave a little shrug. "'Pain in the butt', maybe?"

"I see you know her well," Keegan said. "And I see you have an impressive vocabulary."

The woman let her shoulders sag. She seemed a little more at ease. "I'm an English teacher," she said. "And an avid reader."

"I studied English in college," Keegan said.

"Yes," she said. "Mrs. Dodd informed me of that fact. You went to USC. She told me all about you, Jim Keegan."

Keegan nodded. "She didn't tell you my GPA, did she?" he said. "Because it wasn't impressive."

"That's one of the few things your dossier didn't cover," the woman said. She held her hand out over the armrest for him to shake. "Since you're the one being blindsided, I'm guessing she didn't tell you a thing about me," she said. "My name's Helen. Helen Stark."

Keegan shook her hand. "Helen Stark the English teacher," he said. "I'm really sorry about the set-up."

The woman settled back in her chair and looked down at the field. She seemed to have reclaimed most of her composure. "No complaints here," she said. "I'm at the World Series, Drysdale's pitching, and we're already up two games to zip." She pushed the sunglasses back up to the bridge of her nose. "You and I could end up mortal enemies, and I'll still chalk this up as a win."

Keegan liked her droll humor and the glimpses she gave him of that crooked smile. Maybe Mrs. Dodd knew what she was doing. "You like baseball?" he asked.

"Love it," Helen said. "I grew up listening to Red Barber with my dad. The old man was a huge Brooklyn fan. If only he'd lived to see them move out here. He'd be thrilled to know I'm here."

"I'm a recent addition to the bandwagon," Keegan admitted. "I wasn't a huge Brooklyn fan, but it's good to have a team in LA."

For a minute or two, they both looked down at the field not speaking. Someone a few rows ahead of them turned on a transistor radio, and Vin Scully's voice took up his companionable game-day chatter. "...a bea-u-tiful October day in Chavez Ravine for baseball..."

"I hope Mrs. Dodd didn't talk me up too much," Keegan said. "What else did she tell you?"

Helen turned to face him. "Well, she told me you were her boss," she said. "You used to write for *The Times*. Now you're some kind of detective."

"Did she tell you I was a grumpy old recluse?" he asked. "She thinks I need to get out more."

"She *did* mention that."

"*Really*?" Keegan said. He'd been mostly joking. "She said I was a grumpy recluse?"

Helen smiled and looked back at the field. "'Curmudgeonly' was the word she used," she said, "but we both know what that means." She folded her arms. "She just wanted me to know what I was getting into."

"And?"

"I'm here, aren't I?"

Organ music came on over the loudspeakers, and everyone stood for the national anthem. When it was done, and everyone sat back down, Helen folded her hands in her lap.

"So," Keegan said, trying to get the conversation going again, "in a fair world, what would Mrs. Dodd have told me about you?"

"Let's see," Helen said. "She'd have told you that I teach at an all boys' school in Westlake."

"Which one?"

"Saint Matthew's Academy."

"Wow," Keegan said. "Good school." Saint Matthew's was famously elite—all Latin mottoes and school ties and ivy vines trailing over quaint brick-front buildings. If you were the favored son of a movie mogul or a Hollywood star, you probably went to Saint Matthew's. Hell, Danny Church had probably squandered a year or two there, sneaking cigarettes behind the gym and managing not to learn a thing.

Helen nodded and shrugged at the same time. "It's a good school," she allowed. "But the students are all trust fund brats." She tipped her sunglasses down again and looked at Keegan over them. "Did you know that Saint Matthew was the patron saint of bankers?" she said. "That should tell you what we're up against. Still, we do with the little charmers what we can."

Keegan nodded. He liked this Helen Stark. He liked her poise, her droll intelligence. "What else would she have told me?"

"She would have told you I'm single." She looked out at the field then, perhaps a little embarrassed. "She'd *definitely* have told you that," she said.

Keegan laughed. A good portion of the anger he should be feeling for Mrs. Dodd had drained away now.

The players took the field. The crowd stood and clapped. Don Drysdale trudged out to the pitching mound in his gleaming white home uniform. His head was bent low in concentration. He stood on the mound and kicked the dirt around. He stretched out and threw a few warm-up pitches. The crowd noise died down, and, one by one, everyone took their seats again.

In a few minutes, Tony Kubek entered the batter's box, knocking dirt from his cleats with the bat. Game Three was underway.

DRYSDALE PITCHED THE full nine innings. Ron Fairly caught the last out, back against the bullpen's gate, to end the game. The Dodgers won with a single run scored. They could sweep the Series with another win tomorrow.

Keegan and Helen climbed the steps together and then joined the bigger river of people heading down the ramps to the exits. Helen held his arm to keep them from getting separated in all the jostling. Her hand felt small and warm through the fabric of his jacket.

Down in the parking lot, Keegan walked her to her car, stealing sidelong glances as they talked. It turned out she drove a red Plymouth Valiant, sturdy and understated, perfect for a teacher, Keegan thought. He jotted her phone number on the back of a receipt with a blue ballpoint pen she dug out of her glove box. They made a dinner date for next Friday, eight o'clock at Jackson's, a fancy place on Sunset Keegan had been wanting to try. He would have Mrs. Dodd make the reservations.

"I can come by your place at seven-thirty," he offered. "If you live next to Mrs. Dodd, it's on the way."

Helen looked at him evenly and then shook her head. "You know, I'd really prefer to find my own way there," she said. "How about I just meet you there at eight?"

CHAPTER SIX

ON SUNDAY MORNING, the kitchen phone rang, just as Keegan was at the counter, spooning ground coffee into the percolator. He glanced at his wrist—a reflex—but he'd left his Timex on the bedside table. It was much too early for a phone call, though. He knew that much. And it was Sunday, for God's sake. Who would be calling him at home at this ungodly hour? He glanced over the phone. There was no way Danny Church could have gotten hold of his unlisted number, was there?

He looked down at the coffee, spoon in his hand. He'd lost count of how many spoons he'd already added, dammit. He put the coffee spoon down on the counter, went to the phone, and picked it up. "Yes," he said into the receiver. "Hello?" His voice was brusque, he knew, but he didn't much care.

"Mr. Keegan," a woman's voice said. "Is this Mr. Keegan?" The woman, whoever she was, sounded distraught. Whatever this call was about, it was serious.

Keegan pulled out one of the chairs and sat down at the kitchen table. "Yeah," he said, "it's Jim Keegan. Who's calling?"

The dog, having heard his voice, trotted into the kitchen now and lay down under the table at his feet.

"It's Mildred Zinnia," the voice on the phone said. "You know, with—eh—with Ida Fletcher?"

Keegan covered the mouthpiece with his palm, so Zinnia wouldn't hear his sigh. He'd been out to report to the old lady just yesterday morning—a *Saturday*—and now the old lady was calling him in on a Sunday. Perhaps those who were rich enough to never work had no concept of what a weekend was. He uncovered the phone again.

"Yes, yes," Keegan said into the mouthpiece, making no attempt to mask the displeasure in his voice. "And what does Mrs. Fletcher need from me on this fine Sunday morning?"

"Well, that's just it," Zinnia said. "I'm not sure where Mrs. Fletcher is."

Nora was giving herself a vigorous scratch under the table now. He could hear the jingle of her collar.

"Are you at the hotel?" Keegan said. "She's not there with you?"

Zinnia seemed not to have heard his question. "I'm worried something's happened," she said. Keegan had never really heard the woman speak before, but her voice seemed genuinely distraught. "Something terrible," she added.

The dog stopped scratching and nudged Keegan's shin with her nose. He reached down between his knees and rubbed her head. "Okay," he said into the phone. "Let's slow down. Tell me exactly what happened."

"They were going to Catalina," Zinnia said. "Frank was sailing them over." When she said the man's name, her voice had a crack in it. "Mrs. Fletcher has a house out on the island—I don't know if she told you that. I've been calling there over and over. There's no answer. I'm worried that they never arrived."

Keegan thought of Danny Church and his game of *warm-warmer-hot*. The buzzer-beating answer he'd arrived at before Keegan could get off the phone: *She's heading out to Catalina!* If the old lady was sailing over there to get away from her nephew, Keegan had unwittingly led the kid straight to her.

"They should have docked last night," Zinnia was saying,

her voice rushed and urgent. "I keep calling the house, and no one picks up. I've already tried three times this morning."

Keegan could imagine the old lady fleeing to the island to elude her ne'er-do-well nephew, only to pick up the phone and find him on the other end. *I didn't hear it from you, James.* "Maybe there's another reason they're not picking up the phone," he said.

"I've just got a bad feeling about it," Zinnia said.

Keegan thought of the boat tied up at the Newport house's dock. *The Seven of Swords.* "Look," Keegan said, "it's too early to panic. It got pretty windy last night. Maybe they turned back. Maybe they didn't sail at all. They could have just spent the night down in Newport Beach."

"I tried there too," Zinnia said. "I called there twice. I'm just so worried. It isn't like them."

Keegan turned and looked at the window over the sink. From what he could see, it was a bright, clear day outside. "I tell you what," he said, "I'll drive down to Newport. I'll see if the boat is still tied up there. You keep trying the Catalina number. I'll call you from the beach house when I see what's up."

He hung up the phone, took a quick shower, and dressed. It was a reasonable plan, he thought. He could get down to Newport Beach and back before lunch in the light weekend traffic. He'd take the dog along with him. With any luck, he'd figure out what happened to Frank and the old lady and be back home in time to catch the Dodgers game on TV.

KEEGAN PULLED UP to the guard shack at the entrance to Waverly Lane before it was even ten o'clock. Vogel was on duty again, and, when Keegan rolled down the window, Nora scrambled across his lap to say hello to her old friend. He held Nora's collar to keep her from scrambling out the window.

'Return to Sender' was playing inside the guard shack on

a tinny transistor radio. Vogel turned down the volume and leaned out the window.

"Jim Keegan," Keegan said, though he was sure the guard remembered him—or at least remembered Nora. "And guest." He scratched the dog behind her ear.

The guard's face brightened. "Donovan's replacement," he said. "How's your Sunday going, sir?"

"Well, I think the Dodgers are going to sweep the Series tonight," he said, "so I'm not going to complain."

Vogel grinned. "Koufax got fifteen strikeouts in that first game," he said. "He's going to be invincible tonight if his arm's rested." He pushed a button somewhere inside his shack and the gate arm raised. "Head right on through, sir."

KEEGAN FOUND A long black Cadillac Fleetwood parked on the circular gravel drive, close to the big house's front door. He pulled up behind it and got out of his MG. The dog scrambled across the driver's seat and tried to hop out after him, but he blocked her way. "You wait in the car until I see if the coast is clear," he told her. He rolled down the window a few inches and closed the door with the dog inside.

He went over to the Cadillac and found the driver's side door locked. He bent and looked in through the window. The car was at least a decade old. It was the early fifties model, with the old side-by-side headlights—but the glossy leather interior was black and pristine, perfectly immaculate. It might have just rolled off the dealer's showroom floor. He tried to look in through the back windows, but they were tinted too dark to see, even when he cupped his hands against the smoky glass.

Back in his own car, Nora pressed her nose to the window crack and gave him a bark. "Sorry, girl," he called back to her. "I'll only be a minute." He climbed the front porch steps, fumbling with the ring of keys, and knocked on the door. He waited and knocked again before he unlocked the deadbolt.

He pushed the door open a crack. "Hello?" he called into the house. "Mrs. Fletcher? Frank? Anyone home?"

He slipped in and stood in the front hallway, looking up to the turn in the staircase and the upper landing. "Hello?" he called out. "Anyone here?"

There was no answer, no movement, just the same leaden silence as before. He tried the light switch on the wall beside the door, and the dangling entryway lamp lit up. She'd had the electricity turned back on. He looked around the dim entryway. Nothing had changed. The dust still lay even and undisturbed on the hallway table, though the phone there looked like it had been dusted off.

Everything in the front room was the same as when he saw it last, as well. The same with the dining room. He found a single emptied coffee mug in the kitchen sink and a filter full of damp grounds in the trash can—another small sign that someone had been here since he'd last visited. He opened the kitchen's back door and headed down the sloping lawn to the waterfront.

The tide was lower than when he'd been here last. There was a gentle slope of ribbed sand beyond the lawn now. The dock was empty, but he walked out along it anyway. The decking bobbed and shifted under his weight. At the far end, he stood shielding his eyes and looking out across the sheltered bay at the distant line of riprap that marked the edge of the breakwater. Beyond that was open ocean. Sunlight glittered off the water's choppy surface. The old lady and Frank the Boxer had cast off. That much seemed clear. Now he just had to figure out if they ever arrived on the island.

Keegan let the dog out of the car before he went back inside the house, that way she could run around the garden. He dialed Zinnia's number at the Chateau Marmont from the hallway telephone. He watched Nora through the open front doorway as she followed a trail of scent across the rangy lawn and disappeared out of sight. When Zinnia picked up, she seemed no less distressed than when he'd talked to her earlier. She told him there was no sign of Ida Fletcher anywhere.

"Well, there's a car parked here, and the boat is gone," Keegan said. "So they definitely headed over." He looked out the open front door, but Nora was nowhere in sight. All he could see was the long slope of lawn and the shaggy privacy hedge on the far end of the garden. His client had up and vanished on him. What was the next step?

He told Zinnia he'd head downtown to his office. He'd make some calls from there, see what he could find out from the Avalon Harbormaster. If there was any news, she could reach him at his office number for the next couple of hours.

It would still give him time to get home and watch Game Four on TV.

At the guard's shack, Vogel smiled and waved him out, but Keegan pulled to a stop and rolled the car's window down. Vogel lowered the radio's volume again and came to the window.

"Were you on duty yesterday when Mrs. Fletcher came in?" Keegan asked him. "You know the big Fleetwood."

"Yeah," Vogel told him. "I saw the car around three. The big Italian guy was driving."

"Yeah, good old Frank," Keegan said. "Did anyone come back out?"

"Not on my shift."

"Did you talk to the old lady when they came in?"

Vogel shook his head. "She's never much of a talker," he said. "But I got the impression the driver was on his own yesterday. The windows on that thing are tinted so dark, it's hard to tell, though. Maybe she was back there."

"What made you think Frank was alone?"

"Boss Radio," Vogel said, as if that should mean something to Keegan.

"Boss what?"

"*KHJ*," Vogel said. "The Italian guy had it on the car radio. Pretty loud, too." Vogel ducked back inside and cranked up the radio.

Louie Louie, oh baby, me gotta go.

"It's what I listen to in here," Vogel said, speaking louder now to be heard over the din of music. "It's top 40. He had it playing in the car. Wouldn't have thought it was the old lady's kinda thing."

Keegan thought of the Chateau Marmont bungalow and the smell of marijuana in the air. "The old lady might surprise you," Keegan told him. He reached past Nora into the glove compartment where he kept a box of his business cards. He pressed one on the car window's sill and jotted his home number on the back with a ballpoint pen. He fished a ten-dollar bill from his wallet and folded it around the business card. "Do me a favor," he said, passing it to Vogel. "Call me at these numbers if either of them turns up. Some people are getting worried about them."

Vogel pocketed the cash and looked down at the business card, nodding. "Sure thing, Mr. Keegan."

THE DOG SEEMED disappointed to get up to the sixth floor and find the office empty. Still, she slunk under Mrs. Dodd's desk and curled up on the old pillow she kept down. Keegan got Ida Fletcher's strongbox from the office safe and put it on his desk in the inner office. He'd need the details of Ida Fletcher's boat and the address of her house on Catalina. He unlocked the box and spread out the papers on his desk, under the fluorescent lights, making sure he knew where everything was.

He found the thick Los Angeles Central phone book in the stack of books on top of the file cabinets and dialed the Avalon Harbor. After that he tried the Coast Guard, then anyone else he could think of. He worked the phone for an hour to no avail.

He was a civilian, after all, and it was a Sunday. No one with any authority felt inclined to give him the time of day. There was only so much he could do on his own. He looked at his watch. It was an hour from game time.

There was only one real option left. He'd have to swallow his pride and call Lieutenant Moore to ask for a favor. He thought of the Lieutenant at the Ambassador Hotel, blocking his way into Donovan's send-off party. *We need to get past this*, he'd told Keegan. *Give me a call when you're ready. I'll buy you a beer.* A beer or a Sunday-afternoon favor. To Keegan they seemed roughly equivalent.

The Lieutenant's wife answered on the third ring, and Keegan waited, drumming his fingers on his desk, until Moore's voice came on the line.

"The elusive Jim Keegan," he said, making a big deal of it. "I didn't think you'd actually ever call." Keegan could hear birds singing in the background. He could imagine the man in his shirtsleeves on some sunny patio, stretched out on a chaise lounge with the *Sunday Times* crossword, feeling easy and guiltless.

"Don't get too excited," Keegan said. He found himself sliding into their old glib repartee without really intending to. "I'm only calling because I need a favor."

"Still, I'll take it," the Lieutenant said. He kept the tone bright and jovial, still pretending like nothing had happened— like a woman had never washed up on the beach with a bullet in her. "Not that I haven't done you enough favors over the years, Jimmy. What is it you need this time?"

Keegan gave the Lieutenant a quick rundown of the situation: Ida Fletcher and her bodyguard unaccounted for, the empty Newport house, the missing boat. "I called the Catalina harbormaster, but that was a no go," he said. "They won't tell me anything." He moved the phone from one ear to the other. "And someone needs to swing by the house over there to do a welfare check."

The Lieutenant sighed into the phone, like he was mulling the information over. "Yeah, the harbormaster is going to be pretty tight-lipped," he said. "A lot of celebrities tie up their sailboats there. Movie stars who don't want to be bothered."

"But the harbormaster will talk to *you*, right?" Keegan said. "Big shot with the LAPD."

"I appreciate your faith in me, Jimmy," the Lieutenant said, "but Catalina is LA County Sheriff's Department. I'm pretty much a civilian myself when it comes to those guys."

"Come on, Lou," Keegan wheedled. "Aren't you guys in blue all some big fraternity? Isn't there some deputy you know over there who owes you a favor?"

Moore sighed again. "You know it's a Sunday, right?" he said. "You know the World Series is on in about an hour?"

"I wouldn't be asking if it wasn't important," Keegan said. It was true. He would have happily gone the rest of his life without dialing this particular number, without burying this particular hatchet.

He heard a small groan on the other end of the line, like Moore was reluctantly getting to his feet. "What's the name of the old lady's boat?"

Keegan shuffled through the papers on his desktop until he found the boat's title. "*Seven of Swords*," he said.

"Like the tarot card?"

Tarot card? It had never occurred to Keegan to wonder what the name might mean. "If you say so," he said.

He could hear movement on the other end of the line, like the Lieutenant was headed back inside his house, carrying the phone.

"And where do you want the welfare check?" Moore asked.

Keegan found the deed for Ida Fletcher's Avalon house and read him the address: 13 Tradewinds Lane. It was settled. Moore would make some calls and get back to Keegan in a few hours.

"Call me at home, Lou," Keegan said, as a little dig, before he hung up the phone. "I'll be taking it easy, watching the game."

THE PHONE IN Keegan's kitchen rang a few minutes after the game's final out. It had been a sweep. LA beat New York 2–1, in a low-scoring pitcher's duel. The Dodgers won the Series in four straight games, and even all the way up here on the hill, Keegan could hear the commotion—bugles and car horns and firecrackers—down in the valley. He switched off the television set before he went into the kitchen to pick up the ringing phone.

"I don't have a whole lot of news for you, Jimmy," the Lieutenant told him.

According to the harbormaster, *The Seven of Swords* hadn't docked in Avalon. The captain of the Catalina Sheriff's station sent a deputy by the old lady's house on Tradewinds Lane. The front gate was chained shut, but the deputy climbed over and banged on the door. There was no answer. He checked with the house next door, and the couple living there said the house had been empty for months. If the old lady had arrived on Catalina, she'd done it pretty stealthily.

"I checked with the Coast Guard too," the Lieutenant went on. "No SOS calls or incident reports all day. Looks like you'll just have to wait and see."

"Thanks, Lou."

"Give me a call at the station tomorrow and touch base," the Lieutenant said. "Something might come in overnight."

IT MADE NO sense that Ida Fletcher and Frank the Boxer would have gone over to the Bel Air mansion—especially after the way they reacted when Keegan had told them Danny Church seemed to be staying there—but it was the only other place Keegan could think of where the old lady might have gone. It was a long shot, but he had to rule it out.

Sure, the old lady had made it clear that she didn't want Keegan to have anything to do with her nephew, but the situation had changed. The house on Monticello Drive belonged to her, and Keegan would have to rule it out as a possibility. If he ran into Danny Church there, it wouldn't really be his fault.

Keegan locked the dog in the house—it would be dark before he got back home—and headed down the hill. He took Santa Monica Boulevard through Beverly Hills. Down here, the World Series celebration seemed to be going on full tilt. At every bar, customers spilled out onto the sidewalks and into the street, all of them wearing blue. Just past the country club, a couple of drunken men reeled along the road's centerline, wrapped in an American flag. To them, all the blaring car horns around them were just part of the celebration. Keegan changed lanes to keep out of their way. The sun was barely setting, and bedlam already reigned. Tomorrow would be a hangover Monday in Los Angeles, a total write-off.

Keegan turned onto the long, dusky shadows of Beverly Glen and turned on his headlights. When he got to the address on Monticello Drive, he found the big front gate standing wide. He pulled through and paused at the foot of the drive, idling. The massive house was dark. The cobblestone driveway was empty. At least he wouldn't have to deal with the nephew.

Keegan pulled up the car to the foot of the front steps and parked. He climbed the broad front steps, key ring jingling in his hand. The lamps on the portico were dark and none of the front windows were lit. He knocked on the big front door anyway and pressed the doorbell a few times for good measure. There was no answer, no sound from inside. He fumbled with the ring of keys in the gathering darkness. He knew it was large and bronze-colored, but, with so little light, it was hard to make anything out. He was still searching for the right key when a pair of headlights turned off Monticello, going much too fast, and bounced up onto the long drive. The lights swept across the front of the house, sending shadows skittering across the entryway.

Keegan watched the red Jaguar career over the cobblestones, engine gunning. It lurched to a stop behind his MG. The driver's door opened, and Danny Church scrambled out like he was late for something. "James!" he shouted with game-show-host enthusiasm. He wore a black turtleneck under a tailored gray blazer. Again, the clothes looked expensive but rumpled. The outfit, the car, the foppish persona—it all struck Keegan as part of the Danny Church affectation, the charming scoundrel, the loveable cad.

"You're just the man I wanted to see!" the kid said, jogging up the front steps. "I've been trying to call old Aunt Ida out on Catalina like you suggested."

Keegan shook his head wearily. The last thing he needed was for the old lady, wherever she was, to hear that he'd been aiding and abetting her nephew. "Look, Danny, I didn't suggest any such thing," he said. "I never *said* she was on Catalina."

"Right! Right! Mum's the word!" The nephew made the lock-the-mouth-and-throw-away-the-key gesture, like he and Keegan were partners in crime.

Keegan gave him a pained shake of the head.

"No one picks up out there, though," the kid rattled on obliviously. "The phone just keeps ringing."

Church took Keegan's hand and wrung it, and Keegan felt a deep sense of misgiving. It was a mistake to come out here. Here he was, after all, face to face with the man he had promised his client he'd avoid. "Look, I just came to look the place over," Keegan said. "It's part of my job."

"Indeed, it is," Church said merrily. He stepped past Keegan, key already in hand, and unlocked the door. "Sorry I wasn't here to greet you," Church prattled on, pushing the door open. "I just stepped out for a bite of dinner." He reached inside the house and switched on the big lamps on either side of the door and the foyer lights inside. "The Bouzy Rouge," he said. "'A bit of Old France on Sunset'—except that it's nowhere near Sunset. It's right out there on Stone Canyon. Ever been?"

He felt a prick of suspicion. Something about Church naming the restaurant, telling Keegan where to find it, didn't sit right. It was never a good omen when someone volunteered more information than they had been asked for. In Keegan's long experience, there was no surer sign of a lie.

"I must have driven right past it on the way here," Keegan said. "Never been inside, though. I'm sure it's out of my price range."

Church stood to one side. He bowed and swept out his hand, inviting Keegan inside. "Come in, come in," he said. "Go about your business. We'll have a drink together when you're done."

Keegan stepped through to the white-tiled foyer with its high, glimmering chandelier.

"That place was my favorite growing up," Church continued as he closed the door behind them and twisted the deadbolt lock. "The restaurant, I mean. It was my go-to birthday destination. It might be the reason I moved to France in the first place."

Again, volunteering information no one had asked for—a bright red flag. The kid seemed intent on convincing Keegan about where he'd just been. But if he was lying about the restaurant, where *had* he been?

"You'll have to join me there some night," Church went on. "As an aspiring restaurateur myself, I'd love to hear what you think of the place."

Keegan nodded slowly. "Yeah," he said with no hint of enthusiasm. "We'll have to do that." It wasn't just Church's lie that bothered Keegan; the kid was acting strange in other ways. He seemed even more manic and scattered than the last time Keegan had talked to him. But his glibness felt forced now, contrived. It was a show put on for Keegan. Church was clearly hiding something.

Keegan looked around the formal entryway. It was lit up brightly, but the rest of the house was in shadows. He peered through the dark arches at the far end of the foyer and up the sweeping double staircase. The place felt like a dark, empty shell, a series of comfortless, cavernous rooms. He turned to squarely face the nephew and looked him in the eye. "I'm going to have to take a look around," he said firmly. "It's just part of what your aunt hired me to do."

Church nodded. He seemed eager to cooperate. "Very well, James," he said. He made an odd salute—all hand flourish and a click of the heels. In certain company, the gesture might have passed for droll and charming, but the affectation only heightened Keegan's sense of unease.

"I'm going upstairs," Keegan said, watching the kid for any reaction.

"And I shall retire to the billiard room," Church answered back. "*You* make your rounds, and *I* will make our drinks. What say we reconnoiter in…" He pulled back the sleeve of his blazer and glanced at his wristwatch, a Rolex. "What? Five minutes?" He turned and headed along the dark hallway, switching on lights as he made his way. "We can compare notes and plan our next steps," he called out without looking back. His voice echoed in the vaulted space.

Keegan turned to the big sweeping staircase. He had no idea what he might be looking for. There was no plan, just a sense that something here wasn't right. On the upper landing, he ran his hand along the wall, feeling for a light switch. He found it, and a row of wall-sconce lamps suddenly lit up a grand hallway with a dozen or so doors scattered along it on either side.

He made his way along the hall, ducking his head into each room in turn, flipping the wall switches to find broad, bare spaces with no signs of life. Sure, there were beds and dressers and nightstands, but the rooms felt forsaken. Just like the house in Newport, there was nothing personal here—no keepsakes, no fondly placed curios, no silver-framed photos on bedside tables. The rooms felt scrubbed of any clue as to who might have lived here.

Keegan easily found the room Church was squatting in by the smell of his cigarettes and the rumpled linens. The three open suitcases stood lined up against the wall along with a banded leather trunk. But even this room felt *occupied* rather than *lived in*.

Keegan thought of the nephew's dismay when he'd realized the old family portrait had been moved. *You don't suppose I've fallen out of favor?* Well, the painting wasn't in any of these rooms, but neither was anything else that was personal or idiosyncratic. Perhaps the whole world had fallen out of old Aunt Ida's favor.

When Keegan came back downstairs, he found the nephew smoking in the billiard room again. He was sitting on a barstool, one elbow on the marble bar top, staring into the middle distance. At first, he didn't seem to see Keegan standing in the doorway, but when Keegan cleared his throat, the other man roused himself, instantly, to his usual high spirits—as if a light switch had been flipped on.

"My late, lamented uncle was quite a connoisseur of the finer things," the kid said. It was as if he'd scripted the line during Keegan's absence. Two small crystal tumblers lay on the bar top now, brimful with whiskey. He picked up one of the glasses and held it out to Keegan. "Single malt. Speyside," he said. "Eighteen years. Only the best."

Keegan walked over and took the drink from him. The glass, whatever it was made of, felt surprisingly leaden in his hand. He raised it to his nose and sniffed. "Is it scotch?"

"Is it scotch!" the nephew said. "Moray by way of Glen Haggis. You can practically taste the tartan." He picked up his own glass and raised it to his lips, looking over it at Keegan, like he was waiting for him to do the same.

"Cheers," Keegan said and took a sip. It was smoky and mellow. He'd emptied a lot of whiskey bottles over the years, but he'd never tasted anything like this. It was warm caramel and seawater on the tongue. He looked around the room, glass in hand. A constellation of billiard balls dotted the pool table, with a cue angled across the green felt. A newspaper lay on the floor next to a wingback chair. A few empty glasses occupied one end of the fireplace mantel. The nephew had been making himself at home, and he was clearly used to someone picking up after him.

Church set his glass on the bar. He pivoted to face Keegan and took a drag from one of his French cigarettes. "So, James," he said, watching Keegan through the rising smoke. "As a comrade, what light can you shed on my situation? I can't help but feel that the old dear has been avoiding me."

The old dear had, in fact, disappeared completely—but how much did the kid already know? Keegan took another sip of the scotch and savored the flavor on his tongue. He needed time to measure his words. He looked at the nephew, trying to gauge what he did or didn't know. "I'm sure she'll get in touch with you when she's ready," he said carefully. "You have to appreciate the situation I'm in."

Church tilted his head forward a little and looked up at Keegan from under a pair of dark, sculpted eyebrows. "I don't want to read too much into your words," he said. "But I get the impression you've spoken to her since we last met. Am I wrong?"

Keegan didn't answer. He took another long, slow sip of the scotch.

Church nodded. He swiveled suddenly and picked up his own glass. He downed what was left in a single gulp and clinked the heavy glass down on the bar top. He then made a slow pivot back around to face Keegan. Was that a sly smile on his face? "It's almost as if the old dear vanished into thin air," he said, dark eyes glinting.

OUTSIDE THE MANSION, Keegan paused, his hand on his MG's door handle. He glanced back at the big house. There was no sign of the nephew at any of the dark front windows. The kid was probably still back in the billiard room, smoking another Gauloise and further depleting his late uncle's store of fine spirits.

Keegan walked around to the front of the red Jaguar. He

pressed his palm on the car's long hood and drew it quickly away. It had been parked out here nearly half an hour, but the hood was still scalding. There was no way Church had only driven a quarter mile back from a restaurant on Stone Canyon. Wherever he'd been before Keegan arrived, it was a good many miles away, far enough to get the engine good and hot. Keegan saw a small rectangle of paper tucked under the base of the driver's side windshield wiper. He tugged it loose. It was smaller than a postage stamp, heavy white paper with a number stamped on it in red ink: 213.

Keegan looked up at the blind, dark windows of Ida Fletcher's mansion. The nephew was lying—that much was clear—but where had he really been tonight? And what did it have to do with the old lady's disappearance?

KEEGAN PULLED INTO the Bouzy Rouge's parking lot on his way back down to Santa Monica Boulevard. The mullioned windows were all dark, and there were no other cars in the parking lot. The light from his headlamps bounced across the red-painted facade and the ivy trellis. He put on the parking brake and pushed open the door of his MG. He left the car idling and went up to the entry alcove. A menu was posted, under glass, next to the paneled front door—all French script, with no prices listed. Along the top were listed the restaurant's hours of operation.

The Bouzy Rouge was closed on Sundays—a Catholic blue-law family, no doubt.

CHAPTER SEVEN

THE BEDSIDE PHONE woke Keegan from a deep sleep. It was daylight. He rolled over and looked at the alarm clock on the bedside table. Nine-twenty. He picked up the receiver.

It was Lieutenant Moore on the line. "Nursing a hangover, Jimmy?" Moore asked. "I called the office—thinking this was a workday—but your secretary said you weren't in. Hell, I'll bet half the baseball fans in town called in sick today."

Keegan yawned and sat up. "No hangover," he said. "I had just the one scotch last night, but it was a hell of a good one." He swung his feet down to the cold wooden floor. "So, did you find my old lady and her sailboat?"

The Lieutenant didn't answer right away. Keegan could hear typewriters and phones ringing in the background. He held the phone to his ear, waiting.

"That bodyguard you told me about," Moore said. He paused, like he was searching his desk for something he'd written down. "Frank Romano?"

Keegan nodded. Frank the Boxer. "What about him?"

"You think you'd recognize him?"

"Like in a lineup?"

The Lieutenant paused again. "Like on a morgue slab," he said.

Keegan looked at the bright bedroom window. The curtains were drawn, but the morning slat of light lit up the whole room. "Shit," Keegan said. "Really?"

"Yeah, a body washed up this morning. Playa del Rey. I haven't been down to see him, but he sounds like he's your guy. They say he's got the cauliflower ears. A lot of tattoos. Doesn't look like he's been in the water long."

Keegan thought of Frank, jogging after him with that last envelope of cash. *Think of it as a bonus*, he'd said. *Just keep the kid at bay a while until you hear from her.* Keegan had liked the guy. His good humor had helped round off the old lady's sharp corners. Could the man really be dead?

"The thing is, Jimmy," Moore went on, "since we don't know where Ida Fletcher is, we're going to need someone to make a provisional ID on the body. Think you'd be up for that on a Monday morning?"

Keegan thought of the nephew last night at the big house in Bel Air. Where had he been? What the hell had he done? *It's almost as if the old dear vanished into thin air.*

"Yeah," Keegan said. "I could do that. I mean, I didn't know him well, but I know what he looks like. You at the morgue now?"

"Not at the moment," the Lieutenant said. "I just got the call a few minutes ago, and there are one or two other crimes going unsolved in Los Angeles at the moment. Think you could meet me down there in an hour?"

BACK WHEN HE covered crime for *The Times*, Keegan had pretty much held an all-access pass to the LAPD. The brass loved him, from Parker on down. The truth was, Keegan had made the department look pretty good after a few decades of bad press—the Black Dahlia, Brenda Allen, Bloody Christmas. For years, Keegan typed up article after article about beat-cop heroes whisking muggers or murderers off the southland streets. Each story had been a fresh salve for the LAPD's healing wounds.

As far as the cops were concerned, Keegan could do no wrong. He was free to go anywhere, talk to anyone. File cabinets and evidence lockers were thrown open. Crime-scene tape was lifted, and he was invited to duck under and take in the gore to his heart's content. He'd be shown to a chair behind the two-way mirror and handed a Styrofoam cup of weak coffee to witness interrogations.

All of which meant he knew the old building on First Street inside out. But—by chance or by design—he'd never been down to the morgue before. The prospect of going there this morning had him feeling more unsettled than he would have guessed. Before he left the house, he'd brewed a pot of coffee and then didn't pour himself a cup. He took Wilshire Boulevard on the drive over, though Beverly would have been quicker. He parked his MG in a downtown lot and rolled a window down a crack for the dog. She'd be fine; he'd only be gone a few minutes. At least he hoped it would only be a few minutes. He locked the car and took his time heading up Temple Street.

When he climbed the steps and came through the old building's big, heavy doors, Lieutenant Moore was already waiting for him, sitting on an ornate wooden bench in the grand marbled lobby. When he saw Keegan, the Lieutenant rose and walked in his direction with his signature smooth and carefree stride. Gray bodies on steel tables were all in a day's work for the man.

"Jimmy." The Lieutenant's voice echoed along the high-ceilinged colonnade. "Thanks for coming down." He held out his hand, and Keegan shook it.

"You know me, Lou," Keegan said bleakly. "Always happy to ID the bloated corpse of someone I know."

THE MORGUE WAS below street level, down an austere steel staircase, where the public wasn't welcome. Here the marble floors and ornate coffered ceilings gave way to worn linoleum tile and long racks of fluorescent lights that held a sickly flicker. The two of them fell silent as they approached the battered steel doors at the end of the hallway. The scuffle of their feet echoed in a way that seemed impossibly loud to Keegan. The beating of his heart also seemed too loud.

The feeling of foreboding surprised Keegan. After all, he was no stranger to crime scenes. He'd seen plenty of dead bodies in his day. Why did this moment, as the Lieutenant pushed back the steel door for him, feel so—well—so *portentous*?

Inside, three of the six steel tables were occupied, human shapes lurking under threadbare, graying sheets. The chemical sting of antiseptics in the air burned at his eyes and made it unpleasant to breathe. The coroner on duty led them down to the farthest table, looking all the while at his steel-cased clipboard of curling forms.

"Haven't got far with this one," he said, eyes still on his paperwork, "but there's water in the lungs, so I doubt it's much of a mystery." He flipped a page. "There's a contusion on the back of his head, but no corresponding skull fracture, so..." He finally looked up from his forms and seemed to catch something in Keegan's expression. He stopped talking and stood straighter. He closed the lid on his clipboard and hugged it to his chest. "Sorry," he told Keegan. Though he didn't make it clear what he was sorry about.

Keegan looked down at the cloth-covered shape on the table and steeled himself. He knew—before he'd set foot in it—that the room would be cold. But he was unprepared for the rawness of it. He felt the chill in his bones. It made his face tighten and his legs shiver. Keegan had liked Frank. The man had seemed down to earth, unfazed and unaffected— the kind of guy you'd be happy to meet at Cole's some afternoon for a French dip and a glass of beer. The coroner seemed to be waiting for a signal from Keegan, so Keegan took a steadying breath and nodded grimly.

The man pulled back a corner of the sheet to reveal a head propped up with a crescent-shaped wooden block. The skin was blue-gray and the eyelids were swollen, but there was no doubt who the dead man was.

There was Frank the Boxer's twisted nose, the one notched eyebrow, the crumpled ears. Keegan felt a bit lightheaded, so he looked at Lieutenant Moore instead. "Yeah," he said, his voice sounding thin in his own ears. "That's him. That's Frank Romano. I can get you his details when I go to the office. It's all in the old lady's will." It struck him that he was staring at the Lieutenant too long. He didn't want to look again at the dead man's inert face.

Moore gave the coroner a nod and, in Keegan's peripheral vision, the man pulled the sheet back up over Frank the Boxer's ruined face. It seemed to break the spell. Keegan looked down again at the blockish human shape under the sheet. "The guy was strong as a bull," he told the Lieutenant. "If *he* didn't survive whatever happened to him, I don't suppose there's much hope for the old lady."

Moore shrugged and put a hand on Keegan's back, steering him towards the door. "Doesn't seem likely."

Keegan turned back and nodded a thanks to the coroner—he was just doing his job—then let the Lieutenant usher him to the double doors. "Think we'll find her body?"

Again, Moore shrugged. "It's a big ocean, Jimmy," he said.

As they climbed the staircase, Keegan still felt the cold tremor in his legs. It would be good to get back out on Temple, into the sun and the traffic and all the living world. "What happens if the old lady's body never washes up?" he asked the Lieutenant.

"She'll have to be declared dead."

Keegan nodded. "Doesn't that take seven years?" he said, his voice echoing in the stairwell. "What happens to all her money until then?"

The Lieutenant stopped at the top of the stairs and pushed open the door. "It can be done pretty quickly in a case like this," he said.

They were back in the high-ceilinged ground-floor portico

now. Orange light angled in through the arched windows, lighting up dust motes in the heavy, sluggish air.

Moore dug his hands in his pockets and jingled the loose change there. "If the old lady had pulled a Judge Crater and just up and vanished—sure, we'd have to wait around. But in a case like this—where it seems obvious there was an accident—it can be done in a few weeks. Somebody needs to file a petition." He looked at Keegan and then looked a little harder—like he'd read some apprehension in his face. "It won't be a major problem, Jimmy," he said. "And it shouldn't be your headache. Just leave it to the lawyers."

WHEN KEEGAN CAME in the office, Mrs. Dodd watched him coyly as he unclipped the dog's leash and hung it on the hat rack. It was only then that Keegan remembered Helen Stark and the ambush date Mrs. Dodd had engineered. That was only two days ago, but their afternoon at Dodger Stadium already seemed like the distant past. Mrs. Dodd wasn't up to speed. She didn't know there was an extra three thousand dollars sitting in the office safe. She didn't know that Ida Fletcher had gone missing on a sailing trip over to Catalina or that Keegan had just come from seeing Frank the Boxer on a morgue slab. She didn't know that the nephew was hiding something about where he was the day it all happened. Hell, Keegan had a lot more on his mind at the moment than his afternoon with Helen Stark, attractive though she had been.

Mrs. Dodd pretended to hunt in one of her desk drawers for something, careful not to make eye contact with Keegan. "Apparently, you made a good impression," she said offhandedly, with that nasal Queens accent. "Which, honestly, surprised me a little."

Keegan didn't even bother taking off his jacket. He dropped down onto the wooden bench against the wall, where clients waited to be let into the inner office. He leaned back and crossed his legs. "Remember Frank?" he said.

His abrupt tone made Mrs. Dodd look up from what she was pretending to do.

"I told you about the guy," Keegan said. "He was the old lady's bodyguard. I met him up at the Chateau Marmont."

"The boxer?" she asked.

"Yeah, that one," Keegan said. "Well, I just came from identifying his body in the morgue. Looks like the old lady had a boating accident over the weekend. So, I've got a lot on my mind this morning."

Mrs. Dodd abandoned her pretense of searching her desk. She sat up straight and looked at Keegan, eyebrows raised. "Wait," she said, "the old lady and the bodyguard are dead?"

"It certainly looks that way," Keegan said. "They set sail for Catalina Saturday and never arrived there. And I've got a sneaking suspicion the nephew had something to do with it."

"With the boating accident?" she said. "How?"

Keegan sighed and leaned his head back to rest on the wall. That was the real question, wasn't it? "Hell, I don't know," he admitted. "But I saw him the night after the two of them went missing. He was in a big hurry to get into the house. He was talking a mile a minute, and he lied to me about where he'd been."

"Holy crap," Mrs. Dodd said. It was the closest Keegan had ever heard her come to cussing. "So, what do we do?"

Keegan sat straighter and looked back at her from the bench. There were a lot of loose ends, and he'd have to start tying them up right away. First, he'd have to head out to the Chateau Marmont. That much was certain. Zinnia needed to hear what had happened—and it was the kind of news that should be delivered in person. After that, he'd call the lawyers, he supposed.

It was all so sudden. He'd just started working for the old lady, and already everything had fallen apart into a grand, unholy mess. He'd been paid a year's salary to run interference for Ida Fletcher, and the old lady was dead inside a week.

Even old Donovan couldn't have screwed up the situation so badly.

"I need to go to the hotel and let the old lady's companion know what's happened," he told Mrs. Dodd. He groaned as he got up from the bench. "Keep an eye on the dog for me?"

Mrs. Dodd, he noticed, had gone a little pale. He'd sucked all the fun out of her Monday morning. She nodded. "Of course," she said. "Anything you need."

Keegan went and opened the door. "Oh," he said, turning back, "if the nephew calls, give him some line. Tell him I'm out of town for a few days. Tell him I can't be reached. Just make something up. I don't want to talk to him again until I've figured a few things out."

WHEN KEEGAN CAME through the Chateau Marmont's lobby door, the bow-tied concierge was on duty behind the front desk. He was bent over the phone book yellow pages, probably hunting something down for a hotel guest—a stand-by chauffer, perhaps, or a poodle groomer who made house calls. Keegan must have groaned audibly because the man looked up from his work and scowled. The last thing Keegan needed this morning was more runaround from the hotel sycophant. He trudged up to the desk.

The concierge regarded Keegan dourly though his little round glasses. The tiny smudged lenses magnified his glower.

"I need to see Miss Zinnia," Keegan told him, resignedly. "She's in Ida Fletcher's bungalow."

"I'm afraid—"

Keegan held up his hand like a traffic cop, cutting the man off. "I know, I know," he said. "I've heard your spiel before. You can't tell me who's staying in this dump, and there's a phone outside Schwab's." He nodded over at the glass French doors that led out to the hotel's courtyard. "With all the alcoholic screenwriters you've got holed up in here, you should get someone to write you some fresh material."

The concierge reared up stiffly—like someone had dropped an ice cube down the back of his shirt. It was clear he wasn't used to being talked to like that. "I'm sure I don't know what—"

"First of all," Keegan said loudly, talking over the other man, "I *don't* want to come into your lousy hotel. Just tell Zinnia I'm across the street at Schwab's. I'll be at the lunch counter. Tell her it's important. She should come right away."

The other man's face had grown red. He seemed unable to speak.

Keegan gave his head a derisive shake and then turned away and headed for the door. He could hear a kind of furious sputtering behind him as he walked. He pulled the door open and then looked back over his shoulder at the concierge. "If you want us to bring you back a sandwich," he said, "just give Zinnia the details. We can settle up later." He stepped out into all the sunlight and traffic.

FROM HIS STOOL at Schwab's lunch counter, Keegan saw Zinnia through the big front window. She paused on the sidewalk outside, peering up at the neon sign above the alcove.

Keegan felt a small surge of sympathy for her. She looked so woefully out of place standing there on the famously stylish Sunset Strip—a tiny, plain woman bundled in a frumpy housedress.

She pulled the door open, and the bell above it jingled. She came inside the drugstore, looking around herself, as if she'd never visited such a place before. Keegan raised himself up on his stool and waved her over. She came and sat down next to him.

When he asked, she told him she hadn't eaten breakfast, but that she wasn't at all hungry. The two of them would be taking up counter space, so they'd have to buy something. It was too early for lunch, so Keegan caught the counter girl's eye and ordered them both a coffee and a slice of cherry pie. Zinnia made no objection.

This was the closest Keegan had ever been to Zinnia, and it looked like she hadn't slept at all the night before. He could see the glassiness of her eyes and their red-rimmed lids. She wore no makeup, so he could see a scattering of pimples below her hairline and the vertical creases that were beginning to form on her lips. She sat holding her purse on her knees primly, tensely waiting for him to tell her whatever news he'd brought. She seemed downtrodden and brittle.

Keegan didn't want the counter girl to interrupt them while they were talking. He thought he'd wait until the coffee and pie were on the counter in front of them before he gave Zinnia the news. This was the part of the job Keegan most hated: the report. As a detective, he was hired to find information, but the information he dug up was seldom happy. He'd never grown cozy with breaking bad news; there was no painless way to do it. He didn't mind waiting another minute while the Schwab's girl plated a couple of pie slices and poured them coffee. Keegan waited until she was out of earshot and then swiveled on his stool to face Zinnia.

"It's bad," he told her, choosing his words carefully. "We don't know exactly what happened, but the boat isn't in Newport, and it never arrived in Avalon."

Zinnia stared at his mouth as he spoke. She seemed to have trouble grasping the meaning of his words, and he felt another surge of sympathy for her.

"And I'm afraid Frank turned up dead," he told her.

Zinnia looked up at his eyes then. "*Frank?*" she said. The shattered expression on her face made Keegan stumble.

"And things don't look good for Mrs. Fletcher," he plowed on, clumsily. "She's missing at sea."

Sudden tears welled up in Zinnia's tired eyes. One dribbled down her cheek, and she didn't bother to wipe it away.

"There's no Coast Guard report," Keegan floundered

on, "but it seems like the boat went down somewhere out in the channel."

"Frank is dead?" Zinnia said miserably. "Frank Romano?" Her voice sounded tiny, vanquished.

There was something about the expression on her face that threw Keegan off. He felt like he was missing some key element of the situation. "I saw the body," he told her, distracted. "I'm sorry."

Zinnia looked beyond him then, over his shoulder. "Frank's dead," she said. It wasn't a question.

Keegan watched Zinnia's face go through a series of alterations, helpless to help her. "That can't be right," she said. "We were going to go away."

Keegan nodded, not sure what she was saying. "And Mrs. Fletcher is—"

He stopped mid-sentence, caught up short. In a flash, he understood what he'd been missing all along: Frank and Zinnia had been lovers—with or without their employer's knowledge or blessing. He slumped a little on the stool and stared at the woman beside him. The blood had drained entirely from Zinnia's face. She might have been a body on a slab. She might have been a ghost.

Keegan should have seen this coming. He should have understood what kind of news he was bringing her. But how could he have known about their liaison? That was the way it always was with people, he had learned: the closer you looked, the messier and more complicated they turned out to be.

Zinnia gasped twice and then dissolved into a fit of sobbing, which she made no effort to hide.

Keegan put his hands on her shoulders, in an awkward gesture of comfort, while she cried and gulped for air. What a fool he'd turned out to be. Cowed by a glorified hotel clerk, he'd made poor Zinnia meet him out here in public—in Schwab's Pharmacy, of all places—so he could break her heart where everyone could witness it.

The girl behind the counter had just refilled a coffee cup

at the far end of the counter and was headed in their direction with the carafe held high. When she saw Zinnia's unchecked sobbing, she stopped in her tracks and then backed away again.

Others around the place were starting to notice Zinnia as well. A couple sharing a club sandwich at one of the tables turned in their direction. A woman back by the magazine racks shot Keegan an angry look, assuming he must have done something churlish. At least it wasn't the lunch rush yet, Keegan thought. At least he hadn't brought the poor woman here when the place was packed with spectators. Zinnia's breakdown was becoming a scene, and he needed to get her out of there before someone tried to intervene.

He rifled his trouser pockets and left a wad of cash on the counter without bothering to count it. Holding Zinnia by the shoulders, he got her up off the stool and then tucked her purse under one arm. He steered her between the tables and outside to the sidewalk.

When they had safely crossed Sunset Boulevard at the corner light, he moved her along the busy sidewalk, staring down any passerby who dared take a second look at them. He ushered Zinnia into the Chateau Marmont's lobby. She was keening loudly by this point, blind with grief, crying with a small child's abandon.

The concierge glowered in Keegan's direction but, for once, made no move to stop him as he steered the weeping woman—she was a paying resident, after all—toward the French doors and through them.

Keegan found the bungalow's gate and front door both unlocked; Zinnia had come away without securing them. He guided her through the door and sat her down in her usual spot at the kitchen table. He went to the kitchenette and poured her a coffee mug of tap water—for no purpose he could explain, other than the need to do *something*. He hunted down a box of Kleenex from a bedroom nightstand and set it on the table within reach.

Despite Keegan's clumsy ministrations, Zinnia cried,

unable to speak, for a good half-hour longer. When she stopped, abruptly exhausted, she stared blank-eyed at the door, which Keegan had left standing wide in his rush to get her inside. She still seemed unable yet to speak.

"I'm going to have to leave you here," Keegan told her gently. He was standing at her side, bent to her level, pressing both palms on the kitchen tabletop. "You can call my office if you need me. I just have to call the lawyers—and somebody needs to talk to the nephew."

Zinnia snapped her head up. "*No*," she said fiercely. It was her first word spoken since they'd left the drugstore's lunch counter. She pressed a damp hand on top of one of Keegan's. "Don't talk to that—that—*boy*," she said, as though that were the most stinging insult she could come up with for him. "This was all his fault."

Keegan thought of the scorching car hood and the kid's lie about the Bouzy Rouge. "Well, the police know he's in town," he said. "He's officially next of kin. They're going to call him if I don't."

"*Let* them," she said, her voice full of spite. "None of us should have the least thing to do with him." She looked at Keegan then, eyes damp and fiery red. "It's what they would have wanted."

Keegan straightened up. There would be no contradicting her. He nodded.

WHEN HE LEFT her, he walked through the Chateau Marmont's courtyard, past the empty pool, feeling like too much of this unholy mess had been his doing. He'd brought the news about the nephew's arrival, setting the whole thing in motion. Then, without meaning to—without even knowing the fact himself—he'd tipped the nephew off that the old lady was on her way to Catalina.

Would it even be possible? he thought as he approached the lobby's French doors. Could the nephew have waited offshore somehow? Could he have intercepted the sailboat out there in the dark open waters at night? The idea hardened in his stomach, like a small, indigestible stone. He paused with his hand on the door handle. It had happened once before, where his best intentions and his lack of understanding had cost a woman her life.

Were Ida Fletcher and Frank the Boxer two more souls to add to his reckoning?

CHAPTER EIGHT

KEEGAN HEARD THE phone in the outer office that afternoon. It rang twice before Mrs. Dodd picked it up. The documents from Ida Fletcher's strongbox were strewn out over his desk, and he was trying to sort them out in his head, to get a sense of how many loose ends he'd have to tie up before all this was someone else's problem.

First, he'd set the will off to one side—that was clearly the most important of these documents, and he was happy to know it wouldn't be his responsibility much longer. By this afternoon it would be the lawyers' headache, and the lawyers would have to deal with Danny Church and Zinnia and whoever else held a stake in the old lady's estate as well.

He'd then sorted through the rest of the papers, pleased to see how many of them—deeds and titles, insurance papers and tax returns—could also be handed off to the old lady's white-shoe attorneys. He was grateful he'd majored in English and had never gone to law school. In a few days, he'd be clear of this whole mess.

Mrs. Dodd rapped on the inner office door. She opened it a little and stuck her head in. "Hey, boss," she said. "You-know-who is on the phone."

Keegan, in fact, didn't know who—and he was about to

tell Mrs. Dodd as much, when it occurred to him who she must mean. He looked down at the phone on the corner of his desk where one of the line buttons was blinking yellow. Danny Church was on hold. He'd no doubt heard the news and called to talk to *James*, his old friend and confidant. Why had Keegan given the kid his card in the first place?

"I know you didn't want me to put him through before," Mrs. Dodd was saying, "but has that changed? I mean, with the old lady out of the picture, isn't *he* sort of our client now, as her next of kin?"

Keegan looked down at the stacks of documents on his desk. A fortune of property and assets and cash, and almost all of it would be going to the nephew. *You don't suppose I've fallen out of favor, do you?* Keegan didn't like Danny Church. The kid was a cad, a gadabout, a narcissist—but could he really be a killer?

"I wish you hadn't put it quite like that," Keegan said. "But, yeah, you're probably right. I suppose I should talk to him." He picked up the phone's receiver and paused with an index finger hovering over the blinking button. He thought of all the money locked up in the outer office safe. The old lady had given it to him in good faith to do a job for her. He couldn't wash his hands of Ida Fletcher just yet, not in good conscience. If the old lady had wanted her nephew to get her fortune, he'd have to see it through. And if the kid had murdered his aunt, Keegan would need to make things right.

He sighed and pressed the button.

DANNY CHURCH COULDN'T hide the excitement in his voice over the phone. Sure, he said all the *de rigueur* things about the old dear having lived a good, long life and her being in a better place—but there was an edge of eagerness to his words. The kid sounded, in fact, like he'd already begun celebrating his good fortune with his late, lamented uncle's stock of single-malt scotches. His voice rose and fell in giddy, lubricated cadences. He was even more voluble and flighty than usual.

The Sheriff's Department had tracked him down and broken the news that morning, while Keegan was out at the Chateau Marmont. They'd told him that Frank's body had been found; that the old lady was missing, presumed dead; that the Coast Guard had found some wreckage, late that morning, drifting in the north-flowing current off Malibu. It was the right kind of boat, they'd told him—the same make and model as *The Seven of Swords*. It wouldn't take long for a positive ID.

As he listened, Keegan knew the question that was coming, but the nephew was taking a few minutes to get around to it. At least his privileged upbringing had taught the kid to be discreet. In polite circles, a few minutes of small talk preceded the big talk.

"How long before the old dear can be declared legally dead?" the kid finally asked. "I'm only asking because of the funeral arrangements and so on."

Keegan nodded. Yeah sure, he thought, the flowers and the black armband and the obit in the newspaper—*that's* what the kid's got on his mind. He tried to keep his voice neutral as he spoke. "My understanding is that—given the facts of the case—it shouldn't take too long," he said. He picked a ballpoint pen and tapped it on the edge of his desk. "But that's all up to the lawyers."

How would you even *find* another boat at sea? How would you go about sinking it and making it look like an accident? Did the kid even know how to sail? And, if he'd just arrived back in California, would he even have had access to a boat?

"Well then, James," the nephew went jauntily on. "I suppose I should let you go. I appreciate all you've done for me since I arrived on your doorstep, as it were. I suppose the next step is to give Mr. Burritt a ring, and he'll let us know where to go from here. You wouldn't happen to have his number handy?"

"Burritt?" Keegan said. He glanced around the papers littering his desk. He couldn't remember ever coming across the name.

"Milton Burritt?" the kid said. "My aunt's lawyer?"

Keegan pulled the will in front of him. *Roland Dion and Associates*, it read along the top of the paper, *Attorneys at Law*. He flipped through the pages, skimming for any reference to *Burritt*.

"That's not the attorney who drew up the will," Keegan said into the phone.

"It's *not*?" the kid said. He paused a few seconds, clearly surprised. It was the first real break in his torrent of words since Keegan had picked up the phone. "But Mr. Burritt has been the family lawyer—well, since before I was born. He's an old family friend."

Keegan looked down at the stack of oversized legal parchment, creased twice and bound with a paperclip. He picked it up and leaned back in his chair. He squinted at the fine print, trying to make out the firm's address: 22 Heeser Place, Santa Monica, California. He knew that address. It was the building where old Donovan had rented an office—a big, breezy building just up the hill from the pier, all steel and plate glass.

Looked at one way, it made perfect sense that a paranoid old lady might have changed lawyers. A single sideways glance or an ill-chosen word could have turned her against this Milton Burritt—old family friend or not. And, if Burritt had become the target of Ida Fletcher's dark suspicions, she might have asked Donovan to help her find a new attorney. Old Donovan, following the path of least resistance, would have conserved his energy by simply picking a lawyer from the lobby directory in his own building: Roland Dion and Associates. It would have required as little effort as possible on Donovan's part, so it made perfect sense. Hell, it almost felt inevitable.

"All I can tell you is that it's a new will," Keegan said. "Your aunt had it done up a couple of months ago. She used a lawyer called Roland Dion."

There was a longer pause on the line now, a deathly, calculating silence. A truck rumbled by down below Keegan's office window. He allowed himself a small smile. It felt good to know the kid was flustered—wondering if he had, indeed, fallen out of the old dear's favor.

"A new will?" Church finally said. The sentence was just three words long, Keegan noted, but the man's dry voice took its time with it.

"Look, this is for the lawyers to work out," Keegan said, regretting the words even as he was saying them. "But, between you and me, I don't think she changed anything major. Pretty much everything she had is coming to you."

Keegan heard a hiss of breath on the other end of the line. "*James*," Church said finally, his voice swelling with gratitude, "you're a good man. I'm grateful to have someone like you in my corner. You're about the best friend I have these days."

Keegan winced. He wasn't in Church's corner, and he damn sure wasn't his friend. "Look," Keegan said into the phone, "I need to run all this stuff over to the lawyer anyway. I'll do it first thing in the morning, and I'll give him your number. I'll tell him to give you a call. You can get all the details from him."

THAT NIGHT, LONG after midnight, Nora stood in the bedroom doorway, barking. She seemed too scared to go out into the living room, too unsettled to go back to sleep. Keegan shushed her and wrapped his head in a pillow, but, of course, she just kept barking.

Keegan gave up. He groaned and rolled out of bed. He picked up the dog, carried her out into the living room, and turned on the lamp to show her no one was there. "You shouldn't listen to Mrs. Dodd," he told the dog, his voice creaky from sleep. He could feel her rapid-fire heartbeat in his arms. "There are no such things as ghosts."

She gave a little whimper and wagged her tail.

He switched off the lamp again and carried the dog back into the bedroom. He kicked the door shut behind them and set her at the foot of the mattress where she liked to sleep. He sat down on the edge of the bed.

"That woman's a bad influence on you," he told the dog. "She'll have you reading your horoscope soon." He lay down, but his heart had picked up its pace. He knew he probably wouldn't get back to sleep. He put one arm behind his head and looked up at the ceiling.

If he *were* to be haunted by an apparition, whose ghost would it be?

His mother, of course, had died in this very room a little over a year ago—but she had always been a quiet soul. She'd never raised much ruckus when she was alive, so why would she do it now?

Eve, perhaps—but he refused to let his mind traipse down that avenue of thought. It was too well trod already, and it only led to darkness.

Hell, it could be Frank or Ida Fletcher at this point—back from the other side to make sure Keegan avenged their deaths. Or perhaps to avenge *Keegan* for putting the murderous nephew on their trail. If a ghost could ride an elevator, why couldn't one look Keegan up in the white pages and float on over to the listed address?

Keegan reached down and ran his hand along the dog's dense, curly fur. She'd stopped trembling now, and her breath was slowing, deepening. At least one of them might get back to sleep tonight.

THE LOBBY DIRECTORY at 22 Heeser showed that Roland Dion and Associates occupied a suite up on the building's third floor. Donovan's old office had been in 302, so Keegan had been right: when the old lady had asked Donovan to find her a new lawyer, he hadn't even got on the elevator. It would have been just like him. The man spared no effort when it came to avoiding effort. For him, laziness was a single-minded pursuit, every shortcut tirelessly run down and wrestled into submission. What would retirement even look like for someone like Donovan? Other than waking up every day in a new city, was there any noticeable difference to his life?

Keegan stepped onto the one open elevator with Ida Fletcher's strongbox tucked under his arm. On the third-floor hallway, he passed Donovan's old office on the way to Dion's suite. Keegan paused to look at the new gold lettering that had been painted on the pebbled glass panel of 302. The office now belonged to a certified public accountant. Out with the old.

The law offices of Roland Dion and Associates were at the very end of the hallway and took up half the third floor. Keegan went into the reception area and gave his name to the woman behind the desk. He told her someone should be expecting him; he'd called ahead.

The receptionist was direct and officious—a young redhead, brimming with professional poise, in a no-nonsense skirt and blouse. Keegan guessed she probably never talked about haunted elevators or ambushed her boss with blind dates or sat in the office reading movie magazines when no one was there to look over her shoulder. With a graceful sweep of her hand from the other side of the counter, she invited Keegan to have a seat on one of the stylish leather chairs arranged against the floor-to-ceiling windows across the room. Someone would be with him in just a moment.

Keegan sat down and propped the strongbox on his knees. The chair, he had to admit, was much more comfortable than the wooden bench clients waited on in his own office. A better secretary and better furniture—perhaps Keegan should have gone to law school after all.

Roland Dion's office also seemed incredibly busy, with phones ringing and the steady clatter of electric typewriters. Out the big plate-glass window behind him—past all the palm trees and red-tile roofs—Keegan could make out the turquoise stucco of the Georgian Hotel, and, beyond it, the pier's Ferris wheel. His own office windows looked down on a Sixth Street barber shop and realtor's office.

Keegan waited only a couple of minutes before Roland Dion himself came rushing out from the back offices to greet him. Keegan did an involuntary double take when he first saw the man. He tried to cover it up by fumbling with the strongbox as he got to his feet, and then he stooped to shake the lawyer's hand.

Dion was short. He was, in fact, astonishingly short. He was the kind of short that probably drew constant double takes from those who met him—followed, no doubt, by Keegan's exact brand of flustered backpedaling.

He was dressed in a perfectly tailored bespoke suit, navy blue with a yellow silk tie, and he had pale translucent skin—all of which combined to give Keegan the unfortunate impression of a ventriloquist dummy. Dion waved Keegan through the door into the back offices and then led him past a number of closed doors—the advertised *Associates*, Keegan guessed.

Keegan followed behind, gripping the strongbox with both hands and trying not to look down at the baseball-sized bald spot in the smaller man's combed-over hair. They entered a big corner office. Two of the walls were floor-to-ceiling glass, with dizzying views of terracotta roofs and the distant sweep of azure water. It was a lot to take in.

A pair of black wingback chairs sat facing Dion's oversized desk. The little man waved at them and went behind the desk to his own high-backed executive chair. It swiveled as he sat down on it.

Keegan sat on the nearest of the two chairs and set the strongbox in the other. He crossed his legs and looked across the desk at the lawyer. Now that they were both sitting, their height difference had vanished. Did Dion have some kind of platform back there?

The lawyer folded his boyish hands on top of his desk and offered Keegan an indulgent frown. "I was so sorry to hear about Mrs. Fletcher's passing," he said in a reedy tenor voice. "I'm sure she will be greatly missed."

Keegan nodded at the cliché. It was the kind of perfunctory sentiment you had to offer in situations like this. *So sorry for your loss. Time heals all wounds.* Yes, perhaps the old lady would be greatly missed—but not by either of them.

"Did you know her well?" Keegan asked.

The question seemed to fluster the lawyer. He pressed both hands down on his desktop blotter, like a schoolkid caught in a lie. "I met her just the once," he admitted, "at her hotel. She was a relatively new client to our firm."

Keegan nodded. It was just as he had guessed. "Mike introduced you to her, I assume?" he asked.

"Michael Donovan?" Dion said, brightening a little. "Why, yes. Mr. Donovan and I work together on occasion. You know him?"

Keegan nodded. "Old Donovan and I go way back," he said. "He was my predecessor in this job with Mrs. Fletcher." Keegan reached over and picked up the strongbox in the chair next to him and set it on his knees. "In fact, he recommended me to Mrs. Fletcher when he moved away last month."

Dion cocked his head. It seemed news to him that Donovan had left town. Had he failed to notice that the man was no longer in the building? That his name had vanished from the lobby directory? That a CPA had moved into office 302?

The lawyer tented his tiny fingers. "Well then, we both owe Mr. Donovan a debt of gratitude," he said. "Mrs. Fletcher was among our firm's biggest clients."

Keegan thought of the envelopes of cash back in his office. "Yeah, mine too," he said. "Any idea why the old lady fired the family lawyer and came to you? I think the lawyer's name was Burritt."

Dion nodded. He straightened up and fiddled a little with his yellow tie. There were, of course, lawyer-client rules about confidentiality, and the man seemed to be choosing his words carefully. "She came to believe there were financial irregularities," he said, after that most pregnant pause.

"But you didn't believe her?"

The lawyer put on a polite smile. "Milton Burritt enjoys a sterling reputation in the California Bar," he said. Again, he paused to perfect his wording. "And I was given to understand that our client sometimes had her own notions."

If *notions* were a euphemism for *delusions*, Keegan was given to understand the exact same thing. He lifted the strongbox from his knees and set it on Dion's desk. He pulled the key ring from his trouser pocket, unlocked the box, and lifted the steel lid. "I was holding these for her in my office safe," Keegan said. "As far as I can tell, this is all your headache now." He turned the box in Dion's direction and pushed it across the large desktop in his direction.

Keegan sat back in the chair. Was that it? Would it really be so easy to get clear of this mess?

Roland Dion pulled the box closer and started taking out the documents one by one. He made a big production of putting on his reading glasses and tilting his head back, sorting the papers into four or five piles on his desktop. Breath whistled though his nose as he worked. Behind him, through the big plate-glass windows, a flock of brown pelicans crossed the sky in a *V*, left to right, way out along the water's edge.

There didn't seem anything else for Keegan to do. He glanced at his wristwatch. He'd wait here silently a polite ten minutes while the lawyer worked. Then, if he didn't seem to be needed, he'd make some excuse to leave. He looked beyond Roland Dion again, out the window at the vast, sun-flecked swath of the Pacific Ocean. The gray hulking outline of Catalina Island lay profiled on the far horizon.

The thought struck him, cold and unexpected as a rogue wave: somewhere in that field of glimmering blue was Ida

Fletcher's watery grave. That was the exact stretch of water where Frank the Boxer died. He thought of the man's gray hulking body, supine on the steel table, profiled by the coroner's sheet.

How would you even go about it? How would you intercept a little sailboat out on that vast open ocean? How would you get aboard? How would you sink it?

Roland Dion's voice seemed to come to Keegan from a great distance. "It all seems fairly straightforward," the lawyer was saying. "First, we file a petition with the State and wait for a declaratory judgment." He pressed his small, childlike hand down on one of the stacks of paper. "With an affidavit from Miss Zinnia and the wreckage and the body that already came ashore, it shouldn't take long," he said. "After that, the State forwards a court order to the registrar to issue a death certificate, and we're free to execute the will. It's just a matter of filing the right paperwork."

Keegan nodded. He hadn't quite followed the lawyer's train of thought—he'd been derailed by the man's use of the word *we*. "Is there anything you need from me?" he said.

Roland Dion looked him over from behind his massive desk. "Well, since you're Michael Donovan's replacement, there are a few loose ends I'd like you to help us with," he said. His hand hovered over the stacks of paper. "For one thing, I notice there isn't a copy of the original will in here," he said. "The one she had before she came to me. That would come in handy. Do you have any idea where it might be?"

"Everything she gave me is in the box," Keegan said.

"Well, tracking down the original document would be a big help," Dion said. "I wouldn't want to tangle with Milton Burritt in probate if it can be avoided. I'm sure there are some notes about it in our files, but the original document itself would be a great help." At that point, he stopped talking and pushed a button on his intercom. He told someone on the other end to bring him everything from the files on Ida Fletcher. He sat back in his elevated chair and gave Keegan a boyish smile. He seemed pleased with himself, to be acting so officiously.

"We had Mr. Donovan on retainer," Dion said, folding his hands on his desk blotter, "and we can do the same with you. It will be good to have someone familiar with the case to—"

There was a smart rap on the door. The ginger receptionist entered, holding a stack of manila file folders with both hands. She must have had them all ready to go before she was even asked. Without a word, she set them on the lawyer's desk, graced Keegan with an efficient smile, and slipped back out, quietly closing the door behind her. No sass, no gossip, no bickering. Everything poised and professional.

The lawyer opened the files and consulted his notes. "Yes, yes, here are the notes," he said. "A woman who went by Madame Lena was cut out of the will entirely." He glanced at Keegan now over his glasses and then looked back down at his notes. "Her share was then split between Romano and Zinnia and a former employee called Lillian Cole."

"*Madame* Lena?" Keegan said. "What kind of a name is that?"

The tiny lawyer made a face. The subject seemed distasteful to him. "I was given to understand that was her professional name," Dion said. "She was an advisor to Mrs. Fletcher. A *spiritual* advisor, she might call herself."

"And what might *we* call her?"

The lawyer sighed. He looked at Keegan over his reading glasses again. It seemed to pain him to speak plainly, without the emollients of legal jargon. "We would probably call her a *medium*," he said.

"As in flickering candles and crystal balls?"

"I'm not sure of the accoutrements," Dion admitted, "but yes. I suppose that would be a fair assessment." He looked back down at his notes. "Apparently, our client came to distrust the woman." He turned a page and ran a small finger down the lines of typed texts. "You would be tasked with tracking down this Lillian Cole and informing her of

Mrs. Fletcher's generosity," he told Keegan. "What with Mr. Romano's death before the will's execution, her share will likely be even greater than our client originally intended."

Keegan nodded. A simple skip-trace. That kind of job was bread and butter for a PI. All it required was to find someone. Sure, it could sometimes be tricky if the person in question was trying not to be found. In this case, though, no one would be hiding. People might cover their tracks to avoid alimony or child-support payments, but no one ever hid from a six-figure windfall.

"Sure," Keegan said, "I can find her. Shouldn't be too difficult. Anything else?"

"Just locating the original will," the lawyer said, closing the file he'd been consulting. "Maybe Miss Zinnia knows where it is."

"Sure," Keegan said, "I'll get right on that. I guess I should keep the key ring for now. I'll need to check the houses."

The lawyer said something in return, but Keegan wasn't listening. His mind was still on the fortune teller. Ida Fletcher was clearly afraid of her nephew. If the old lady had unburdened herself to anyone about what was going on with him, it would be this *spiritual advisor* with her crystal ball. "I think I'll track down the fortune teller too," Keegan said. "Someone should let her know what happened."

The other man nodded. He seemed doubtful but unwilling to put up much of an argument. "If you think it advisable," he said.

CHAPTER NINE

WHEN KEEGAN GOT back to the office that afternoon, he called an old acquaintance in LAPD vice and got Donovan's new phone number out in Tempe.

"How's the easy life?" Keegan asked when Donovan picked up.

"It's a paradox, Jimmy," Donovan told him. His voice was somber, reflective. It was as if he'd been giving this very question a great deal of thought. "You spend your whole life as a working stiff looking forward to Saturday. It's the only thing that keeps you going." He started coughing, and the sound was suddenly muffled, like he'd covered the mouthpiece with his palm to spare Keegan the eruption. In a few seconds, he came back on the line, breathing raggedly. "But then you retire," he said. "And suddenly *every* day is a Saturday." He sighed into the phone. "It turns out to be a living hell."

"That's a damn shame," Keegan offered. "Maybe you could take up a hobby. Stamp collecting? Ham radio? There's got to be something you can do out there in the desert." He hoped that would be enough small talk. He was never much good at idle chitchat. He hadn't been trained in courtly etiquette like Danny Church. "But, Mike," he said, "here's the reason I'm calling." He gave Donovan a quick rundown of all that had happened since that night they'd talked by the Ambassador's pool—the nephew, the sinking boat, Frank Romano dead and the old lady about to be declared so.

"Wow," Donovan said, when he had finished his recitation. "I turn my back for five minutes."

"And to top it off, I got hired by Roland Dion," Keegan said. "Your old friend on the third floor."

Donovan whistled into the phone. "You don't mess around, Jimmy," he said. "I give you Ida Fletcher, and you swoop in and scoop up the little man too. You're just helping yourself to everything I left behind." He let loose with one of his wheezing laughs. He seemed overly happy just to be talking to someone on the phone.

"He's the reason I called," Keegan pressed on. "Dion wants me to track down Lillian Cole. You don't have any idea where I could find her, do you?"

Donovan was still puffing a little. "Who the hell is Lillian Cole?" he managed to say.

"I was hoping *you'd* know," Keegan said. "Her name's in the will." He leaned back in his chair and swung his heels up onto the desk. "She was on the old lady's staff, but I guess she retired a while back. With Frank out of the picture, she'll be splitting half a million with that Zinnia woman."

"*Mildred Zinnia*," Donovan said wistfully, like the name conjured up fond memories. "I had a bit of a thing for that girl. Why, if I was twenty years younger…" He let the thought trail off and chuckled. "You keep your hands off her, Jimmy," he said. "Leave me with something to remember."

Keegan thought about how he'd steered poor Zinnia, blind with tears, across Sunset to the Chateau Marmont. Donovan clearly hadn't known about her and Frank the Boxer, either. "Sure thing," he said. "She's all yours, Donovan. But this Lillian *Cole*? You don't know *anything* about her? I'm supposed to track her down and deliver the good news."

Donovan breathed into the phone. "I think I know who you mean," he said. "I never met the woman. She was up and gone before I got hired on. She was some kind of long-term housekeeper or companion to the old girl. Went to live up in Portland with her daughter, I think someone said. Shouldn't be too hard to track her down."

Portland. That was all the lead Keegan really needed. He knew a PI up there, a good one, and he could give her a call as soon as he got off the phone with Donovan. Sue Belk was her name. She could probably track down this Lillian in a day or two.

Keegan smiled. Old Donovan had come through, after all. He pictured the man, plump and florid, stretched out on the poolside chair with his whiskey and cigar. He wasn't so bad, old Mike Donovan. They should have spent more time together when they had the chance.

"According to the will," Keegan said, "you've got a chunk of money coming your way too, once the old lady gets declared. Ten thousand bucks would buy a hell of a nice ham radio."

Donovan laughed. "I know it," he said. "I was there when she signed the damn will." He chuckled wheezily. "Now, don't swoop in and steal that ten grand from me too, Jimmy."

KEEGAN FOUND SUE Belk's number in his Rolodex and dialed her number. It wasn't yet five, so he might still catch her in the office. Sue had had a place in Carlsbad for as long as Keegan could remember, then moved up to Portland a few years ago for a change of scenery. She sounded happy to hear Keegan's voice when she picked up. She sounded even happier to hear there'd be a paycheck in it for her, if she could follow up on his skip-trace.

"The woman's name is Lillian Cole," Keegan told her. "Spelled just the way you'd expect. Sounds like she's pretty elderly. She might be staying with her daughter. Used to live down here in LA until she retired a year or two ago." That was it. That was the sum total of what Keegan had to offer her. "It's not a lot to go on, I know," he said.

"At least her name's not Jane Smith," Sue told him. "Portland's no sprawling metropolis. There won't be more than a handful of Lillian Coles in town. Just give me a day or two to beat the bushes."

There was something brittle-sounding in Sue's smoker's voice now, and Keegan wished he had a better job to send her way. Maybe he could pad the bill for her a little before he passed her invoice along to Roland Dion.

"So, how much does the old dame stand to inherit?" Sue wanted to know.

"Around fifty thousand," Keegan told her. "As far as I can tell."

Sue whistled on the other end of the line. "In that case, I can probably find you as many Lillian Coles as you want."

Keegan laughed. "Just one of them will do nicely," he said.

WHEN MRS. DODD made it to the office the following morning—more than half an hour late, Keegan noted—the dog darted from under his desk and skittered out to greet her. Keegan had been busy jotting Sue Belk's billing details on an invoice sheet with a ballpoint pen.

Mrs. Dodd took her time hanging up her coat. She took the cover off her typewriter and sharpened a few pencils before she appeared in Keegan's doorway with the dog peering around her legs. "What have you got for us to do today, boss?" she wanted to know.

Keegan set his pen down. "Not a whole lot," Keegan said. "I'm working a skip-trace for somebody in the old lady's will. Otherwise, we're pretty much done with Ida Fletcher. It's all in the lawyers' hands now." He thought of Roland Dion, boosted up on the other side of his aircraft-carrier desk, Ida Fletcher's papers sorted into piles around him. "You ever hear of someone called Madame Lena?" Keegan asked. "I should probably give her a call too. She was in the old will. When word gets out about the old lady's death…" He wasn't sure how to end the sentence, so he didn't. The truth was, he just wanted to find out what the fortune teller knew about the old lady's private life.

Ida Fletcher had probably confided *something* to her about her no-good nephew in Europe, the one who frightened her.

"*Madame Lena?*" Mrs. Dodd said, pronouncing the words with some distaste. "She some kind of foreigner?"

Keegan shook his head. "She's some kind of fortune teller," he said. "Worked for the old lady. I guess they had a falling out."

Mrs. Dodd took on a stern look. She stood a little straighter and folded her arms in front of her. She shook her head. "I don't think so, boss," she said, as though it were her call to make. "You leave that stuff alone. Don't be messing with any psychic. It isn't safe to dabble with the occult."

"Just seems like someone should tell her what happened," Keegan said reasonably. "It's the least we—"

"If she's really a psychic, she already knows," Mrs. Dodd said, cutting him off. "Don't go monkeying around with that kind of thing. I mean it."

Haunted elevators and horoscopes—and now fortune tellers. Mrs. Dodd's superstitions were proliferating like a magician's rabbits. "You really think she's going to put a curse on me over the phone?"

"I'm just saying not to take any chances," she said. Then, as if the matter were settled, "So, what do you need me to do this morning?"

"I don't know," Keegan said. "Just answer the phone and pretend to look busy if I come out there. The usual."

"You got it, boss," she said.

Keegan thought the discussion had ended, but Mrs. Dodd still hovered in the doorway. "Is there something else?" Keegan asked.

"I understand you've got a date this weekend," Mrs. Dodd said. "I hope you're taking her somewhere nice."

Keegan thought of Helen Stark at Dodger Stadium with her sun hat and crooked smile. He'd got her phone number, but he hadn't yet called. He'd been too distracted. "We're meeting at Jackson's, if you must know," Keegan said.

"That place on Wilshire Boulevard?" Mrs. Dodd said. She

frowned appraisingly and nodded. "That should do. Not too cheap for a first date. Not too formal. You got a reservation?"

Keegan sighed. It had slipped his mind. "Not yet."

"Why don't I get on *that* then," Mrs. Dodd said.

"Sure," he told her. "Eight o'clock."

The dog seemed to have grown bored with their conversation. She wandered into the inner office and lay down on the floor between them. Keegan picked up his pen and went back to filling out the invoice.

Mrs. Dodd still stood in the doorway. "Flowers?" she asked him when he looked up at her again.

"What?"

"Maybe we should send Helen flowers while I'm at it."

"*We?*" Keegan said. "You're not planning on tagging along on the date, are you?"

She gave him a look of weary patience. "I just want you to do this right," she said. "She's a nice girl, and I don't want you screwing it up."

"If it's okay with you," Keegan said, "I have a lot work to do." He pointed at the single invoice sheet on his desk with the tip of his ballpoint. The image was less than compelling, he knew.

Mrs. Dodd sighed heavily. "Jackson's at eight," she said. "I'll get right on it." She finally disappeared from the doorway. The dog got up and trotted after her.

"That's going to be a table for *two*," Keegan called out, loud enough for Mrs. Dodd to hear.

Her deadpan voice came to him from the outer office. "That's funny, boss," she said. "That's real funny. But you should try to save the charm for the date."

It was still a quarter of an hour before quitting time, but Mrs. Dodd was already packed up and ready to go when Keegan came out of his inner office. The dust cover was pulled over her typewriter, and her purse was on the desk's edge, ready for her to grab as she headed out the door.

Keegan couldn't blame her. It had been a painfully slow day, with only a couple of phone calls coming in and no new jobs on the horizon. More than once, Keegan had wandered out to catch Mrs. Dodd slipping one of her movie magazines back into her desk's top drawer. There didn't seem any point in keeping her there another fifteen minutes, just for appearances. There was nothing for her to do.

Keegan shook his head in mock annoyance. "Go on home," he told her. "Get a jump on traffic. Give Wendell my best."

"You sure, boss?" Mrs. Dodd asked. She seemed coiled and ready to jump up from her desk as soon as he delivered his answer.

"Yeah," he told her. "Go ahead. I'll lock up."

When Mrs. Dodd was out the door, Keegan closed the blinds in the window next to her desk. He went into the inner office and did the same and then turned off the overhead lights. The dog jogged after him.

In the outer office, Keegan got his jacket off the rack by the door. He was about to pull it on when the phone on Mrs. Dodd's desk rang. He looked at it, debating with himself whether to answer as it rang twice more. It wasn't yet five, so the office was supposed to still be open. It might be Sue Belk, with news of the elusive Lillian Cole.

He hung his jacket back up and sat down at Mrs. Dodd's desk. He picked up the receiver and pressed the lit button. "Jim Keegan," he said into the phone.

"James?" the voice on the other end said. "Am I talking to James?"

James? Only Danny Church ever called him that, but it clearly wasn't the kid on the line. This voice sounded older, deeper. It conveyed the settled weight of authority.

"Yeah, this is Jim Keegan," Keegan said. "Who's calling?"

"My name's Burritt," the voice said. "Milton Burritt." He spoke as though the fact of his name held great importance. "Look, *James*, I appreciate how you've been looking out for Danny. I only just heard from him today. I had no idea he was back in California." Keegan heard a phone ring loudly on the other end of the line, but Burritt's voice didn't pause or acknowledge it in any way. "I've known Danny Church since he was born, and—*well*—let's just say the boy can use all the guidance he can get."

"I'm really just a professional acquaintance," Keegan said. "But he did mention you. You were Ida Fletcher's attorney. The old family friend."

"Yes, I've known the Fletchers more than forty years," Burritt said. "Been their attorney nearly all that time. So, I was more than a little surprised to hear that Ida might have changed her will." His voice dropped in volume, like they were going off the record. "I've got to say I find the timing a little suspicious, it coming so close to her—"

"Yeah, Mr. Burritt," Keegan said, trying to cut him off. "You'll need to talk to a man called Roland Dion. He's the lawyer who did the new will. He's got all Ida Fletcher's papers now."

"Dion?" Burritt said. "I'm afraid I've never heard of him."

"Well, he's heard of you."

"Yes, well…" Burritt didn't finish the thought. He seemed to assume everyone had heard of him.

"Well, I passed all the papers off to him," Keegan said. "So, you should probably—"

"Yes, James, I gathered all that from Danny," Burritt went on. "But I thought I'd call you first, since we're both looking out for Danny's interests. I thought maybe you could give me the lay of the land before I stormed the ramparts as it were. I'm usually pressed for time, but I'm dining tonight at nine, if you'd care to join me."

THE SOUTH BAY Yachting Club lay in a bosky, sheltered corner of Newport Bay overlooking a marina. A young white-jacketed valet—very blond, very tanned—manned a tiny desk at the foot of the steps outside the entryway. He straightened up as Keegan's headlights approached, but Keegan just drove past him without slowing. He'd be damned if he was going to tip some surfer kid a dollar just to park his car.

He chose a far, empty corner of the lot, under a row of young eucalyptus trees, where his MG would be out of the way. He locked the car and walked back to the club's entrance. Wind was coming in off the bay, briny and damp and cool. A Coupe de Ville pulled up in front of the valet stand, and the kid in the white jacket got busy opening doors and tearing tickets, so Keegan slipped past him and climbed the front steps under the awning to the big oak doors.

The young maître d' inside could have doubled for the Chateau Marmont's concierge. It wasn't that they looked the same—this one had a squarish face and a precision haircut that might have been clipped from a Vitalis ad. It was more that the two of them manned their stations with a similar air of haughty purpose. They were brothers in a cause.

Keegan, however, had come prepared. He had had a sense of what to expect from a place like Milton Burritt's yacht club. He'd swung by his bungalow to drop off the dog, shave a second time, and change into a clean shirt. He'd put on his newest sports coat and his most expensive Botany tie. Still, somehow, this gatekeeper had pegged him right away as the kind of person he'd been installed here to keep at bay.

"My name should be on your list," Keegan said for the second time. "I just spoke with him on the phone. He's expecting me."

"And what is the name of the party you came to meet?" the man asked, all the while looking over Keegan's shoulder at the doorway, as though expecting someone of greater consequence.

"Burritt," Keegan said. "Milton Burritt. He said he'd be here for dinner."

At the mention of Burritt's name, the young man's eyes snapped back to Keegan. "Oh," he said. "I'm sorry, sir. Mr. Burritt told me he was expecting a guest. I just didn't think it would…" The young man didn't finish the sentence, so

Keegan would never learn in what ways he'd fallen short of the maître d's lofty expectations.

Instead, the young man turned toward the dining room, as if he expected Keegan to follow him. With a flick of his hand, he signaled to another, younger man to keep an eye on the door for him. Heaven forbid someone else as unsuitable as Keegan should wander in from the street without Milton Burritt's express invitation.

Keegan followed the maître d' down a short hallway. As he passed a wide arch, he glanced into a large, nautically themed barroom. Couples and foursomes sat around small round tables—an impressive crowd for a weeknight. The air was filled with boisterous, liquor-lubricated chatter. The décor was all burnished wood and brass-work, with painted buoys and burgee flags hung along the ceiling. A jazz trio was setting up in one corner. Keegan stopped walking.

There sat Danny Church at the bar. He was perched sideways on a barstool, an empty martini glass at his elbow. His jacket was draped over the back of his chair and his polo shirt was dazzlingly white. He seemed caught up in an animated conversation with another man a couple of barstools away. He didn't see Keegan in the archway, and for that Keegan was grateful.

Keegan picked up his pace and caught up with the maître d', who had yet to look back to see if Keegan was indeed following him. They passed into a large, dimly lit dining room. Though the bar was just a few yards away, this room was somehow hushed and sedate, cut off from the clamor. The conversation here held to a polite murmur, soft enough that Keegan could hear the clinking of glasses, the scrape of silverware on good china. At every table, a candle guttered in a crystal holder.

The maître d' led Keegan between all the tables to the vast room's farthest corner. There Milton Burritt, a florid white-haired man, sat in a large booth with a much younger woman. In any other context, Keegan would have taken them for father and daughter. But they were pressed too closely together, especially for a big leather booth that seemed designed for a party of eight. The way the man sat—spread out and smugly possessive—gave Keegan the impression that this was Burritt's usual table, a reserved outpost where he could sit in the shadows and keep an eye on everyone who came and went.

The maître d' offered Burritt an obsequious bow and then gave Keegan a curt nod. He headed back across the dining room without a word to anyone.

Milton Burritt didn't get up. He just gestured to the far end of the large booth. They might have shaken hands, but the table was too large to do it without considerable effort, so the lawyer brushed away the formality with an assured smile and a quick flick of his hand. He was clearly used to calling the shots, to being obeyed.

Keegan slid into the leather high-backed booth and looked at the couple opposite. Milton Burritt's voice boomed when he introduced himself and his young wife. He spoke with volume and careful enunciation, as if he might be addressing an open court. Burritt was in his late sixties, Keegan guessed—thick and prosperous in a pinstripe suit that was cut to disguise his bulk. The whiteness of his close-cropped hair stood out sharply above his ruddy, capillary-mapped cheeks.

Mrs. Burritt, on the other hand, was thin, well kept, and much, much too young—she probably hadn't yet reached thirty. Her sculpted hair was honey-blonde and the dress she wore showed off her smooth pale shoulders. Her eyes were bright, but they were disengaged, as though her thoughts were somewhere far away from this dim booth in this swanky yacht club. On the whole, she would not have been out of place on the cover of one of Mrs. Dodd's *Photoplay* movie magazines.

Burritt turned to her. "James and I just need to talk a little business before dinner, if that's okay with you." He didn't wait to find out if it *was* okay with her. He just turned back to Keegan. "Have you *had* dinner, James?" Burritt asked, his voice much too loud. "We'd be happy for you to join us."

Keegan was pretty sure he couldn't afford a meal in a place

like this, and he didn't want to feel beholden to Burritt if the man offered to cover his check. "I already ate," he lied. "Nine o'clock is a little late for me."

A waiter came and set two drinks in front of the couple, something amber in an etched crystal tumbler for him, something tall and pinkish and fruity for her. "How about a drink, then, James?" Burritt wanted to know. He tapped the rim of the glass that had just been set down in front of him. "Bruno makes a whiskey sour that is unsurpassed."

Again, Keegan thought it best to decline. Liquor on an empty stomach was never a good idea. "No thanks," he told the waiter. He turned to Burritt. "I'm driving," he explained.

Burritt grinned, as if this might have been a wonderful quip on Keegan's part, and he released the waiting server with an offhand nod. He lifted the whiskey sour to his lips and took a generous sip. Candlelight glinted off the carved crystal.

Here was a man, Keegan suspected, who never had to worry about getting pulled over for driving under the influence. Any officer foolish enough to stop him for erratic driving on PCH would surely regret it more than Milton Burritt ever would.

Burritt set down the drink on the tablecloth and tented his fingers together in front of him, ready for the case to commence. "Now, this alleged new will," Burritt said, his words carefully intoned for the jury's benefit. "What can you tell me about it? Did Ida make significant changes to the last one I drew up for her?"

Alleged? Keegan thought. "I couldn't tell you," he said. "I wasn't there when she made the new will, and I haven't seen the old one."

"It wasn't among her papers?"

Keegan shook his head. "Mrs. Fletcher gave me a box of papers, but that wasn't in it," Keegan said. "Just the new will. Would that make a difference?"

Burritt shrugged and adjusted his silk tie. "It might give us a little leverage if the original signed copy of the previous will can't be produced," he said. "We might be able to use its absence to slow probate down—if that turns out to be in our interest." He smiled and leaned forward. He let his voice drop. "So maybe keep it out of sight?" he said, like he thought Keegan had buried the evidence, a favor for their mutual friend Danny Church.

Keegan bristled. "I honestly haven't seen the original will." He said it clearly, for the record.

Burritt nodded knowingly, like he was happy to play along. He pressed himself back against the leather booth. "But perhaps we're getting ahead of ourselves, James," he said, his voice full and booming again. "How well were Danny's interests represented in this new will?"

"I'm no lawyer," Keegan said, "but I think the kid will do okay. There was a lump sum—a hundred grand—to be split between some of Mrs. Fletcher's staff. As far as I can tell, everything else goes to the nephew."

Burritt dismissed the mention of a hundred thousand dollars with a wave of his hand, as if such a sum were negligible. Hell, a man like him might tip the valet that much for chasing down his Bentley and having it idling out front when he came through the door. "But you understand why I'm asking, don't you, James?" Burritt said. "Do you see why I'm a little suspicious? A new will with a new lawyer just a couple of months before she died?" An unctuous smile lit up the man's reddened face. "I'm sure, like me, you want Danny to get his due." He tilted his head forward a little as he regarded Keegan from across the table. "Am I right, James?"

Keegan thought of Danny Church out in the bar, laughing and chatting and slapping backs. He thought of the kid's scorching car hood, his fake alibi, the old lady who died trying to escape him. "Yes," Keegan said evenly. "I do want Danny to get what's coming to him." He nodded over at the dining room's entrance. "You know, I might have seen him at the bar on the way in." He watched the other man closely. "Is he a member here?"

Burritt nodded with an air of patient sagacity, as if such

facts had already been stipulated and read into the record. They needn't be trotted out again. "Of *course* he is," Burritt said. "Since birth. His uncle was a charter member."

Keegan imagined Frank at the helm of *The Seven of Swords* on the dark water, the lights of Avalon Bay ahead of him on the horizon. "So, Danny knows how to sail a boat?"

Burritt chuckled and slapped the tabletop, jingling the ice in the glasses. "Good lord, yes," he said. "Why, Danny raced in Port Phillip Bay in '56."

Keegan nodded, though he had no idea what the sentence meant. It was enough for him to know that Danny Church could sail. How hard would it be to intercept a small boat like *The Seven of Swords* on its way to Avalon? How hard would it be to sink it?

"Danny grew up on the marina out there," Burritt was saying. "He's 'born to the brine', as they say."

"And he has his own boat?"

The question seemed to catch Burritt off guard, like a query from the bench he hadn't anticipated. "Well, maybe not one of his own," he said. "He's been away a good long while. But you don't have to rent a slip to be a member here." He waved vaguely around the dim room as if to indicate that this yachting club might contain more surgeons than sailors, more bankers than actual boatmen.

"But he could get out on the ocean if he wanted to go for a spin," Keegan said.

"Well, yes," Burritt said. "I suppose he could."

The whole time the two of them were talking, Burritt's young wife kept glancing sideways, across the dining room to the entryway, as if hoping to catch a familiar face that might come to her rescue. Burritt barely acknowledged her, rarely glanced in her direction. He seemed to regard her as a decorous prop, part of a well-appointed night out—like the crystal candle holder on the tablecloth or the ornately folded napkins.

A waiter arrived with a pair of plates, and Burritt's trophy wife brightened considerably. He set them down on the table, bowed, and then backed away. Milton Burritt smiled down at the oozing steak before him. He grunted softly and picked up his silverware.

"Lillian Cole," Keegan said. "She was one of the staff members mentioned in the new will. Any idea where I could find her?"

"I know who you mean," Burritt said. He stabbed the steak with a fork and made an incision. A clear, pinkish fluid oozed from the meat. "But I really know nothing about the woman."

"How about someone who goes by the name Madame Lena?" Keegan said. "Ever hear of her?"

Burritt nodded indulgently. "She was an advisor of sorts," he said. He lifted a wedge of meat to his lips.

"She was a fortune teller," Keegan said.

Burritt nodded again. He regarded Keegan as he chewed and swallowed. His lips were slick with drippings now. "Ida Fletcher could be a trusting soul," he said.

"Until she wasn't," Keegan said.

Burritt paused a beat. He rested both fists on either side of his plate, the knife and fork jutting upward, while he considered Keegan's words. He nodded. Apparently, he would allow Keegan's testimony to stand without objection. "You're right about that, James," he said. "The woman—God bless her soul—could be a little capricious."

WHEN KEEGAN PASSED the big archway on his way out, the barroom was a bit less noisy. The jazz trio was playing a sleepy version of 'All of Me'. The nephew was still parked on the same barstool, though the others around him were empty now. Church sat with his back turned to the archway, a fresh martini on the bar top. He was talking to one of the two bartenders, a hulking, balding man with a garland of silvery hair at his temples.

The big man seemed to be half listening while the kid prattled on. He did absolutely nothing to hide his indifference. He polished a stemware glass with a white cloth and slipped it into the overhead rack. The bartender seemed disproportionately large for the job, a giant among all those bottles and glasses, a bull in a china shop. Then again, Keegan thought, maybe he was the perfect hire, barkeep and bouncer in one package—that is, if a place as refined as the South Bay Yachting Club ever had a need for muscle.

The blond valet jumped up from his stool when Keegan came out through the club's front doors. He loped toward Keegan like a friendly Golden Retriever, but Keegan just shook his head and looked past him. He'd be getting his own car, thank you very much.

The parking lot was much darker now than when Keegan arrived. The lamps gave off a sickly buzz and drained the colors from the cars parked underneath them. Every paint job appeared to be just a slightly different shade of jaundiced gray. The wind coming in off the bay was much colder now too.

An idea came to him, and he glanced behind him at the club's entrance. A foursome was waiting at the valet stand, and the blond kid was jogging down a row of cars, looking for theirs. Keegan reached out as he passed a parked Buick Riviera and tugged out the slip of paper that had been tucked under the windshield wiper. He walked a bit farther before he looked down at what he had in his hand: a paper stub the size of a postage stamp, numbered in red ink, just like the one he'd found on Church's Jaguar the day after Ida Fletcher went missing. It had been a valet's ticket. The nephew hadn't been dining at the Bouzy Rouge. He'd been here at the marina, and he'd lied to Keegan about that fact.

Keegan unlocked his car and got in. This trip had been a qualified success. He was no closer to finding Lillian Cole—the actual job he'd been tasked with—but he'd learned a little more about Danny Church. The kid could sail. And he'd been at the marina the night his aunt went missing. Keegan could only make out the foggiest outline of the supposed crime, but it was getting clearer in his head. Church could have waited out on the bay for his Aunt Ida's boat to leave her home dock. He could have slipped in behind her, running without lights. He could have followed her, at a distance, out past the breakwater into the open sea. It might easily have happened that way. All the kid would have had to do was find a boat to use.

Keegan started up his MG and pulled on the headlight switch, lighting up a line of eucalyptus trunks. He was about to put his car in gear when a rectangle of light skimmed across the dumpsters and bushes along the side of the club and then vanished—a door opening and closing. A large shape lumbered across the dark lawn and stopped at the railing that overlooked the marina. There was no mistaking the huge, shambling shape: it was the bartender from inside, the one Danny Church had just been talking to. Keegan turned off the engine and killed the headlights. He got out, closed the car door quietly, and slipped across the parking lot. He skirted the edge of the lot, staying near the line of trees.

The bartender struck a match and held it to a cigarette. His big, meaty face lit up like a jack-o'-lantern for a few seconds and then vanished into darkness again when he shook out the match.

The big man turned when he heard Keegan's footsteps coming up behind him. He stepped away from the railing and squared off, standing akimbo. Keegan waved to him, doing his best to look harmless. He dug his hands into his pockets like someone innocuous, out for an evening stroll. Nothing to see here. No reason to raise an alarm.

The barkeep folded his arms in front of himself and stood with his feet apart. He was as broad and imposing as the invisible breakwater far out on the horizon. In the dim light, Keegan made out a white shirt and black tie under a gray vest with a pocket square—the club's uniform for bartenders, he guessed. The man's engraved nametag read BRUNO.

"You're the barkeep," Keegan said, keeping his voice bright and casual. "I hear you make a whiskey sour that is unsurpassed."

The big man shot him a sardonic look, like he was on his

break and shouldn't have to deal with club members. He had to tolerate the chitchat behind the bar, but not out here behind the dumpsters. He turned away and faced the dark marina, hunching over and leaning on the railing.

Keegan came and stood next to him. "The truth is, I'm not a member," Keegan said. "I wouldn't know an anchor from an anvil." Keegan put both his hands on the railing. "And, hell," he said, "who am I kidding? There's no way I could afford it. I'm just a PI." He looked at the side of the big man's face. "A woman named Ida Fletcher hired me to keep an eye on things for her. You ever hear of her?"

Bruno shrugged. "Sure, I heard of her," he said with little enthusiasm. His voice was a low rumble, like waves breaking over riprap. "She's the old dame who drowned last week."

Word traveled fast. "Well, the kid in there at the bar?" Keegan pressed on. "The one who I'm guessing won't stop talking your ear off? Well, that's her nephew. And he stands to inherit a bundle."

The big man turned to face Keegan and waited solemnly. He took another drag on his cigarette and watched Keegan through the smoke.

Keegan tried to gauge how much to say and how much to hold back. "The truth is, I don't like the kid," Keegan said. "Not even a little. I don't trust him, and—well—I think he had something to do with what happened to the old lady."

The news didn't faze the big man. He nodded and leaned an elbow on the top of the railing. "The kid's been standing a lot of rounds," he said. He flicked ash from his cigarette onto the ground between them. "He's running up a big tab in the old lady's name," he said. "So, yeah, he acts like he's got a lot of money. Or at least expects to get some soon."

Keegan nodded. This Bruno was a man he could work with. He might be employed by the rich and mighty, but he was no sycophant. The Chateau Marmont could use a guy like Bruno. Keegan nodded out at the dark marina. "You know if he has a boat out there?"

The big man shrugged and gestured back at the building's side door with the hand that held the cigarette. "The bar closes at 1:00 a.m.," he said, "so I'm generally out of here around two."

"And?"

"And some nights the kid's Jaguar is still in the parking lot." He looked steadily at Keegan. "Make of that what you will," he said. "But to me that means he's got a berth somewhere nearby."

Keegan nodded. That would explain the unclaimed valet ticket under the windshield wiper. He turned and looked out over the dark marina. Bare masts tilted in the moonlight. Rigging clanged softly. Boarding piers creaked on the flowing tide. Only a few lights were on in the boat cabins. The knot in Keegan's stomach cinched tighter. Somewhere out there was the boat Danny Church used to kill his aunt.

Keegan got out his wallet. He found a ten in among all the ones. He tugged it out and then found a business card that had his home number written on the back. "What nights do you work, Bruno?"

The bartender looked at the ten, unimpressed. In a place like the South Bay Yachting Club, he'd obviously seen bigger tips.

Keegan grinned. "Yeah, I know," he said. "But I'm a working man like you. It's all I can afford."

The big man gave him a wry smile and shrugged. He took the money and slipped it into his trouser pocket. "I'm here every night but Monday," he said.

Keegan nodded. "If it gets past midnight some night, and the kid's still sitting at the bar running his mouth and running a tab," Keegan said, "call the number on the back and give me a heads up. I want to see where he goes when he leaves."

The bartender held the card up to the light. "James Keegan," he said, sounding the words out slowly, like he wasn't much of a reader.

"Call me Jim," Keegan said. "Nobody I like calls me James."

CHAPTER TEN

EARLY THE NEXT morning, Keegan parked in the usual lot on Sixth Street, but instead of going to his office, he took the dog on a leisurely stroll over to Pershing Square, letting her sniff all the lampposts and hydrants and sidewalk trees she wanted along the way. It was a brisk, breezy morning, and the cool night air still lingered in the shadows of the tall buildings. The sun had not yet risen high enough to burn it away.

There weren't many people in the park when they arrived, just a few hunched men on the benches, bundled in overcoats. They had probably slept here. The three flags atop the Biltmore Hotel rippled and snapped in the wind. Sycamore leaves and a few loose newspaper pages had blown against the Beethoven statue pedestal. Autumn had arrived in Los Angeles.

Keegan let the dog have her way. He followed her around the fountain, and she led him with her nose to the brickwork, trailing invisible lines of scent. He let her pee on the lawn under a date palm before he finally gave her leash a tug and led her over to Lusk's newsstand.

Lusk watched the two of them approach and shook his head with mock disdain. When Keegan was within speaking distance, Lusk nodded down at the dog. "Some kind of big hunting dog would make sense," he said. "A chocolate Lab maybe, or an Irish Setter." He leaned forward lazily, elbows on his plywood counter. "But *that* thing belongs in an Audrey Hepburn movie," he said. "It doesn't help your image any."

"Yeah, but she's a terrier," Keegan said, looking down at the dog. "It's the attitude that counts. That right there is eighteen-and-a-half pounds of pure tenacity."

The dog got busy scratching behind her ear with a hind paw, moaning indulgently—which didn't do much to buttress Keegan's claim.

Lusk shook his head. "You keep telling yourself that, buddy," he said. He leaned back in his chair and folded his arms across his chest. "So, what brings you by my little corner of the world before lunchtime?"

Keegan tugged the dog's leash and brought her closer to Lusk's stand. It seemed like a long shot, but he might as well ask. Lusk's connections covered more of this town than the Red Car lines. "You ever hear of a woman who goes by the name Madame Lena?"

"The fortune teller?"

Keegan stood a little straighter, surprised. "Yeah," he said. "You actually know who she is?"

Lusk shrugged. "What is it you want to know about her?" he asked.

"Do you know where I can find her?"

Lusk sat back in his chair and looked at Keegan sourly. "It'll cost you a dime," he announced.

Keegan rocked back on his heels. It was an unusually small price to pay for a good lead, especially from Kipper Lusk. He dug the loose change from his pocket, shook it on his hand, and then set two nickels on Lusk's plywood counter.

Lusk swept them into his palm and dropped them in his till. He leaned out, grabbed a copy of the *LA Times* from its rack, and handed it to Keegan.

Keegan took it and gave it a look. SPACE SENTRIES, the banner headline read. U.S. ATOMIC WATCHDOGS IN ORBIT. "What's this for?" he asked.

"Madame Lena's got a classified ad in there every damn day of the week," Lusk told him.

"Really?"

"*Yes*, really."

Keegan pulled out the paper's back section and tucked the rest under his arm. He flipped through the pages.

"Look under P," Lusk told him. "'Personal Advisors'."

Keegan found the section and folded back the paper. The ad was small, not even a full column inch. How had Lusk even known it would be there?

Mme Lena

Reader & Advisor on all matters. Has the
power to help humanity. Can influence
the actions of anyone, anywhere. Will
answer one question by phone.
1692 Nella Vista Dr. AX5-2124

"Thanks, Kip," Keegan said. "You really know your newspaper."

Lusk shrugged. "Not a hell of a lot to do in here all day," he said.

"Still," Keegan said, "it's a small ad. I'm impressed you remembered it."

"I'm no fancy detective," Lusk said. "But I'm observant."

Keegan nodded, thought a moment, and then grinned. "You *called* her," he said, "didn't you?"

Lusk looked off down Hill Street toward Sixth. "I don't know what you're talking about," he said.

"It was your jinx, wasn't it?" Keegan said, his grin widening. "You broke a bunch of lousy mirrors, and then you called a fortune teller to see if she could reverse the curse."

"She's not a fortune teller," Lusk said sulkily, "she's a *personal advisor*." He sat back in his chair and crossed his arms. "So, okay, maybe I talked to her on the phone," he admitted. "Just the once."

"Calling a fortune teller because you broke some mirrors," Keegan said, still smirking. He tucked the classified section under his arm with the rest of the paper and tapped the side of his head with a finger. "You're a man of rare insights, Kip. A real intellect."

"Go ahead," Lusk said dourly, "laugh all you want. You're the one who came sniffing around my newsstand to find out about the woman." He sighed and shook his head, arms still crossed. "This right here?" he said. "The way you treat an old friend? It's eighteen-and-a-half pounds of pure bullshit."

In his office, Keegan clipped out Madame Lena's ad with a pair of scissors, a scrap of newsprint smaller than a matchbook cover. He tucked the paper in the corner of his desk blotter and then stared down at it. *Personal advisor.* The idea seemed even more promising than Keegan had hoped. If anyone knew what private worries Ida Fletcher had about her nephew, it would be this woman. He picked up his desk phone and dialed. He listened while it rang a few times, and then an answering service picked up.

"Tell the Madame I'd like her to call me at her earliest convenience," Keegan told the woman on the line. "Though I'm sure she already senses that."

The woman on the line didn't seem to get the joke. "I'm sorry," she said, all business. "I should say what?"

"Nothing," Keegan told her. "Just tell her to give me a call. Today, if she can." He gave the woman his name and office number and then waited while she wrote it down and repeated it back.

The phone rang after Mrs. Dodd had left for lunch and Keegan picked it up, assuming it would be Madame Lena. It was Sue Belk up in Portland.

"Found the daughter out in Saint John's," Belk told him.

"But she hasn't heard from Lillian in a few months. Said she thought she was still down there in LA. Didn't know anything about a retirement."

A dead end. But if Lillian Colle was still in LA, Keegan could probably track her down himself. Word of Ida Fletcher's demise would reach her eventually—hell, even Bruno the Barkeep had heard the news. Lillian Cole would come out of the woodwork, especially if she thought there was a chance she was in the old lady's will. "Did you tell the daughter there was money involved?" Keegan asked.

"I didn't say how much," Belk told him. "But I said it would be in her mom's interest to give you a call right away."

Keegan could hear the crumple of papers on the line. Belk had done what she could. He'd make sure Dion paid her well.

"Say, what's the weather like down there these days?" Belk asked, her voice suddenly a little wistful. "I miss the sun."

Keegan glanced over his shoulder at the window. "Bright," he said. "Clear and windy. What's it like up there?"

"Showers and downpours with a chance of rain," she said. "Why I ever came up here, I don't know."

THE CALL FROM Madame Lena finally came early Friday morning. Mrs. Dodd sent it through to Keegan's inner office phone without complaint or commentary. She seemed eager to pass the woman off to him and wash her hands of any involvement with the occult. No dabbling with the spirit world for her.

"Do you have a question you would like to ask?" Madame Lena said as soon as Keegan picked up the line. She spoke with a faint accent, like an actress in a B-movie tasked with sounding exotic. *Come with me to the casbah.* "The first question is free," she went on, "and I can answer it over the phone."

Keegan tugged out the clipped newspaper ad he'd tucked into the corner of his blotter. *Will answer one question by phone.* As far as gimmicks went, it wasn't half bad. It had, after all, worked on Kipper Lusk.

"You can spare me the spiel," Keegan told her. "I don't have a question. That's not why I called."

"But of *course* you have a question, Mr. Kee-*gon*." She pronounced the name all wrong, but she plowed on with such confidence that it didn't occur to Keegan to go back and correct her. "Everyone has questions. It is only human to wonder."

"That might well be," Keegan said, "but I'm calling on a different matter. I need some information about one of your former clients." He slipped the ad back in his blotter and picked up a ballpoint pen. His notebook was already open and waiting.

"But you *do* have a question," Madame Lena insisted, brushing his words aside. "It is a question that can only be answered by someone who communes with other realms. There is no reason to hold it back, Mr. Kee-*gon*. I already have the answer you need."

She was good, Keegan had to admit. There was something to her headlong self-assurance that came across as compelling—and, if he were being honest, it put him a little on the defensive. He set the pen down on his desk, tipped back his chair, and swung his feet up. "So, *you* have an answer," he said, "even though *I* don't have a question?"

"In fact, I do," Madame Lena said, unfazed.

Keegan smiled and ran a hand back through his hair. "An answer from other realms?"

"You are not fooling anyone," she said. Her voice sounded impatient now, as if *Keegan* were the one wasting time with tiresome mind games. "And here is your answer, Mr. Kee-*gon*," she said. "The young woman wants you to know that she forgives you. She knows that what happened was not your fault."

Keegan swung his legs down from his desk and rocked forward in his chair. He pictured Eve sitting in the big chair in the cottage living room, her feet tucked up under her. They had sipped that good Bordeaux from his mother's Royal Doulton teacups. They had talked glibly of travel and romance and wine cellars. Neither of them had imagined the blind, deadly turns just ahead of them.

"Did you hear me, Mr. Kee-*gon*?" Madame Lena was asking.

Keegan stared blankly down at the empty page in his open notebook. It would be pure folly to give this woman's words any credence. This was the same cheap gimmick any carnival soothsayer might use. It was the stuff of horoscopes—the good-chance guess. What man Keegan's age *wouldn't* have a young woman in his life he'd want forgiveness from?

Still, she'd caught him off guard, and he didn't like it. *Don't go messing with her*, Mrs. Dodd had warned him. Well, damn that Mrs. Dodd and her haunted elevators. Keegan rubbed his face and willed his thoughts to slow down. "I don't know what you mean," he said—but his voice sounded timid and tinny, even in his own head. "I don't know any young women."

Madame Lena paused on the other end of the line. He could only hear her breathing. It was as if she were listening while someone whispered into the woman's ear. "She is in your house," the woman said finally. Her voice was a little more tentative now, as though she were relaying a message that she, herself, didn't quite comprehend.

Keegan opened and closed his free hand. "I'm afraid you're all wrong," he said. "I live alone."

Nora trotted into view in the open doorway, looking like she'd just wakened from a nap on the oval rug next to Mrs. Dodd's desk. She sniffed the air in Keegan's inner office and then backed away, out of sight again.

"Yes and no," the psychic told him airily. "You live alone, but also you do not."

"It's a tiny house," Keegan said. "If there was a young woman in it, I'd probably have noticed her by now."

Again, a long pause and the woman's breathing over the line. She seemed to be listening to a voice Keegan couldn't overhear. "You refuse to see her," Madame Lena reported. "But she visits there nonetheless."

Keegan picked up the pen again and tapped it on his desktop. This phone call was getting away from him. "Look, I'm not really a customer," he said. "I'm an investigator. I just need some information about one of your clients, that's all. It's the only reason I called."

"If you have more questions, an appointment will be required," Madame Lena informed him, her voice suddenly cool and businesslike. "I could fit you in tonight, if you would like."

WHEN KEEGAN HUNG up, he sat in the dimly lit office with his palms pressed down on the desktop, trying to collect his thoughts. This unsettled mood he was in—it was nothing. He was just tired. Who wouldn't feel a little unnerved after a week like the one he'd had? A dead man on a steel table. A dog barking at empty chairs. A superstitious fusspot manning the desk in his outer office. It was October, that was all. It was the season for weirdness and flights of fancy. And Madame Lena? She was nothing but a sideshow act—just a lot of smoke and broken mirrors.

Keegan got up and went to the window and pulled up the blinds to let more light in the gloomy room. Down below, Sixth Street was bright and clogged with morning traffic. A blue World Series banner hung from the awning in front of the barber shop across the way. A bicycle messenger slipped between a passing red car and van that was double parked.

It was just another bright and workaday Los Angeles morning out there. Keegan had seen a million of them. There was nothing in the least uncanny about it.

KEEGAN CLOSED THE office early that afternoon. If he was going to get to Madame Lena's address out in East Whittier during rush hour, he'd have to give himself time.

Mrs. Dodd was only too happy to accommodate him. She

was never one to complain about a weekend starting early. "You sure you can make it all the way out there and back to Jackson's in time for your date?" she said as he was pulling on his jacket.

"There's plenty of time," he told her. "You just don't want me to go."

She nodded. "I will not pretend," she told him. "I don't like it at all." She stood by the door with her arms folded, looking, somehow, both worried and petulant. "You sure you know what you're getting into, boss?"

"It's just an interview," Keegan said. "I interview people all the time."

"You know what I mean," she said. "It's not a good idea to mess with that kind of stuff. *Madame Lena's* kind of stuff."

"What stuff might that be?" Keegan asked, just to goad her a little.

"The *occult*," she told him. She spread her arms out in front of herself. "There. I said it. Make fun of me if you want. *You* should take it more seriously."

"I'm a grown man," Keegan reminded her. "Ghosts and goblins and Bloody Mary—that stuff's all kids' play. Stories you tell at sleepovers. You realize they sell Ouija boards at Toys 'R' Us, right?"

Mrs. Dodd shrugged. "They sell rat poison in grocery stores," she said. "That doesn't mean you should make a meal of it." Her purse was on the corner of her desk. She picked it up and pulled the strap over her shoulder. "Don't tempt fate, is all I'm saying." She began to pull the door open. "It isn't safe—whether or not you believe in it."

Keegan took the dog's leash down from the hat rack. "Don't worry," he said. "Nothing's going to happen."

Mrs. Dodd turned back and looked him up and down. She pushed the door shut again. "Something's *already* happened," she said. "You've been acting all weird since you got off the phone with that Madame this morning. You don't think I noticed it? I don't know what she said to you, but it definitely got you spooked."

The dog, seer of ghosts, was sniffing the base of the door now, waiting to go out.

"She didn't spook me," Keegan said.

Mrs. Dodd stepped closer. "I know you, boss," she said. "I know when something fazes you. You try to be all smooth and slick, but stuff gets to you sometimes. And you're not very good at hiding it."

He shook his head and called Nora over. He bent to clip the leash on the dog's collar.

"This isn't trick-or-treat," Mrs. Dodd told him. She adjusted the purse strap on her shoulder. "I've got a real bad feeling about this Madame Lena," she said. "Nothing good is going to come from seeing her. I just know it's going to turn out badly."

"So now *you're* clairvoyant too?" he said.

Mrs. Dodd sighed, like he was being contrary. She gave him a weary, dismissive shake of the head and went to the door. "Be nice to Helen tonight," she said. "That girl deserves a lot better than you."

The dog lunged forward as soon as the door was open, but Keegan held her back with the leash. He waited until Mrs. Dodd closed the door behind her. He'd just linger here a minute longer until she was on the elevator.

THE FRIDAY AFTERNOON traffic, headed out of town for the weekend, was heavy, but Keegan was driving south, and most of it was northbound. It was only a little after five now, and his exit from the 101 was coming up.

He'd dropped the dog off at the cottage, washed his face, and changed his clothes. He put on the same sports coat and Botany tie he'd worn to meet Milton Burritt. It had been years since he'd gone on an actual date, and he wasn't sure if the apprehension he felt was because he was meeting Helen for dinner or because Mrs. Dodd had gotten under his skin with all her worry about Madame Lena.

In a few minutes, he was on Whittier Boulevard, driving through the nondescript postwar housing tracts of Montebello and Pico Rivera, with all their corner gas stations and strip mall storefronts. He'd get to Madame Lena's early, he guessed, which was fine with him. It would give him a chance to gather his thoughts in the parking lot before he went inside her office.

The plan was simple: he'd humor the woman, see what he could find out about the old lady and her nephew, and be done with the Madame. He'd have plenty of time to head back up the 101 to Jackson's before eight o'clock—and, with any luck, he'd arrive with a good story to tell Helen over dinner: his meeting with the soothsayer. It would be like something out of *Macbeth*. She'd appreciate that.

KEEGAN HAD EXPECTED Madame Lena's place of business to be a storefront shop, or maybe a shabby office suite at the top of some stairs off a busy boulevard, but the directions he'd jotted in his notebook took him to narrow suburban streets full of modest houses. The same four models of small tract homes repeated again and again down both sides of the street. He pulled over in front of a playground and unfolded one of the glove-box maps to make sure he was heading to the right address. He was. He continued on, driving slowly.

He turned onto Madame Lena's street, Nella Vista Drive, and slowed the MG as he checked the numbers affixed to the curbside mailboxes. And there it was, number 1692. The only thing that set this small house apart from its neighbors was the neon sign burning in the window by the door, in front of the drawn curtains: the word *Psychic*, written in crimson cursive script against a blue quarter moon.

Cars were parked at the curb on both sides of the road, so Keegan drove to the end of the block and make a wide U-turn in the intersection. He came back along the street, looking for a space, and backed into an empty spot across the street from Madame Lena's, between two different models of station wagon. He turned off the engine and consulted his watch. He was a good fifteen minutes early. He'd have to wait.

The sun was just dipping below the horizon behind him. Tall jacaranda trees lined both sides of the street, their gaunt, arthritic branches merging above the asphalt. With all the modest, well-kept starter homes, this looked like the kind of neighborhood that would be full of young families: stickball in the streets, bicycles abandoned on front lawns, hopscotch chalked on front drives. In a few weeks, these sidewalks would be awash with trick-or-treaters.

Keegan glanced across at Madame Lena's house, where the neon light burned in the front window. None of the interior lamps were on, despite the dying daylight. The house was close and dark and sinister. It seemed to gather in more than its share of shadows from the towering trees. What did these neighbors think of their suburban soothsayer? On Halloween night, did the children flock to the *psychic* house or flee it? Keegan checked his watch again. Nine more minutes.

The young woman wants you to know that she forgives you. Keegan liked to think he was immune to superstition, that he'd grown wise to every con and shortcut in the book. And Madame Lena's trick was just another of the same. He knew how quickly the mind jumped to its own conclusions, filling in the missing details. Madame Lena was nothing more than the Zoltar machine at a penny arcade. The preprinted card says an old woman is watching over you, and your mind lunges right away to your dead grandmother. Her routine on the phone was the same ruse; it was plain as a pikestaff. Madame Lena had mumbled something about a young woman—and Keegan's mind had plunged through the ice, plummeting straight to Eve. He'd be a fool to let such a cheap gimmick throw him off.

Keegan checked his watch. He'd be damned if he was going to spend five more minutes sitting out here in his car talking to himself. The last of the daylight had fled from the sky by now. He took the keys from the ignition and squeezed them in his fist. He got out of the car and crossed the dark, quiet street. Perhaps arriving a few minutes early would be to his advantage. Maybe he'd catch the psychic off guard.

He passed a row of trimmed rosemary bushes, climbed the porch steps, and paused to steel himself. He was reaching out to press the doorbell, when the door swung open. Madame Lena must have been watching him through the crack in the curtains. She'd seen him sitting in his car, talking to himself and looking like a fool. She'd seen him checking his watch and climbing her porch steps mumbling. So much for his element of surprise.

In the doorway's shadows, Madame Lena's face was side-lit by the red neon sign. It was a ghoulish effect, like a bloodstain splashed across her cheek. The woman was in her sixties, Keegan guessed, with silvery hair that hung past her shoulders. She wore large hoop earrings and a shapeless black robe that swept the floor. Even the gold amulet that dangled on a chain around her neck struck Keegan as cliché. In a way, her getup soothed his nerves. Here was a stereotype from a low-budget movie, a bit-player gypsy sent over from central casting. *Abbott and Costello Meet the Psychic*. There was nothing here but charade.

"Evening," he said. "I'm Jim Keegan."

The woman smiled at him serenely. "I know who you are, Mr. *Kee*-gon," she said, her accent even more pronounced now than it had been over the phone.

This was no more sinister than Halloween in Hollywood, Keegan thought—except here the costumed trick-or-treater was on the wrong side of the door.

"Come in, Mr. *Kee*-gon," she said, stepping back to let him enter.

Keegan stepped into the gloomy lit front room. Again, it felt like a set-dresser's stereotype: candles and beads, oval tables and wingback armchairs, lampshades draped in gauze. A table in the center of the room was bracketed by two oval-backed chairs. A small wood fire crackled in the grate, but the house still felt unnaturally cold. The air smelled of sandalwood incense. The only thing missing, as far as Keegan could see, was a crystal ball.

Madame Lena closed the door behind them and directed Keegan into one of the chairs at the table. An oversized deck of tarot cards and an unlit candelabrum waited on the black tablecloth.

"Like I said on the phone," Keegan said, "I'm not really here to have my fortune told. I just have a few questions about Ida Fletcher." Keegan pulled out the nearest chair and sat in it. He folded his hands on the table. "Don't worry," he said. "I'll pay you just the same. You can bill me your usual fee."

Instead of taking the other seat, Madame Lena crossed to the fireplace. She took a wood taper stick from a vase on the mantel and bent to light it in the flames. She came back to the table and began to light the candelabrum's three candles, one by one, with ritualistic flourish. It was all part of her show, Keegan sensed.

"Like I said," Keegan told her, "you don't need to do all that on my account. I'm not here for a reading."

Madame Lena ignored him. She touched the flame to the final wick, tossed the taper into the fireplace, and took her seat across from him. Her dark eyes glimmered in the candlelight. She picked up the stack of large tarot cards. Without shuffling them, she began to lay out a row on the black tablecloth in front of her.

"I'm actually a private eye," Keegan said, trying to get her to look up at him. "I'm just here for information."

She added one last card to the row and set the deck down in the table's center, next to the candelabrum base.

"You see, I was hired by Ida Fletcher," Keegan pressed on, feeling like he was in danger of ceding control of the situation if he didn't assert himself more. "I understand she used to be one of your clients."

Madame Lena pondered the cards a few seconds, as if

parsing what she saw there, and finally lifted her head. "And how may I be of assistance?"

Now that Keegan had her attention, her gaze felt somehow too direct, a little unsettling. He glanced down at the cards on the tabletop. The room seemed impossibly chilly, colder than the night had been outside. "How long did you know Mrs. Fletcher?"

"Many, many years," Madame Lena said airily. "Since before the war."

"So, she must have consulted you about a lot of personal things."

"Indeed."

"Did she ever talk about her nephew?" Keegan said. "A kid by the name of Danny Church?"

"Naturally," Madame Lena said. Her every answer was clipped, reticent—like a hostile witness under oath.

"Did Mrs. Fletcher have any worries about him?" Keegan asked. "Was there any kind of conflict? Any animosity?"

Madame Lena bowed her head a little. It was hard to know if she was composing her answer or consulting the tarot cards. "Mrs. Fletcher loved her nephew," she said, choosing her words carefully. "Like a mother, she made the child her life's center. It was a great difficulty for her when he moved away."

Keegan nodded. That didn't square with the Ida Fletcher he knew. Either the psychic was being coy, or something big had happened between the old lady and her nephew since she'd fallen out with her psychic. "I didn't know the woman well, myself," he admitted, "but she had a reputation for— let's say—turning against people?"

Madame Lena continued to gaze down at her cards. She seemed determined to reveal nothing. Her circumspect manner was maddening. "She is indeed a complicated woman," Madame Lena allowed.

Keegan noted her use of present tense and pressed on. "Do you know any reason Mrs. Fletcher wouldn't want to see him?" he asked. "Was she scared of him?"

"Of course not," Madame Lena said. "She loved her nephew."

Keegan thought of the old lady's shocked face when he'd told her Danny Church was in town. Alarm had electrified the whole room at the mere mention of his name. What had Church done to turn her against him? "Well, the two of them must have had some kind of falling out," Keegan said. "Any idea what might have caused it?"

"Falling out?" she said. She was still gazing down at the skulls and scythes and hooded figures splayed out on the tablecloth—still concentrating on them, though nothing about them had changed.

Keegan felt a surge of irritation. This whole visit had been a mistake. He wanted to reach across and sweep the row of cards off the table onto the floor. "*Yes*," he said hotly. "The two of them had a *falling out*. You know—like the one she had with you."

Madame Lena looked up from her cards, her gaze still cloaked in an otherworldly serenity. "She and I had no falling out."

"She stopped coming to see you," Keegan said, leaning forward. "She took you out of her will." He pressed down his hands on the tabletop on either side of the stack of unused tarot cards. "You *did* know you were in her will at one point, didn't you? Or did your gifts fail you on that point?"

"I was led to believe as much."

"But she cut you off," Keegan said. "She wrote a new will. You're not getting a penny now. I'd call that a falling out."

Madame Lena looked at Keegan, as if a little pained by his tone, a little offended by his disbelief. Again, she tilted her head down. "I know you are a skeptic, Mr. *Kee*-gon," she said, looking at the cards and not at him. "I can truly see your future in these cards. But only in glimpses." She straightened one of the cards, a robed man bearing a lantern. "You'll soon travel across the ocean," she said, as if reading what was plainly printed there. "You live alone, very high up, but your house is haunted by a spirit." She tilted her head, as if trying to bring the vision into better focus. "It is a young woman. A short name. From the Bible."

Eve, Keegan thought, his heart thudding. *Her name was Eve*. The room seemed to be listing to one side now. He reached out and held the edge of the small table with both hands to steady himself. The air felt raw and chilled against his face. The incense was clouding his thoughts. How did this woman know about Eve?

Madame Lena gathered the cards into a stack and tapped them straight on the tabletop. "For you, I see only glimpses of your future," she said, eyeing him with cruel detachment. "But my own destiny I see with great clarity."

"And what is it you see?

"When all is said and done," she said, "I will be in Ida Fletcher's will."

"That's not possible," Keegan said, his voice dry. "Has anyone told you what happened to her?" He watched her closely. He found himself hoping she wouldn't answer him.

"No one has told me," she said. "But still I know."

"And what is it that you know?" he asked.

Madame Lena gazed placidly back at him, candlelight glimmering in her dark eyes. "We *both* know she is dead, Mr. *Kee*-gon," Madame Lena said. "We both know she is at the bottom of the sea."

CHAPTER ELEVEN

KEEGAN CROSSED NELLA Vista Drive to his MG in a trance, lightheaded and rattled. He stood beside his MG, fumbling too long with the keys before he could get in the driver's seat. He then gazed numbly out through the windshield.

The streetlamps and all the spindly jacaranda branches crosshatched the scene with shadows. His hands felt numb, and he sat holding the keys, squeezing them in his fist. He stared out at the dark street, trying to think of what it was he should do next. His thoughts seeped out in every direction. He couldn't even focus on the simple, mindless task of putting the key in the ignition and starting up his car. What was wrong with him? He looked across the street at Madame Lena's house, just in time to see the neon sign go dark.

How had she known about Ida Fletcher's drowning? Keegan hadn't said anything on the phone, and the story hadn't hit the papers; he'd checked for it more than once. Having the gossip spread among Newport Beach's yacht clubs was one thing, but how had the story made it out to East Whittier? And then there was the spirit in his house, the woman with the short biblical name. How could Madame Lena have known that his dog kept him up at night, barking at empty chairs?

He managed to get the key into the ignition and started up the engine. He pulled away from the curb and crept along the dark street, driving much too slowly. The gaunt, bare branches he passed under sent shadows writhing in his peripheral vision, like wily black serpents. He was a fool to let his imagination run so rampant. He switched on the radio and found the news on KNX. But the voices only cluttered his thinking more. After a block or two, he turned the radio off again.

Keegan lost his way getting back to the 101. First, he'd turned the wrong way on Slauson Avenue and had to backtrack. Then he missed the freeway entrance and didn't realize his mistake until he was passing the Chrysler Plant in Maywood. He kept finding himself looking out through the windshield at carpet stores and auto dealerships and donut shops, completely disoriented—as if he'd been dropped down on the spot without having driven here himself. He should pull over, get the map from his glove box, figure out where he was—but he was overwhelmed by a strange restlessness, a deep-rooted urge to just keep moving.

Madame Lena had told him he was being haunted. God, if the woman only knew. Eve had been buried up in San Francisco's Holy Cross, he'd heard. There had been a small funeral, but he'd been ordered not to leave town until the investigation wound up. First her uncle was killed, then Eve herself—and Keegan had been at the center of it all.

And now, a year later, he was adding to his total, racking up the tally. Ida Fletcher and Frank the Boxer had made the mistake of trusting him as well. He was some kind of poison. A human plague. A grim reaper in a JC Penney sports coat.

He pulled to a stop at a red light and looked around: an elementary school parking lot and a Phillips 66; a pair of phone booths and an abandoned bicycle chained to a bus stop bench. None of it was familiar. He glanced at his wristwatch. It was coming up on eight-thirty, and he had no idea where he was. Helen would be waiting at the restaurant for him now, growing more offended by the minute. If only she knew about his poison touch. She'd be better off keeping her distance. He'd be better off staying out of her way.

HE PULLED INTO the carport and cut the engine. When he opened the driver's side door, the phone was already ringing inside the cottage. He sighed. It would be Helen, calling to see what had happened. Or Mrs. Dodd, calling to give him a piece of her mind. Either way, he was in no hurry to get in the house, and the phone stopped ringing before he'd got the key in the door.

It was near midnight now, and he'd never made it as far as Jackson's. He'd driven around for a while, ended up cruising along the coast highway past all the crab shacks and the arcades. The piers were all lit up against the black ocean, like Viking funeral ships set ablaze. On his way back home, he stopped for a whiskey at a place down on Wilshire, but it was a Saturday night, and the place was too crowded, the atmosphere too raucous for his desolate mood. He slipped out after one drink, leaving a lump of crumpled bills on the bar top, and brought himself home.

The dog was ecstatic to see him, and she followed him through the kitchen to the back door, running ahead of him and then back to him, quivering with elation. He paused at the fridge to get a can of beer and a can opener, and then he opened the back door. The dog sprinted out into the dark backyard, and he followed her, pausing to switch on the back porchlight.

She'd been cooped up too long, so Keegan let her make a slow circuit of the yard, sniffing at the ground, peeing more often than seemed necessary. He stood by the low back fence and looked down at the dark Ormsby estate. He punched open the beer and slipped the can opener into his pocket.

He downed half the beer in two long quaffs, and then the phone started ringing again. It had to be Mrs. Dodd, calling to berate him for standing Helen up. Well, he had it coming, didn't he? And it would be better if she got it off her chest tonight, rather than bringing it to work on Monday. He downed the rest of the beer and called the dog over. The two of them went inside to face the music.

He set the empty beer can on the kitchen table and picked up the phone. "If you're calling me to tell me what a bastard I am, I already have a good—"

A gruff voice cut him off. "This Keegan?" the voice wanted to know.

Keegan looked at the dark window over the sink. "It is," Keegan said. "Who is this?"

"Bruno," the voice said. "You know, South Bay Yachting Club."

Bruno the Barkeep, Keegan thought. Bruno the Unsurpassed. "So, the kid's there right now?"

"Drinking sidecars and talking like an avalanche," Bruno said. "Doesn't look like he's planning on leaving any time soon, but I'll be throwing his ass out in about forty-five minutes. So, if you want to see where he goes, this is your chance."

"Yeah, okay," Keegan said. "I'll be right down. Try to keep him talking."

"'*Utterly fascinating, Mr. Church*,'" the bartender deadpanned in a deep monotone. "'*Please tell me more*.' Yeah, I think I can manage that."

Keegan quickly dumped a full can of Alpo into Nora's bowl and filled her water bowl at the kitchen sink. He locked her up in the cottage while she was still distracted with dinner. She'd be okay. She'd probably be curled up asleep at the foot of the bed before he got his car down to PCH.

THE VALET'S STAND was abandoned for the night when Keegan rolled up in front of the South Bay Yachting Club. Only a scattering of cars remained in the dark parking lot—a big Lincoln, an Aston Martin, a couple of Cadillacs, and, he was happy to see, the nephew's red Jaguar parked well out of the way in the deep shadow of a eucalyptus tree.

He backed into a space as far from the Jaguar as he could and still have a clear view of both the car and the club's entrance. He checked his watch. Bruno would kick Church out in ten or twenty minutes. One by one, the other cars cleared the parking lot—couples and foursomes talking in loud, martini-amplified voices. Soon the Jaguar was the only car left. The light in the club's front entrance went out, then the lights in the side windows. Still, there was no sign of Danny Church. Keegan checked his watch again. It was after one. Any minute now.

The front door of the club opened with a horizontal sweep of light, and the nephew came out into the entryway. Someone inside pulled the door shut again. Church ambled down the steps, past the valet stand, and over to the Jaguar. He seemed a little unsteady on his feet, like he was treading a pitching deck. He got out his keys and opened the driver's side door. He ducked his head inside.

If he took off in the car, Keegan would follow to see where he was headed. If he didn't, it would mean he had a boat in the marina where he could spend the night. Either way, Keegan had to be ready. He held the key in the ignition and put his foot on the brake. That was a mistake. The bushes behind him lit up scarlet in the rearview mirror. He yanked his foot off the pedal, like he'd been scalded.

Danny Church straightened up and looked in his direction, so Keegan ducked down a little in the car. Damn. Would the kid remember what kind of car Keegan drove? What the hell could Keegan possibly say if the kid recognized his MG and strode over to say hello? *Why, James! What in heaven's name are you doing at my club at this ungodly hour?*

But Church didn't seem to notice him. He just stood beside the Jaguar and tore the cellophane off a blue pack of those French cigarettes he smoked. He shook one loose and put it to his lips. He slipped the pack in his trouser pocket and started patting himself down, looking for his lighter. When the cigarette was lit, he closed the Jaguar's door. He paused to lock it with the key and then tried the handle. It looked like he was planning to leave it parked there overnight.

Church headed toward the club's side yard, where Bruno had taken his smoke break. He passed it and took the steps that led down to the marina. He had a good head start, but Keegan didn't want to get out of his car until the kid was out of sight. He'd come too close to being seen already. Fortunately, Church was still smoking one of his Gauloises. The red glow of the ember would make it easier to keep track of him in the darkness.

Keegan watched as the man's figure disappeared incrementally down the steps, his knees vanishing first, then his waist and shoulders. When his head was out of sight, Keegan opened his car door and slipped out, closing it quietly behind him.

He jogged over to the steps as silently as he could and paused at the top, looking down at the darkened marina. Few lights were on in the moored boats. Beacon lamps from across the bay shimmered on the dark water. White hulls reflected in the black water. He held his breath and peered into the void, watching for movement. And then there it was: a cigarette flared and faded.

It looked like the nephew had turned down the fourth jetty, and he was making his way along it, slow and unsteady. The sidecars he'd had at the bar and the gently rocking dock both seemed to impede his progress. Keegan would have no trouble keeping up.

Keegan crept down the steps, but once he was level with the marina, he could no longer see Church beyond the forest of sailboat masts. He wouldn't be hard to find, though; Keegan knew where he'd turned down. Keegan slipped quietly along the quay to the fourth jetty and stopped to look along it. It was different than the others, much broader abeam and with wider berths. This was where the larger boats tied up—the big luxury yachts with their double decks and their hoisted dinghies. He couldn't see Church now; the kid must have already boarded one of the boats.

Keegan crept slowly along the jetty, listening and watching for any sign of movement. The big hulls loomed high over his head. These weren't the little thirty-footers you'd take up the coast to Santa Barbara for the weekend, hugging the shore. They were floating mansions—the kind of vessel you could sail to Singapore if you had a mind to.

Keegan crept along the jetty, glancing back and forth for any sign of life. A light came on in the farthest boat and then switched off again. Keegan picked up his pace and made his silent way to the end of the jetty. He stood at the final berth, listening. Despite the breeze coming off the bay, he caught the clear scent of tobacco smoke. He waited and then heard muffled music on board. The radio signal swelled and shifted. Someone was working the dial. Elvis sang 'It's Now or Never', and the dial stopped there.

For who knows when we'll meet again this way.

Keegan looked up at the prow. The boat's name was scrolled under the pulpit in gold lettering.

Recess

Newport Beach

BACK AT THE yacht club, Keegan rapped at the side door, waited, and then knocked again more loudly.

The door opened a crack and the giant bartender looked out at him, amused. "I thought it might be you," he said. He pulled the door all the way open. "Did you find what you were looking for?"

"Yeah," Keegan said. "He got on a boat out there. A really big one. *Recess*? You know it?"

The big man nodded. "Yeah, I know it," he said. "I've

worked a couple of private parties aboard the thing. It's got a full bar below decks—as big as the one we've got in here. Belongs to Mr. Burritt."

"*Milton* Burritt," Keegan said. "The lawyer?" He laughed suddenly, unable to hold it in. Bruno gave him a look.

"'*Recess*'," Keegan explained. "I just got the joke."

Bruno shrugged. He wasn't so easily amused.

"Does Burritt take it out much?" Keegan asked.

The bartender shook his head. "Hardly goes aboard it at all as far as I can tell," he said. "It just sits out there. Something to impress."

Keegan thought of Burritt's beautiful too-young wife sitting by his side looking deathly bored while they talked. The *Recess* was Burritt's maritime version of a trophy wife— and he probably neglected them both to similar degrees.

Bruno glanced back inside the club, like he was eager to finish up and go home.

Keegan took the cue. He found a ten-dollar bill in his wallet and passed it to the big man, again knowing it wasn't much of a tip in Bruno's world. "Thanks," he said. "Your assistance has been unsurpassed."

So, IT WAS possible, Keegan thought as he drove up an empty PCH toward the freeway. It was more than just a hunch. Danny Church had access to a boat. He pictured the kid at the helm of the *Recess*, following his aunt's smaller, unsuspecting boat out of the channel into the dark open waters beyond. What happened next was anyone's guess, but a little sailboat like *The Seven of Swords* would have no hope of outrunning Burritt's big motor yacht.

The nephew already had the motive, and now Keegan could prove he had the opportunity.

CHAPTER TWELVE

"So, HE'S BORROWING a boat," the Lieutenant said. "That doesn't prove he did anything wrong."

"Proving things isn't my job," Keegan reminded him. "That's kind of *your* profession. Are you interested in this or not?"

"I'm interested," the Lieutenant allowed. "It's just not a whole lot to go on."

It was Sunday afternoon, and the Lieutenant had agreed to meet Keegan at the Regency Café for a beer while his wife was at her sister's. He'd hear Keegan out about his suspicions concerning Danny Church. Maybe there would be something to it; maybe there wouldn't. He made no promises.

Well, a beer in the afternoon suited Keegan just fine, it turned out. A few hours out of the damn house was just what he needed. They sat at the bar. They'd talked through their first beers and were well along into their second.

"Not a whole lot to go on?" Keegan said. He held his hand above the marble bar top and pulled one finger back with the other hand. "First, we've got the motive," he said. "They had a falling out, and he was worried she'd change the will." He pulled back another finger. "Then we've got opportunity. He's got a boat waiting for him in the marina." He pulled back a third finger. "We've got the fact that old Frank had a bump on the head, like someone had knocked him out before he went in the water."

Keegan gave up counting and rattled off the rest. "We've got the fact that the old lady was terrified of him, for some reason. There's also the fact that he lied to me about where he was the day they went missing." He was getting too worked up, so he took a deep breath and a sip from his beer glass. "I don't know, Lou," he said. "That seems like plenty to me. What more do you want? I can't do my job *and* yours at the same time."

The Lieutenant gave Keegan a smooth, unruffled smile. "Easy, Jimmy," he said. "Let's not get personal." He gave Keegan's arm a pat. "You're jumping over a lot of questions here. The kind of questions a DA is going to have to answer."

Keegan pressed both hands down on the bar top. "Like what, for example?"

"Well, for one, the old lady refused to talk to the kid, right?" He turned sideways on his stool and put one elbow on the bar, looking easy and unflappable. "If she was terrified of him—*as* you say—how did he find out she was sailing over to Catalina?"

Keegan looked away. He took another long sip from his beer and set the glass back down. He turned it slowly on the bar until the Regency logo was facing him. "For the sake of argument," he said, "let's just say he found out somehow."

The Lieutenant shook his head amiably and grinned. "Let's *not* just say that, Jimmy," he said. "It's a giant, glaring hole in this theory of yours—and you'll need to come up with a plausible explanation before we can take it any further."

Keegan took another sip from his beer. He looked up at the rows of bottles lining the shelves behind the bar. He thought of the kid on the phone and his damn *warm-warmer-hot* game. Dammit. "Okay, fine," Keegan said. "For the sake of argument, let's just say he found out from me."

Keegan could feel the Lieutenant's gaze on the side of his face like a spotlight. "*You* told him?" He seemed to be holding in a laugh.

"I didn't *tell* him, Lou," Keegan said. "Not really." It was such a mess, so hard to explain. "I didn't know they were sailing out there myself," he sputtered on. "The kid has a way of talking a person in circles. He keeps up both sides of the damn conversation. It's like you're his ventriloquist dummy or something."

"You *told* him the old lady was sailing to Catalina?"

"Let's just say he came to that conclusion during a conversation we had," Keegan said. "You had to be there, Lou. I never said a word about it. I didn't even *know* that was the old lady's plan until it was too late."

The Lieutenant faced forward on his stool again and reached for his own glass of beer. He was still grinning, and then he started shaking his head. "Well, that *does* fill in one of the holes in your theory," he said. He took a sip of beer and then started laughing. "You might not want to tell me anything more without a lawyer present."

"Hilarious, Lou," Keegan said. "You're a real funny guy."

"Abetting a double homicide," the Lieutenant said, trying to hold back his laughter. "That's twenty-to-life in my town."

"Are you going to take this seriously or not?" Keegan said. "This is murder we're talking about. The kid's going to get away scot-free if someone doesn't do something."

"And what would you like me to do?" Moore said. At least he'd stopped laughing. His voice was cool and earnest now. "If it happened offshore, it's not LAPD's case. And if they were sailing from Newport to Catalina, there's that pesky county line to worry about too." He drew an imaginary border on the bar top with the sides of both hands. "Could be Orange County Sheriff. Could be LA County." He moved his hands farther along the bar. "Hell, with the current, Ventura County might need to be involved." He shook his head. "Whichever way it goes, I can't go sticking my nose in. Not without a lot more evidence."

Keegan swiveled on his stool to face the Lieutenant. He had to make the man understand. "You don't know this kid like I do." His voice came out strident, urgent. "He's a real piece of work. Glib. Smooth. No conscience. No remorse. He's a classic sociopath." He squeezed his fists tight and held them in front of his chest. "He did it, Lou," he said. "I can feel it in my bones."

"I believe you," Moore said. "I believe your bones. But body parts can't be called to testify." The Lieutenant held up his hand to stop Keegan from interrupting. "I'm not saying you're *wrong*," he said. "But I've got rules to follow. You're going to have to bring me a lot more than this before I can go sticking my nose in."

"Like what?" Keegan said. "Bloody footprints on the ocean? Fingerprints on some flounder? It happened on the open sea. What kind of evidence could there be?" He imagined Danny Church's smug, unctuous grin. It sickened him.

The Lieutenant nodded. "Yeah," he said. "It makes it hard. I'm surprised more murders don't happen at sea. If you ever wanted to get away…" He let the thought trail off.

"So then, what would it take for you to be able to do something?"

"I don't know," the Lieutenant said. He sounded a little frustrated himself now, which made Keegan feel a little less dejected. "You ever seen this lawyer's boat? Any damage to it? Anything on board the kid might have used?"

Keegan swiveled back to face the bar. He picked up his beer and took a sip, not really tasting it. His thoughts were running out ahead of him now. He knew exactly where to find Milton Burritt's yacht. If Bruno was right, the old lawyer rarely used it. And if Danny Church were out of the picture some night—out on the town, say, or even just drinking at the yacht club bar—Keegan could slip on and off the *Recess* without anyone being the wiser. Sure, it wasn't quite legal, but what harm could it do to give it a shot?

AT THE KITCHEN table Monday night, Keegan pushed his Swanson's TV dinner away. He'd had the exact same

Salisbury steak meal the night before. It had gone cold by now, and he hadn't made much of a dent in it. He didn't have an appetite these days.

There was a time, not too long ago, when most weeknights he'd have met some old friend at Casa Bonita for Mexican food, or he'd have swung by the Red Lion on the way back to his Mid-Wilshire apartment to grab a burger and see which of the regulars were hanging around in the bar. There was a time when he didn't eat TV dinners straight from their tinfoil trays, when he didn't spend his nights banished up here in his late mother's hilltop cottage—with a terrier as his only company.

Unless, of course, you counted the ghost.

His visit with Madame Lena had affected him more than he could explain. *You live alone, very high up, but your house is haunted by a spirit.* Since the evening he'd gone to see her, he'd left the lights burning all night in the living room and the kitchen. He told himself it was for the dog, but that wasn't the whole truth. The cottage was beginning to feel too populous.

A young woman. A short name. From the Bible. It was especially maddening because Keegan knew exactly how Lena's trick worked. This wasn't Blackstone's floating light bulb. It was a sure-bet guess. Any sideshow palm reader would use it in a cold reading, and it would work ninety percent of the time. Half the women Keegan ever knew had short biblical names. He knew a Ruth, a Martha, a Sarah, and three Marys. Hell, even Mrs. Dodd's first name was Esther.

Madame Lena had nothing to do with his current unnerved state. He was doing it to himself—working himself up, letting his imagination gallop. So, why was he allowing his memories of Eve to haunt him? Maybe it was the isolation. This damn cottage was the last stop on the road, the place where the pavement ran out. And it didn't help that the Ormsby place down below had been dark and empty for a year now. That dark abyss between him and all the city lights just made him feel more cut off.

He got up and put the uneaten dinner on the kitchen

counter. He'd scrape it into the dog's bowl in the morning. He got down a coffee mug and a mostly empty bottle of Jameson and brought them back to the table. He poured what was left into the mug and took a sip.

And then there was Helen. All that day at work, Mrs. Dodd had been shooting him hot glares and giving him the cold shoulder. She never bothered to ask him why he might have stood Helen up on Friday night, but her mood implied that no reason he offered would be sufficient.

And she was right, Keegan knew. He should have apologized to Helen by now. He glanced over at the phone on the wall beside him. The coiled cord was so stretched out, it dangled, twisting, almost to the kitchen tiles. He should, he knew, just pick it up and dial Helen's number. He had it in his wallet, which was out in the living room, right there on the entry table by the front door. He should just march out there right now and get it, and then pick up the phone. He could swallow his pride for once, offer no excuses, ask her to meet him for a drink, try to make it up to her somehow. But even as he gave himself the pep talk, he knew he wouldn't follow through. Instead, he would finish off the whiskey, take the dog out in the yard one last time, and then go to bed—the same old routine. Inertia had become a way of life. Pathetic.

He tilted his head back and swallowed down what was left of the whiskey in one gulp.

ON TUESDAY, MRS. Dodd's strict policy of excommunication continued. She slammed file cabinet drawers. She refused to look at Keegan, even when forced to speak to him. She worked the Remington with such fury, the typebars poked little holes in the papers she left out for Keegan to sign.

By lunchtime, Keegan was itching to flee the office and enjoy the less palpable abuse of the world at large. He hooked the leash on the dog's collar and rode the elevator down to street level. He walked Nora down Sixth Street toward Olive. He'd get something to eat from one of the vendors in Pershing Square.

He bought a hotdog and a bottle of Orange Crush from a cart and took it to an empty bench. The soda was too fizzy; the hotdog was flavorless and difficult to swallow. He gave the last inch to the dog, who wolfed it down without complaint. He sat awhile, enjoying the cool October sunlight.

When it was time to go back to the office, he headed over to Lusk's newsstand instead. Lusk had no customers to wait on, and he watched Keegan approach with a look of droll amusement.

Keegan had a reason for visiting Lusk, but he went to the small rack of paperback novels as a kind of pretense. There wasn't much of a selection there: some Michener, some O'Hara, a row of Harlequin romances, another of pulp westerns. Back in college, he'd devoured novels, reading everything assigned in his literature classes and countless other books as well. Even when he worked at *The Times*, he'd kept up, breezing through whatever got good reviews back in the Calendar section. It would be a good habit to reclaim now in his old age, a way to fill those long evening hours at home. He plucked a copy of *The Grapes of Wrath* from the rack and set it on Lusk's counter. He'd never gotten around to reading it, back when it was in all the bookshop windows.

The purchase seemed to brighten Lusk's mood. He picked up the book and checked the price. "A bargain at a buck ninety-five," he said. "Want a fresh Bic pen to go with it? Lotta stuff you're probably going to want to underline."

"Just the book, thanks," Keegan said. He dug in his pocket for change and counted out eight quarters.

Lusk swiped the coins into his palm and dumped them in the cash drawer. He took out a nickel and put it on top of the book.

Keegan made no move to pick them up. "So, Kipper," he

said, "when you talked to that Madame Lena, was it on the phone—or did you drive out to see her?"

Lusk leaned back in his folding chair and looked Keegan over doubtfully. "I'm supposed to open myself once again to your ridicule?" he said. "Think again, smart guy."

"No ridicule," Keegan promised. "I want to know your thoughts on the woman."

"And why might that be?" Lusk still seemed leery, waiting for the other Florsheim to drop.

Keegan held the dog's leash tighter in his fist. "I went to see her last Friday," he admitted.

Lusk sat back in his folding chair and grinned, immensely pleased with the news. Then he leaned forward and pressed his elbows down on the plywood counter. "*You* went to see *her*?" he said. He was clearly delighted.

"It was business," Keegan said defensively. "And her whole act was pure hokum—all carnival tricks and tarot cards."

Lusk nodded, smiling. Clearly, there was more to the story. "But?" he said.

Keegan sighed. Of course there was a *but. A young woman. A short name. From the Bible.* "She kind of got under my skin with some of the stuff she said."

Lusk pressed his fingertips together and eyed Keegan suspiciously. "Why do I still feel like this is a set-up?"

"It's not a set-up, Kip," Keegan said. "I really want to know what happened with you."

Lusk proceeded with caution. "I called the number," he said. "I told her about the mirrors. Asked her if I was cursed, and if there was some way I could reverse it."

"And?"

"Yes, I was cursed."

"And, let me guess," Keegan said to Lusk, "the trick to erasing the curse was to send her a check, right?" The dog had made a slow orbit of Keegan's legs while he'd been standing there, and Keegan had to step over the leash now to stop himself tripping.

"She only charged me twenty bucks," Lusk said, as if he counted that as a great bargain when it came to curse-removal. "But—yeah—she took care of the problem."

"What did she do?"

Lusk looked beyond Keegan at the park and then back at him again. "Again, I feel like I'm walking into a trap here," he said.

"You're not," Keegan said. "Swear to God. Just tell me what happened."

Lusk rolled his eyes. "She told me to go burn some bay leaves around the house," he said defensively.

"Bay leaves?" Keegan said. "That's it?"

Lusk nodded. "I went to Ralphs and bought a big jar of them. When the wife went to church Sunday morning, I walked from room to room with a Zippo lighter and burned them in a mixing bowl."

"How did *that* go?"

"Smoked up the house something awful," Lusk said, "and I had to buy a new toaster because I told the wife the old one was on the fritz—but you know what?"

"What?"

"Monday afternoon my brother-in-law hit it big. He nailed the trifecta in the fourth race at Santa Anita."

"What does that have to do with your curse?"

"He gave me back the two hundred bucks he borrowed about a million years ago when I was first going out with his sister." Lusk turned both palms up. "The curse, I'd say, has been effectually lifted."

A lady passed by walking three chihuahuas on matching pink leashes, and Nora made a lunge at them. She almost yanked her own leash out of Keegan's grip, and he had to steady himself and drag her back to his side.

"Yeah, well, that's some sound scientific evidence you've got there," Keegan said.

Lusk made a *so-sue-me* gesture. "You asked," he said. "I answered. There's no pleasing you."

Keegan picked up his paperback and his change. He was about to leave, but he had an idea and turned back. He pulled a copy of *Movie Stars* from Lusk's magazine rack and set it on the counter. From the cover, Ann-Margret and Richard Chamberlain smiled up at him. They might have been fraternal twins. He gave Lusk back the nickel and added a couple of dimes.

As a peace offering, the magazine would have to do. He'd leave it on Mrs. Dodd's desk for her to find when she came back from her own lunch break.

ON WEDNESDAY AFTERNOON, Mrs. Dodd's dam finally broke, and she ended her brief but terrible reign of silence. Keegan had taken the dog down to Ida Fletcher's Newport house that morning to make a show of looking for the original will—though he already felt sure it wouldn't be there. The trip was mostly an excuse to get out of the office and away from Mrs. Dodd's wrath. The fact that he'd get to bill Roland Dion for a few more hours only made the prospect more attractive.

After that, they swung by the house in Bel Air. They arrived just as Danny Church was coming down the front steps to the red Jaguar.

"Love to stop and chat," the kid said, "but I was just on my way downtown. Business. My representative has found an empty spot on Sunset he thinks might be perfect."

"For the bistro?"

"The *brasserie*," he corrected. "What brings you to my humble abode?"

Keegan nodded at the grand front steps to the mansion. "I came looking for the old will," he said. "I'm supposed to leave no stone unturned."

"Well, turn the place upside down. I've got nothing to hide," the kid said suavely. He checked his watch. "And help yourself to a drink at the bar. I won't be back until late. Don't wait up." He went around the Jaguar and opened the door.

"Do you know Lillian Cole?" Keegan asked before the kid could duck into the car.

Church straightened up. "Of course I know her. How is the old thing?"

"At large," Keegan said. "I'm supposed to find her. Any idea where I should look?"

The nephew shook his head. "Not a clue," he said. "But I'm sure a man of your rare talents will have no trouble tracking her down." He climbed into the car. "Do give her my best when you see her," he said, and he pulled the door closed.

KEEGAN AND THE dog got back to the office around two in the afternoon and found Mrs. Dodd sitting at her desk wearing her reading glasses. She seemed to have been lying in wait, prepared for an ambush. She started in on Keegan as soon as he came through the door, even before he could hang up the leash. Honestly, it was a relief that the moment had finally arrived.

"Did you lose her phone number?" Mrs. Dodd asked him, apropos of nothing. She swiveled around in her chair to face him, her arms folded across her chest. "Because I've got it, you know. All you have to do is ask."

Keegan took off his blazer and hung it on the coat rack, next to the leash. "I've got her number," he said quietly. It was true. It was in his wallet, jotted in blue ballpoint on an Alpha Beta receipt. He saw it every time he paid for something, each glimpse a fresh prick of his conscience.

"Is your dialing finger broken then?" she went on, acidly. "Because I can go in there and work the phone for you if you're incapacitated."

"It's the middle of the day," he said reasonably. "She'll be in class."

Mrs. Dodd was on a roll now, though. There would be no

stopping her. "Well, if you need me to," she said, "I can drive up to your cottage tonight and hold your hand."

"Give it a rest," he told her. "I'll call her when I'm ready." He turned to go in his office, but she wasn't about to let the subject go so easily.

"And when might that be?" she said to his back. "It's been nearly a week."

Keegan sighed and turned back around in the doorway. "I've been busy," he said. "I've got a lot on my mind."

"*Busy?*" she sputtered. "Boss, I saw you with your feet up on the desk reading Hemingway yesterday afternoon."

"That's not true."

"What do you mean, *not true*?" she said. "I saw you with my own eyes."

"It was Steinbeck," he told her.

Mrs. Dodd let her head fall back dramatically and stared up at the ceiling. "Oh, *please*," she said. "What is it with you men, anyway?" She leveled her scowl at him again. "I don't understand it at all. Wendell would rather saw off his arm with a steak knife than admit he's ever wrong or apologize for something he did."

But it wasn't like that in Keegan's case. She didn't understand. She hadn't seen Frank's body on the morgue's steel table. She hadn't been to visit Madame Lena and her tarot cards. Keegan leaned his weight against the inner office doorjamb. "Look," he said, "I know you like her—hell, I like her too—and I'm sorry I hurt her feelings, but—"

"Oh, boss," she said, cutting him off, "you've got it all wrong. I'm not worried about Helen." She smiled at him ruefully and shook her head. "She's not like you," she said. "People actually enjoy her company. Trust me, she's not sitting at home hoping you'll call. It's *you* who'll be missing out. All because of your stupid male ego." She looked at him over her reading glasses, eyebrows arched. "You don't want to let this opportunity slip by, boss," she said earnestly.

"Believe me, if you had the sense God gave geese, you'd call her tonight."

He didn't.

HE ALMOST CALLED Helen the next night after dinner, though. He'd even fished the receipt out of his wallet and put it on the kitchen table so he'd have the number ready. But then he picked up the Steinbeck novel to read a chapter before he made the call—it would be rude to interrupt the dinner hour—and then he fell asleep on the sofa with the book open on his chest.

THEN FRIDAY NIGHT rolled around. He could have made the call then, but it seemed like the most likely evening to catch Danny Church killing time down at the yacht club bar. If the kid was holding forth under Bruno's watchful eye, it might give Keegan the opportunity to sneak aboard Milton Burritt's boat and see what he could find.

Timing would be important. He would have to wait until it was late enough that no one would be out and about down at the marina; if he was going to trespass, he didn't want witnesses. And he wanted to give himself a least an hour aboard the *Recess* to see what he could find. If he got down to the marina by ten, he'd run little chance of being seen. He could slip on and off the boat and be home by midnight—long before Danny Church ordered his last round of drinks on his late aunt's tab.

A little before nine, Keegan dialed the number for the South Bay Yachting Club from his kitchen phone. "It's Jim Keegan," he said when he finally got Bruno on the line.

Bruno didn't respond.

"You know, the detective," Keegan added.

"Oh, I remember you," the big barkeep said dryly. "The twenty bucks you slipped me made quite the impression."

"Is he there tonight?"

Bruno exhaled into the other end of the phone. "You know," he said, "I'm not supposed to take personal phone calls at work."

Bruno hadn't struck Keegan as the kind to worry much about company policy, but with the man's deadpan delivery, it was hard to know if he was joking. Keegan held his tongue.

"And another thing," Bruno rumbled on, "this club has strict privacy rules. I could lose my job if I told you the kid was here tonight drinking gin gimlets and lecturing everybody about the difference between a *bistro* and a *brasserie*. So, I am not going to breathe a word about the matter to anyone."

Keegan grinned. His life could use more Brunos in it. "Think he'll be there until closing?"

"I'm guessing it would take a crowbar to get the kid off that barstool before I close."

"Thanks," Keegan said. "I owe you."

"Another ten bucks," the big man said wryly. "At this rate, I'll be able to afford a membership in a couple of centuries." He hung up the phone.

KEEGAN COASTED RIGHT past the South Bay Yachting Club's valet. It was an older guy tonight, with a paunch and little interest in Keegan or his passing MG. The rush of arrivals had ended hours ago; he was in the car-fetching business now. Keegan drove up and down a few rows of cars before he spotted Danny Church's red Jaguar, parked in among all the big Cadillacs and Lincolns. He drove to the lot's back corner, where there were a few empty spaces, and pulled in.

He cut the engine and glanced at his watch. It was a little after ten. If Keegan managed to get aboard Milton Burritt's boat, he'd have all the time he needed. It would be midnight before he'd have to worry about Danny Church maybe leaving the bar and stumbling back to sleep it off.

Keegan got out of his car and locked it. Before he left the

cottage, he'd pulled on a black sweater, blue jeans, and a pair of dark tennis shoes for this outing. It would make him nearly invisible in the dark. And, he hoped, he'd look enough like a boat owner to pass muster if someone *did* happen to spot him. He kept well clear of the valet and skirted the parking lot, staying in the trees' shadows. Live music was coming from inside the club tonight. It sounded like a full big-band combo. No mere jazz trio for a Friday night at the South Bay Yachting Club.

Keegan crept past the spot where Bruno took his smoking breaks and came down the long flight of steps to the marina. Lights were on in a few of the boats tonight, weekend sailors bedding down for an early morning departure. Keegan slipped quietly along the quay. Moonlight backlit the angled boat stays. It shimmered on the choppy water that lapped between the jetties. Keegan turned down the fourth dock, where all the most opulent boats were tied up.

One of the big motor yachts seemed to be hosting a party tonight. It lit up the night like an amusement pier. Boisterous laughter and conversation and the sound of a jazz record drowned out the quiet clang and jingle of the other boats' rigging. A woman's voice rang out above the others as Keegan slipped by the boat: "But the colors are gorgeous."

As Keegan neared the end of the pier, the sounds of the party behind him faded. A swell of wind sent a burgee flag rippling above him, high on a bare mast. As he approached the farthest berth, he noticed a pale yellow light glowing behind a few of the portholes on Milton Burritt's yacht—the ones back near the stern. Had Danny Church left the club early? Keegan stopped and watched and listened. He could detect no signs of movement aboard the boat. Perhaps the kid had been careless and left a lamp burning the last time he disembarked. Keegan slipped along the floating pier until he was directly under the *Recess*'s high prow.

He sniffed the air for any hint of French cigarettes but smelled only the dank seaweed brine. He held still again and listened. Music was playing, very faintly, inside Burritt's boat. The kid must be in there, making himself at home, playing the lawyer's phonograph—an inveterate squatter.

Keegan held still and listened a while longer. He heard water running, or maybe it was Milton Burritt's single-malt scotch being poured into a glass. The music grew a little louder, as if someone had turned up the volume: Sinatra's 'My Funny Valentine'.

Stay little valentine, stay.

Each day is Valentine's Day.

Keegan sighed. He'd driven all the way down here, and it would turn out to be the one night Danny Church decided to bed down early. Keegan waited, thinking, while Sinatra's song played through. On the final chorus, a tuneful voice joined in singing.

Is your figure less than Greek?

Is your mouth a little weak?

Keegan froze and listened. The voice was an alto—a woman.

He crouched low and slipped around the side of the boat on the gangway until he could see one of the lit portholes. A swath of blonde hair swept by on the other side of the oval glass, then a profile came into view. It was Milton Burritt's trophy wife. She wasn't sunk in boredom tonight, the way she had been when Keegan first met her in the club. She seemed happy and bright and lissome, moving about inside the boat's cabin, backing Sinatra with a cheery harmony. Keegan stepped back into the darkness.

And then footsteps on hollow wood emerged above the distant party sounds at the far end of the dock. He held his breath and listened among the ambient creaks and clangs and lapping water—then there it was again: someone was walking along the wooden dock. He looked back at the quay, toward the big, bright motor yacht, and saw a silhouetted figure coming down the walkway in his direction.

He glanced around. He was at the dock's farthest end.

There wasn't anywhere to hide. He crossed to the boat moored in the opposite slip and crouched down in its shadow. The empty boat's hull gently rose and fell beside him, groaning a little, but there were no signs of life on board.

He listened as the footfalls—a little uneven—grew louder and more distinct. He caught a scent on the air—that tang of Danny Church's French tobacco—and then the nephew lumbered into view. He turned away from Keegan, along the side of Milton Burritt's big yacht. The kid climbed the boarding stairs, crossed the deck, and disappeared into the cabin. There was a high silvery laugh of delight and then the rumble of the nephew's buttery baritone. It wasn't hard to imagine the couple's embrace.

The shiftless playboy and the bored trophy wife; how had Keegan not seen *that* cliché coming? He thought of how Mrs. Burritt's eyes had kept slipping toward the dining room's entrance the night he had met with her husband. Her secret lover was just down the hall, drinking at the bar. It was just like Zinnia and Frank the Boxer: the closer you looked, the messier and more complicated people turned out to be.

Keegan slipped out of hiding and crept past the big boat's prow, making his getaway. Inside the yacht, Church let out a lusty, muffled laugh. Keegan picked up his pace. It all made perfect sense, now that he thought about it: the nephew's lie about dinner at the Bouzy Rouge, the late nights drinking at the club, his making himself at home on Milton Burritt's boat. The lawyer's neglected yacht was their trysting place. What setting could be more fitting for such a well-heeled affair?

Keegan passed the party boat near the far end of the pier. Someone inside was doing a loud, drunken impression of JFK to unbridled laughter. Keegan walked faster, no longer caring if anyone knew he was there.

He found himself in a sudden dismal mood, and he wasn't looking forward to the long, lonely drive back home. What kind of a man had he become? What kind of a ghoul would feel such deep disappointment when he learned that someone he knew might not be a murderer?

THE LIEUTENANT CALLED Keegan's office early Monday morning. "You dig up anything more on your kid Danny Church?"

Keegan winced. How could he even try to explain what he had found out—and how he'd come to know it? "About that, Lou," he said, feeling enormously foolish. "I might have got way ahead of myself on what was going on with the kid and the boat. I think he was just—"

"Because there's news," the Lieutenant said. "I found a message from the Coast Guard on my desk this morning when I got in the office. I just got off the phone with the guy. They've found more of the boat's wreckage out on the open water. I guess it was about thirty miles offshore, south of the Channel Islands. Some fishing charter spotted it and radioed it in."

Keegan pressed the phone to his ear.

"I don't know all the details," Moore went on. "But they said the boat had been scuttled."

"*Scuttled?*"

"Yeah, I didn't know what it meant either," Moore said. "Apparently, it's when you sink a vessel on purpose."

Keegan stared down at the clutter of loose papers on his desk, trying to fathom what Lou Moore was telling him.

"You were right, Jimmy," the Lieutenant went on, sounding oddly cheerful. "There was definitely foul play. Whatever happened to Ida Fletcher was no accident."

A bus rumbled by down on the street outside Keegan's office window, and he plugged one ear with a finger to drown out the noise. "Whoa," he said into the phone. "Did they find the old lady's body?"

"No body as of yet," Moore said. "But given where they

found the wreckage, the old lady is probably halfway to Maui by now. The current is pretty wild out there."

Keegan rested his forehead on his palm. He'd just spent a weekend convincing himself that he'd been all wrong about Danny Church. And now maybe the nephew *did* kill his aunt after all. Why did that ugly fact make him feel so—well—*pleased*?

"But here's the thing, Jimmy," Moore went on. "The wreckage was pretty far out to sea. It was beyond every local jurisdiction. It'll have to involve the feds now, so it's an even messier situation."

"What does that mean for us?"

"Well, if you give me whatever you can dig up on the nephew—like, I mean, type me up a full report—I'll pass it along to Hoover's crowd. No guarantees they'll be interested, though. They can be difficult to work with."

KEEGAN WENT BACK down to the marina early Tuesday morning to have a look around. The South Bay Yachting Club was not yet open for business. A linen service truck was making a delivery around the back, and he could hear some kind of hammering going on inside the front entrance. Danny Church's red Jaguar wasn't in the empty lot. He was probably back at the mansion on Monticello.

Keegan parked his MG at the far end of the empty lot, under the eucalyptus trees. He didn't really have much of a plan. He'd only seen Milton Burritt's boat at night. He thought he'd walk the dog around the marina in full daylight and see if there was anything he'd missed. He'd make his way to Burritt's boat, look for any telltale signs of damage on the outside. It wouldn't do to sneak aboard, though, not in broad daylight, not with witnesses around, not with a canine accomplice.

The dog had been curled sleeping in the passenger seat the whole way over. When Keegan pulled up the hand brake, she woke and scrambled to the side window to see where they were. Keegan hooked the leash on her collar. He got out the driver's side door and she skittered out behind him. He locked up the car and led her over to the row of trees so she could pee. When she was done, he walked her across the lot and down the long concrete steps to the marina.

Without moonlight and sea breeze, the setting looked sun-bleached and bedraggled, much shabbier than he'd imagined. The wooden planks of the walkways were gray and splintery. The slick brackish water between the boats was rainbowed with oil. On this windless morning, everything smelled like the inside of a tackle box. The dog, at least, seemed to be enjoying the scene.

The sailboats moored on this end of the marina—mostly smaller Pearsons and Albergs—looked frayed and sun-faded. These weren't floating trophies of wealth; they were owned by weekend sailors, the ones who found actual pleasure in their pleasure craft. People who escaped their workaday lives as teachers and insurance agents and beat cops for a Saturday sail up the coast. They'd pack sandwiches and thermoses and life-vests for the kids. Never in their lives would they set foot in the Yachting Club, though it was right up there on the hill staring down at them all.

Keegan walked on and turned down the fourth jetty. Only here—with the wide-spaced slips and the big luxury yachts—did everything look shipshape in the cold light of morning. Every hull was smooth, every line taut, every piece of brass-work polished. A man in a windbreaker and khakis was hosing down the upper deck of a motor yacht. Keegan walked the dog past him without making eye contact. He wanted to look like he belonged here, which meant no gawking. Few people were visible, but he could feel them around him. A radio was playing somewhere. A motor was running. A man coughed. There were plenty of witnesses.

Keegan could see the *Recess* tied up at the dock's far end. He'd check the hull for any sign of damage. Perhaps Danny Church had collided with the smaller sailboat as he ran it down and boarded it. Scrapes could be analyzed. Paint could be matched. He'd have to look it over without seeming to do so.

When Keegan got to the end of the jetty, he walked along the side of the slip, pretending to look at something down in the foul water. From what he could see, the hull was perfectly smooth, perfectly white, perfectly unmarked. He crossed back along the bow and checked the other side. There were no marks there, either.

"Watch out for fishhooks with that one," a woman's voice rang out over the sound of gulls and lapping water.

The sound made Keegan jump, and he turned to find an old woman watching him from the deck of the boat tied up opposite. She wore a shabby blue anorak. Her white hair was tied back in a red bandana.

"How's that?" Keegan asked her.

"The dog," the woman said, nodding down at Nora. "Kids are always leaving fishhooks lying about."

"Keeping a sharp eye," Keegan said, though, of course, he hadn't been thinking about the dog at all. He looked up at the other boat's stern. *Seas the Day.*

The woman came down the deck towards him. She was close enough now that Kegan could get a good look at her. It was hard to guess her age; her face was mapped with deep creases, but maybe it was just from years spent out here in the sun and salt air. She gripped a yellow chamois cloth in one knobby hand.

"This your boat?" Keegan asked. "*Seas the Day?*"

The woman laughed unguardedly. A tooth or two seemed to be missing from her smile. "*Hardly,*" she said. "I'm just a hired hand. People pay me to clean up after them. I'm pretty much the housekeeping staff for a lot of these floating monstrosities." She looked back along the row of large boats, towards the quay. "One of these yours?"

Keegan waved vaguely in the direction of the tinier boats at the marina's far end. "Got a little boat over there," he said. "Nothing to brag about."

The woman nodded and wiped the chrome railing with her chamois. "You didn't look like one of them fat cats," she said sourly. She seemed to harbor little affection for fat cats, so Keegan took it as a compliment.

"I'm just a humble working man, out for a morning stroll," Keegan said. He swept his hand out to indicate the vast boats they were standing among. "So, you know a lot of these big ones?"

"I've worked on a few."

"How about this one here?" he said, jabbing a thumb over his shoulder at the *Recess*. "Ever been aboard?"

She shook her head. "Not one of mine," she said. "Lot of people work on that thing."

Keegan nodded. "I see it here every day on my walks," he said. "Anyone ever take it out?"

"Sure," she said. "Sometimes. Not a whole lot."

"Recently?"

She gripped the chrome railing with her free hand and looked the *Recess* over. She frowned like she was trying to remember. The deep creases of her face grew deeper. "It was gone last weekend. I know that much. Had to be the weekend. I was listening to the Dodgers game while I worked. Gone all day Saturday. Got back sometime Sunday evening."

"You see who was sailing it?"

"No," she said. "Just saw the empty slip." She shielded her eyes with her hand, giving Keegan a closer inspection now that he was asking so many questions. "Say, what's this about?" she said.

"Idle curiosity," Keegan told her.

She narrowed her eyes at him. Something about this situation clearly wasn't kosher. "I didn't catch your name, mister."

Keegan smiled up at her and offered a kind of salute. "Danny Church at your service," he said. He clicked his heels and attempted one of the kid's foppish bows but couldn't quite pull it off. "You've been a big help, ma'am," he rattled off. "Never steered me wrong. Been a good soldier. I didn't hear it from you."

He turned and tugged at the dog's leash and headed back towards land. "Keep those scuppers clear," he called back to the woman over his shoulder as he walked away.

If Danny Church had taken the boat out—and he'd been gone overnight—what was he doing all that time?

THE LIEUTENANT CALLED on the office phone that Friday evening, an hour after Mrs. Dodd had left for the weekend.

"Don't get ahead of yourself," Moore warned, "but you were right. Burritt's boat was definitely in Avalon Harbor the weekend in question."

Keegan leaned back in his chair and grinned. His hunch had been right. He'd wondered if the kid had sailed it to Catalina after whatever he did to his aunt and Frank the Boxer. He thought maybe he'd anchored there overnight and crossed back to the mainland on Sunday. Then he'd have raced back to Monticello Drive just in time for Keegan to catch him—hence the kid's lie about coming from the Bouzy Rouge.

"The boat was in the harbor on Saturday and Sunday night. Water taxi shows one fare going ashore early Saturday morning. Another fare coming back the next day."

"Come on, Lou," Keegan said. "We know what this all means."

The Lieutenant sighed into the phone. "Maybe we do, maybe we don't, Jimmy," he said. "Go easy. There's still not enough for me to butt in. Not yet."

"What more could you possibly need?"

"These things have to be done right," the Lieutenant said. "We can't just start throwing accusations around. These people can afford top-notch lawyers—hell, Burritt *is* one. I, for one, don't want to end up in court for slander."

"But you're with me, right?" Keegan asked. "You think the kid did it."

The Lieutenant sighed again. "I'm not sure what I think just yet," he said. "But, yes, this has got me wondering. It's a pretty big coincidence. Let me sniff around a bit more and get back to you."

IT WAS ALMOST 1:00 a.m. Saturday morning, but Keegan still couldn't sleep. He'd tossed and turned in bed for the better part of an hour before he finally turned on the bedside lamp and picked up *The Grapes of Wrath* paperback from his bedside table. If Steinbeck couldn't put him to sleep at this hour, there was no hope for him.

He got through a few pages and then started to doze off. Mission accomplished. He marked his place and put the book back on the nightstand. He was reaching to turn off the bedside lamp when the dog, who'd been sleeping at the foot of his bed, lifted her head suddenly and pricked her ears. She woofed a half-hearted bark and then listened. She roused herself, jumped off the bed, and trotted out to the living room, issuing a rumbling, throaty growl.

Your house is haunted by a spirit.

Keegan left the light on and got out of bed. Barefoot, he crossed the cold oakwood floor and paused in the doorway. He'd left the living room lamp burning. The dog was staring at the empty chair again. Her hackles bristled. Her body trembled. She held her head low and rumbled. Keegan stepped into the dimly lit living room and stood behind her.

It is a young woman. A short name. From the Bible.

Keegan cleared his throat, already feeling foolish. "I don't know if you've been talking to Madame Lena," he said to the empty room, "but she might have mentioned that I don't believe in ghosts."

At the sound of his voice, the dog, without taking her eyes off the empty chair, backed up and took her place a little behind him and off to one side. He looked down at her. She growled again and then looked up to see his reaction.

Keegan turned back to the chair. "Despite what my secretary might have told you, dogs don't see ghosts either,"

Keegan told it. "I mean, think about it. Why would anyone bother to haunt a dog?"

He was a fool, he knew. It was madness to speak aloud to an empty room, but he had—rooted somewhere deep within him—the wholly irrational conviction that someone was listening, someone could hear him. Was this the feeling some people felt when they prayed?

The chair was his, of course, but it was easy to think of it as *her* chair. He could still picture the careless, loose-limbed way she had occupied it that night: her legs pulled up beneath her, her head thrown back in laughter. He could see the glitter of her eyes in the darkness, her smiling lips damp with wine.

"I didn't know you very long," he said, abandoning all pretense of irony. "But I miss you. I wish you were still around." His hands were tingling now, so he opened them and closed them again. He knew what had to come next. "I am to blame for all that happened," he said. "And I'm sorry." The sentence caught in his throat. Those had never been easy words for him, and they were no easier now, just because he spoke them to an empty room.

No sooner had he finished speaking than the dog turned back and scampered into the bedroom again. Keegan paused and looked at the empty chair. It had seemed so large with Eve in it, sitting sideways, all folded in on herself. He could still imagine her sunny windchime voice in this empty room. He turned and followed Nora into the bedroom. She was already back up on the bed, turning slow circles on the mattress before she lay down again. Whatever had spooked her was entirely forgotten.

Keegan pulled back the covers and lay down again. He reached over and turned off the lamp and rolled away from it on his side. Eve was forever gone, but there was Helen. He thought of her quick, crooked smile, her whip-smart conversation beside him in the stadium stands. If he could apologize to a ghost, he could probably manage it with a living woman.

CHAPTER THIRTEEN

ROLAND DION HAD tasked Keegan with only two jobs: track down Lillian Cole and find Ida Fletcher's old will. In more than a week of spinning his wheels, Keegan had managed to accomplish neither. But Monday morning, he dialed Dion's number from his office phone anyway. The receptionist put Keegan on hold, and he tapped the desktop blotter with a ballpoint pen while he waited.

In a couple of minutes, the lawyer's voice came over the phone. "Jim," he said, "have you made any headway?" His reedy intonation sounded cheery. Just as well. Keegan was angling for something.

"Not yet," Keegan said, trying to sound eager to please. "I looked through the houses in Bel Air and Newport. Nothing there. I was thinking—"

"How about the hotel where she was staying?" Dion said. "Did it have a safe?"

The question took Keegan by surprise. He leaned back in his chair, feeling the air go out of him. He had never thought to ask Zinnia if there was a safe in the hotel bungalow they were renting—though the question should have been obvious. The realization felt like a face slap. Donovan might have been capable of such a lapse—in a place like the Chateau Marmont, *of course* there would be a safe—but not Keegan. Not when his mind was fully on the job. The distractions were getting to him. He was getting sloppy.

"I was going to head out there today," Keegan lied. "But I also had another thought."

"What's that?"

"That I should probably head over to Catalina Island," he said. "I should check out the Avalon house she owned." He kept talking, trying to sell the idea. "Just a quick overnight trip on the ferry should do it. I can keep the costs low."

The phone was silent a few seconds while Dion considered. "Well, it's probably not that important that we find the original will," the lawyer said. "We shouldn't have any problems with—"

"I think Milton Burritt is sniffing around the case," Keegan interrupted. It wasn't a complete lie. Not exactly. "He's an old friend of the nephew's, you know. I think they might want to challenge the will you wrote up." Keegan listened to the silence on the other end of the line. He squeezed the ballpoint in his fist. "If push comes to shove," he said, pushing his own luck, "I don't think we should leave any stone unturned."

"And you think she might have kept the will out there?"

"If it's not in the hotel safe," Keegan said, "it's the only other place I can think to look." He waited, trying to interpret the silence. "I could head out there this week. Give you a full rundown by Friday, end of business."

Dion remained silent a few more seconds. "You know, that's probably a good idea," he said. "We'll cover all our bases."

THAT AFTERNOON, MRS. Dodd came back late from her lunch break. She didn't announce herself, but the dog skittered out from under Keegan's desk to go see her, and then he heard her working the typewriter.

He picked up the phone and called Zinnia at the Chateau

Marmont. Yes, she confirmed, the bungalow had a safe, but she had no idea how to open it. No. She didn't know if Ida Fletcher had ever used it either. She sounded tired. Her voice was faint and impossibly remote. He thought of her weeping openly, his hands on her quaking shoulders, as he guided her along Sunset Boulevard, back to her hotel.

"Why would you need to see the safe?" she asked, wearily. "All her papers were in the strongbox."

"It's just for the lawyers," Keegan told her. "It's a formality. They're trying to track down the old will."

There was a pause. It had been a couple of weeks, but the poor woman still seemed groggy with grief. Her mind was sluggish. What was it like for her to be languishing all alone in that cloistered hotel bungalow?

"Why would the old will matter?" she finally managed to ask.

"It's just routine paperwork," Keegan told her. He tried to sound soothing. "Nothing to worry over. I'll just come by and look, and if it's not there—and I don't think it will be—I'll be out of your hair again in a few minutes."

Again, the woman was silent. Keegan couldn't even hear her breathing. "I'll leave word with Klaus that you're expected," she said. She hung up the phone.

Keegan put the phone back in its cradle. He'd have to go see Zinnia in her grief, and he wasn't sure he could manage it on his own. He went out to the outer office and stood next to Mrs. Dodd's desk. They were talking again now, but she still wasn't happy with him. He had yet to make the promised phone call to Helen.

Keegan cleared this throat. "Did you see the magazine I left for you on Friday?"

Mrs. Dodd's typing didn't pause or even slow. "I got it," she allowed. She hit the typewriter's return bar, a little harder than seemed necessary, and moved on to the next line of typing.

"You ever been inside the Chateau Marmont?" Keegan asked.

Again, Mrs. Dodd's typing didn't lag. "Never heard of it."

"I'd have thought it would be all over those movie gossip magazines."

Mrs. Dodd didn't respond. She didn't look up at him. She didn't speak. She typed, was what she did. The bell on her Remington chimed, and she hit the return bar again.

"You know who I saw there by the swimming pool when I went by there the other week?"

Mrs. Dodd still wouldn't look at him, but her typing lagged a little, so he knew she was listening. Movie-star gossip was the chink in her armor.

"She was in a very fetching blue swimsuit," Keegan said, wanting to draw it out a bit. "Very glamorous. In the company of two handsome young men. They might have been movie stars too, for all I know about Hollywood."

Mrs. Dodd's typing slowed to a stop. She flung her arms down into her lap in a huff but still wouldn't look in Keegan's direction. "*Okay*," she said, sitting very straight in her chair. "*Fine*. Who did you see at the swimming pool?"

Keegan allowed himself a sly smile. "Natalie Wood," he told her.

Mrs. Dodd's head snapped in his direction. "Was one of the boys Warren Beatty?" she wanted to know. "You know Warren Beatty, right? He was in *Splendor in the Grass*? People say they're seeing each other."

"Never heard of him," Keegan said. "But I'll bet he was one of them. I'm heading out there in a few minutes if you want to tag along."

As a gambit, it did the trick. Mrs. Dodd glared at him, then looked at the letter she was typing. "Give me five minutes to finish this," she said. "What'll we do with the dog?"

"We won't be long," Keegan said. "She can wait in the car. We'll roll the window down a crack."

ON THE RIDE over to the Chateau Marmont, Mrs. Dodd made it clear that Keegan still wasn't on her good side. She sat in the passenger seat with the dog in her lap, staring straight ahead through the windshield.

They idled at a stoplight on Sunset, outside Angel's Corner Liquor. Keegan held the wheel with both hands and kept his gaze straight ahead at the blue Pontiac in front of them. He cleared his throat. "For the record," he said, "I like Helen. I enjoyed meeting her. I just got held up at the damn fortune teller that night. I'll call her when I get a chance. I'll apologize."

He waited. In his peripheral vision, he could see Mrs. Dodd stroking the dog's head. It seemed like she wasn't going to answer. The light turned green. Keegan eased down on the accelerator and they pulled ahead through the intersection.

"It's been too long for a phone call," Mrs. Dodd finally replied. "You should apologize in person. What you did was very rude."

Keegan sighed and nodded. She was probably right. At this point, it was something he'd have to do face to face.

They passed the hotel and then turned on Havenhurst to park in the shade of a big magnolia tree. He rolled the driver's side window down a couple of inches before he closed the door on Nora. He and Mrs. Dodd headed back towards Sunset Boulevard and the hotel. He glanced behind them at his MG. The dog was watching them through the back window. She'd be fine.

When he and Mrs. Dodd entered the hotel lobby, the concierge at the front desk didn't even look up from whatever paperwork he was bent over. Zinnia must have called him—or maybe he remembered Keegan steering the weeping woman back to her bungalow the other week. Either way, it was a relief not to have to deal with him. Keegan led Mrs. Dodd straight through the lobby and out through the glass-paneled doors to the garden courtyard without comment or challenge. They might have been invisible. They might have been ghosts.

Mrs. Dodd trailed behind him through the courtyard. She kept lagging, her head swiveling this way and that, afraid she'd miss something. Keegan kept having to wait for her. No one was at the swimming pool today. As they passed it, Keegan felt a little disappointed on her behalf. Natalie Wood was lounging stylishly in some other location today.

The bungalow's gate was open and the front door ajar. Zinnia was waiting for them. Keegan knocked on the doorjamb and called out, "We're here," before he pushed the door wide and waved Mrs. Dodd through into the dim front room.

Mrs. Dodd had never met Zinnia—or Ida Fletcher or Frank the Boxer, for that matter—but of course, Keegan had told her all about them. To her credit, Mrs. Dodd seemed to know exactly how to react, she slipped quickly to the other woman's side on the sofa. After a few minutes of cooing and consoling, she got up to put the kettle on in the little kitchen. Mrs. Dodd might not be as poised and professional as Roland Dion's receptionist, but she was good with people. She was kind and forgiving—unless, of course, those people were Keegan.

"The safe?" Keegan asked Zinnia.

She sat perched on the sofa's edge, looking impossibly small and exposed. She'd been holed up in this shabby bungalow for days, grieving her lost love alone. Keegan realized, only now, that he could have—should have—done more for her.

"It's in the big bedroom," Zinnia answered, her voice sounding weirdly distant.

"And you don't know the combination?"

She shook her head forlornly.

Keegan nodded. "It's just a formality," he said. "I'll call the front desk. It shouldn't take long."

Mrs. Dodd rushed over from the kitchenette carrying a steaming cup of something. She set it down on the end table next to Zinnia. "*I'll* call the front desk," she told Keegan. "This girl probably hasn't eaten in days." She went to the phone in the kitchenette and dialed the operator.

Keegan went back to the bedroom. An antique black Parcells' safe squatted on the closet floor. It had the old brass dial and the three-pronged spindle. It was even more out of date than the safe in Keegan's office. He tried the spindle, just in case, but of course, it wouldn't budge.

He could hear Mrs. Dodd's voice out in the kitchen. He couldn't make out the words, but, even from here, he could sense her displeasure. Her voice was getting progressively louder. He went to the doorway.

"I don't care *what* time it is…" Mrs. Dodd was saying.

Keegan closed the bedroom door and sat on the corner of the bed, smiling. He'd brought the right reinforcements. If anyone could get someone at this contrary hotel to come down here and open the safe, it was Mrs. Dodd. And it felt good to have someone else be the focus of her ire, if only for a few minutes. Keegan waited until the phone call was over before he came out of hiding.

Klaus, himself, arrived at the bungalow's door a few minutes later. Today his bow tie was sapphire blue. He entered in a huff, pushed past Keegan, and headed to the bedroom. Keegan followed him back and found him bent, working the safe's dial. He consulted something written on an index card and then pressed it against his starched shirtfront so Keegan couldn't read it. He spun the spindle and pulled the safe's door open.

The thing looked empty.

The concierge stood, nodded disdainfully to Keegan, and left the bedroom without uttering a word.

"Weren't you *supposed* to bring a sandwich?" Mrs. Dodd voice came to Keegan from the other room. "We *ordered* a sandwich."

Keegan smiled and kneeled down to make sure there was nothing inside the safe. He couldn't hear the concierge answer.

"I don't know," Mrs. Dodd's voice came from the other room. "Some meat, some cheese, some mayo? Surely someone in this dump knows how to make a sandwich. What do you do when Natalie Wood gets hungry?"

Keegan closed the safe again and heard the bungalow's front door pulled shut. He sat down on the edge of the bed again—smiling again. He'd give Mrs. Dodd a few minutes alone with Zinnia. They could talk. Zinnia could eat her sandwich. Keegan would be fine just sitting here, minding his own business.

ON THEIR WAY back through the hotel's courtyard, the swimming pool was still empty, but Mrs. Dodd paid no attention to it this time.

"She's only got to the end of the month," she was saying. "And all the old lady's money is tied up right now. She doesn't have a penny to her name."

"She's going to have more money than you and me and Wendell put together," Keegan said.

"Not right now, she doesn't." Mrs. Dodd stopped walking, which meant Keegan had to stop too. He turned to look at her. She stood akimbo, looking up at him. "Halloween's on Thursday," she said obstinately. "They're going to throw the poor thing out on her ear. Come on, boss. We've got all that cash just sitting in the office safe."

Keegan sighed. "Okay, fine," he said. "We'll pay for another month."

The concierge stiffened when they came back into the lobby. Mrs. Dodd held her hand out to Keegan and he fished in his jacket pocket for a business card. She took it and strode in Klaus's direction. The man swallowed hard; the sapphire bow tie dipped visibly.

Keegan went and stood behind Mrs. Dodd. He had to admit he was rather enjoying himself.

"We're paying for another month on Bungalow One," she said. She slapped the card down on the desk under his nose. "Bill it to our office."

The concierge looked down at the card and nodded. "Yes,

ma'am," he said. He looked up at Keegan, grudgingly. "Thank you, sir."

Keegan smiled. A month at the Chateau Marmont would cost him an arm and a leg—and he might never get reimbursed for it—but it was worth it just to hear the concierge call him *sir*.

ON THE RIDE back to the office, Mrs. Dodd was in much better spirits. She kept up a steady monologue about the hotel and the concierge and poor Zinnia's predicament. Keegan let her talk. It was good that she was venting—because Keegan needed to ask her a favor.

He waited until they were back in the downtown traffic, in the shade of the tall buildings on Figueroa, before he asked. "I'm going to have to head out to Catalina Island this week," he told her. "I can catch the ferry over Wednesday and be back by Thursday evening."

In his peripheral vision, he could see her turn to look at him. "And you need someone to babysit your dog."

That was, indeed, the favor he needed. "I do," he said.

"That's fine," she told him. "You can drop her off at my house tomorrow night." She held the dog and looked out through the windshield.

"Can't you just take her home with you after work tomorrow?"

"Well," Mrs. Dodd said, "you're going to be dropping her off at my house because you're *also* going to go next door to apologize. In person."

Keegan glanced over at her and then looked back at the traffic. Mrs. Dodd may not have had the poise and polish of Roland Dion's redhead, but, in her own way, she knew how to get things done.

IT WAS GETTING close to midnight when Keegan pulled up in front of Mrs. Dodd's house that Wednesday night. The lights were still on in the living room downstairs. Mrs. Dodd's old Hudson was parked in the driveway and her husband's Lancer was at the curb. Keegan parked in front of the Lancer, got out, and walked up the front path, carrying the sleepy dog.

Helen's red Plymouth Valiant was parked in the driveway of the house next door. A lamp burned in that front window as well, a yellow-tinged oval against the blue curtains.

When Keegan rang Mrs. Dodd's doorbell, Nora began wagging her tail and squirming to be let down. She was now fully awake and she knew where she was. Mrs. Dodd looked after her any time Keegan had to leave town. Keegan guessed that Mrs. Dodd spoiled her.

When Mrs. Dodd pulled open the door, the dog wriggled out of Keegan's hold before he could put her on the ground. She jumped up on Mrs. Dodd and then darted around her into the house. Keegan pulled her coiled leash from the pocket of his jacket.

Mrs. Dodd was dressed in a blue bathrobe and a pair of hand-knit pink slippers. The black-and-white television in the living room behind her was tuned to *The Tonight Show*. Johnny Carson was hamming it up in his monologue with the volume turned low. Mrs. Dodd's husband, Wendell, lay snoring in a green recliner.

"Sorry I'm so late," Keegan said.

Mrs. Dodd waved for him to give her the dog's leash, so he did. She hung it on a hook by the door. "I thought for sure you'd chickened out," she told him. "If you had stood that girl up again, I was going to come to your place and beat you to death with your own telephone."

"I don't doubt it," he said. He looked back over his shoulder at the house next door. "You think she's still up?"

Mrs. Dodd shook her head, like he was looking for a coward's exit—which he probably was. "I told her you'd be coming by," she said. "Don't worry. She's a night owl." She looked beyond him at the other house. "And, for God's sake, make it good. You're not going to get another chance with her."

She looked him over then and seemed to feel a little pity. "You can do this, boss," she said. "Just be your best self." She reached out, turned him by the shoulders, and gave him a little push in the direction of Helen's house. She then closed the door on him, and the porchlight went off.

Keegan turned and looked across at the other house. The lawn between the driveways was closely mown and the privet hedge on Helen's side was neatly trimmed. Everything about her house looked practical and elegant—well kept, like the woman herself. He dug his hands into his pockets and made his way across the grass to the other door. He climbed up the porch steps, took a steadying breath, and rang the doorbell.

Inside, he heard footsteps coming along the hallway, and then Helen opened the door. She gave Keegan a nod. The expression on her face was impossible to read. She was barefoot but wore a tweed skirt and a simple cotton blouse. They looked wrinkled, like she'd worn them to work that day.

"I hope it's not too late," he told her.

"She told me you'd be coming by," Helen said. She stepped back from the door, like she expected him to come in, so he did.

"I hope you weren't waiting up," he said.

"Don't flatter yourself," she told him. "I was correcting essays."

He went inside, and she closed the door, and then he followed her along a hallway. At the far end, through an open doorway, Keegan could see a kitchen table. It held two even-looking stacks of papers and a mug of pens and pencils. Whatever she was grading, she was only half finished. A half-empty bottle of sauterne wine sat on the counter beneath a cupboard.

Helen reached through a dark doorway and switched on the lights. She nodded for him to follow her into the room. One wall held floor-to-ceiling bookcases, built on either side of a brick fireplace. The shelves were crowded with neatly arranged hardbacks, an impressive collection. A rosewood beehive clock ticked on the mantel. It was six minutes to midnight. Helen plopped down in a chair, arms folded.

Keegan went over and sat down on a sofa across from her. "I just wanted to apologize for last week," he said.

She nodded in the direction of Mrs. Dodd's house. "I'm guessing someone twisted your arm."

"She did," Keegan admitted. "But I'd been meaning to apologize anyway. I've just been busy."

She didn't speak, only nodded noncommittally, as if the apologizing should commence.

"In my own defense—" Keegan began, but Helen was already shaking her head, so he stopped talking.

"God, no!" she said, eyes smoldering. "Don't even start."

Keegan shifted uncomfortably. "What?" he said. "What did I do?"

"I've been grading essays all night," she said. "Half of them start with 'Webster's dictionary defines…' or 'In today's society…' Three words into them, and I already want to drown myself in the kitchen sink."

"I'm sorry?" Keegan said, confused. "What?"

"I'm saying that if this is supposed to be an apology—a *real* apology—you're off to a pretty crappy start." She stood then and smoothed down her dress. "Why don't you just go on home?" she told him. "Let's forget this whole thing. I have to deal with spoiled boys all day at work."

She started to move toward the door, but Keegan held out his hand, fingers splayed, a plea for her to stop. She was right, he knew. As a former reporter, he should be better with words. He'd come to apologize, and he'd buried his lead.

She paused there by the doorway, looking down at him skeptically, arms folded.

"I'm an asshole," he told her—feeling *that* might be the proper, accurate lead for his story. "I'm selfish and stupid, and I've been holed up in my own damn head so long I've forgotten how to treat people. You deserve better."

The expression on Helen's face went slack, though Keegan

couldn't guess what that meant. Still, she crossed back to her chair and sat down.

Keegan took that as a sign he should continue. "The thing is," he went on, feeling a strange mixture of disquiet and relief, "I got involved with a woman a while ago, and it ended horribly, and I don't know how to get past it. I'm not sure I can."

Helen nodded. "Mrs. Dodd may have mentioned something about that," she said. "The woman who died. She made it sound like it really haunts you."

Keegan nodded. If she only knew. "The woman got murdered," he went on, like he was feeling for something in the darkness. "Shot by some mobster. I know it wasn't technically my fault, but I keep playing the whole thing over and over in my head, and there were so many times when I could have done something different." The words felt compressed—like they were something he'd been holding too tightly inside himself for too long. Something was loosening, threatening to tumble out in an avalanche. "I could have listened to her," he said, shaking his head helplessly. "I could have trusted her. There are so many ways I screwed everything up."

Helen was nodding now, watching him closely, reappraising.

There was so much he wanted to say, so great a burden he felt like he could lay down. In that moment, he felt a glimmer of something like hope—but then Helen stood. He gaped up at her, feeling forsaken.

"No," she told him. "Don't worry. I'm just going into the kitchen to put on some coffee. I'll be right back. I want to hear all about it. We've got all night."

CHAPTER FOURTEEN

JUST PAST THE LA Harbor Lighthouse, the Catalina ferry left the protection of San Pedro's riprap breakwater. The big swells ran under the hull now, and Keegan stood on the starboard deck in the wind, his duffel bag at his feet. The ferry's big engines opened up loud, and the boat lurched forward, making Keegan grab for the railing. As they pulled into the open sea, the wind picked up, too. The spray was cold and damp on the side of Keegan's face.

He knew that if he looked north along the cliffs, he'd see the old Point Fermin Lighthouse. It had been dark since the war, but the shape would be unmistakable, a gabled Victorian home perched up there on the dizzying edge of the bluff, the clapboard painted white.

But he wouldn't look. That escarpment was the site of Keegan's father's suicide—the hushed and heady family secret he'd been raised to overlook. In truth, Keegan barely remembered his father—remembered only the long years of his mother's grief. In his current frame of mind, that was just as well, he reasoned. He had more than enough people now to haunt him.

Instead of looking north, he picked up his bag and went around to the ferry's leeward side, facing south along the coast. A man and a woman were smoking against the railing, so deep in conversation that Keegan felt invisible when he joined them. He set down his duffel. From where he now stood, he could see the docks and cranes and gray hulls of Long Beach. A deep-sea charter boat passed a hundred yards away, heading in to dock. Its deck was crowded with anglers. A cloud of seagulls chased it, shrieking and wheeling and splashing into the boat's wake, chasing after scraps.

He leaned over the rail and looked down at the choppy green sea they were cutting through. If Frank the Boxer had been conscious when he went in the ocean, how long had he kept his head above water before his tangled, heavy clothing pulled him under? How many long minutes had he kicked and splashed, trying to escape his fate? Again, Keegan saw the morgue sheet pulled back; the slack, gray skin of his face; the closed, swollen eyes.

Dammit. He'd hoped the long talk last night with Helen might have soothed his mind a bit, but his thoughts were still in disarray. It was probably because he'd got so little sleep. He'd stayed at Helen's, talking until nearly dawn, and then drove back to his own place full of coffee, mind wired and racing. He was just tired.

Or perhaps Madame Lena was right: he couldn't rest because he was being haunted. By Eve. By Ida Fletcher and Frank the Boxer. By his long-lost father. By his own stubbornness and pride and all his petty failures. And, now that he thought about it, Madame Lena was right about something else as well: *You'll soon travel across the ocean.* He smiled glumly at the boat's port rail and checked his watch.

The crossing would take an hour and a half. But at least he'd brought his book. It was slipped into the outer pocket of his overcoat. He looked in through the misty cabin windows at all the booths in the ferry's brightly lit canteen. He'd buy a bottle of beer at the bar, he decided, and he'd read *The Grapes of Wrath* at one of the tables.

By the time they pulled into Avalon Harbor, he'd only

finished one more chapter of the novel, but he'd emptied three bottles of Budweiser.

It wasn't even four o'clock.

THE TAXI DRIVER who drove him along Crescent Avenue in the direction of his hotel seemed tailor-made for the job. He wore a battered captain's hat and a bright orange Hawaiian shirt. He looked to be in his mid-fifties—Keegan's own age. He was upbeat and rhapsodic, and his devotion for the island he lived on seemed boundless. "Lived out here since I was a teenager," he volunteered to Keegan, within thirty seconds of pulling away from the dock. "Loved every minute of it. Don't miss the mainland one iota."

Keegan looked at him in the rearview mirror and nodded. The beers on the way over had him feeling sluggish and sleepy. "Where's a good place for dinner?" he asked, mostly to keep the cabbie talking.

"Plenty of good restaurants right along Crescent here," the driver said, gesturing at the buildings on either side. "We've got seafood, Italian, Mexican. All great restaurants. Whatever you want." He looked at Keegan in the mirror, as if trying to assess his tastes. "You want a place with a world-class wine list? There's a place up Metropole that's worth the walk."

Keegan smiled ruefully. No one had mistaken him for a wine-list man before. He looked out the driver's side window at the row of kitschy storefronts they were passing—all shells and souvenirs and overpriced ice cream. Half the pedestrians on the sidewalks had cameras dangling around their necks—the worst kind of sightseers, the off-season ones looking for a bargain vacation. Maybe that was why Keegan rarely went anywhere these days: he didn't ever want to be taken for a tourist.

"How about you?" he asked the cabbie. "Where do you eat?"

The driver eyed him in the mirror. "All the restaurants on the island are good," he said warily, like he thought Keegan might be wearing a wire.

Keegan tried again. "Well, let's say a man wanted to get away from all the out-of-towners," he said, nodding at the window. "Just wanted some honest grub and a seat at a bar, someplace no one was going to bother him."

The cabbie sized him up in the mirror again, as if deciding whether or not it was prudent to level with him. He turned his eyes back to the road. "Easy," he finally said. "That would be Duke's. It's all the way up Del Playa as far as you can go." He barked a laugh and shook the steering wheel with both hands. "I'd say, 'You can't miss the place,' but that would be a downright lie. You could walk right by it and never know it's there. Which is why there are never any tourists."

Outside the window, a family of four posed for a photograph in front of a tiled fountain. They looked humdrum and hackneyed and hopelessly out of place.

"That sounds like the place," Keegan said.

THE BEACHCOMBER INN was a good four blocks inland from the sand and water. Keegan hadn't imagined a bay-view veranda or a poolside bar for the six dollars a night he'd be billing Roland Dion and Associates—but he'd allowed himself to expect more than this. The place was shabby and spartan, hunkered in the shade of a larger hotel across the narrow street. Inside the dim lobby, Keegan saw a stack of cheap paper maps at the check-in desk and grabbed one.

The girl at the desk was a wide-eyed brunette who couldn't have graduated high school yet. Her tag said her name was LISA, and she seemed to be all alone here on her shift. She gave him a key to room 12, and he told her he'd find it on his own. She hoped he'd have a pleasant stay on the island.

Room 12 looked out the back of the hotel at a gray cinderblock wall across a six-foot alleyway. This was not the Ambassador. There was no pool at the Beachcomber, no restaurant, no room service. The room's one extravagance was a small electric kettle on the counter, next to the sink, with two chipped coffee mugs. Keegan set his duffel bag by the door and hung his coat over the back of the desk chair.

He sat on the edge of the bed and looked at the paper map he'd taken from the front desk. It was a cartoonish rendering of the town, with all the tourist traps highlighted—the Bird Park, the penny arcade, the glass-bottom boats. The pricey beach-front restaurants were all accounted for, but if there *was* a place called Duke's at the top of Del Playa, it had been left off the map. Perhaps that was a good sign. He found Tradewinds Lane—the street where Ida Fletcher had owned a house—two streets over from his hotel. It ran parallel to Vista Del Mar.

He was tired and a little seasick, so he'd relax for now. He could walk past Ida Fletcher's place on his way to dinner and get the lay of the land before he searched the place in the morning.

He lay back on the bed and kicked his shoes off onto the floor. He propped his head up with both pillows and opened his Steinbeck book, but he hadn't even turned the page when he set it aside, face down to keep his place. The beers he'd had on the ferry and the late night at Helen's place were pulling him down into sleep. A nap was in order, and he could think of no reason to forego such a luxury. He rolled on his side and closed his eyes.

WHEN HE WOKE, the room was dusky, and he was hungry. He tucked *The Grapes of Wrath* under one arm and went down to the lobby to ask young Lisa if there really was a place called Duke's at the top of the hill. When he got downstairs, the front desk was unmanned and the lobby light was out. There was no after-hours Klaus here to keep the riffraff at bay.

Keegan went outside and down the front steps. If Duke's was a wild goose chase, at least he'd get some exercise climbing the hill. It was barely dark, but kids in costume were already out, running along the side streets in small gleeful packs—pirates and princesses and bedsheet ghosts. Keegan had forgotten it was Halloween night.

He took a street parallel to the waterfront and then turned on Tradewinds Lane and headed up the hill. Number 13, Ida Fletcher's island getaway, was dark. The front gate was locked up with a chain and padlock. He'd had no intention of going into the house tonight. He'd even left the old lady's ring of keys in his duffel. The electricity might have been shut off. There was no point in entering the house until tomorrow when the sun was out—but he paused there, looking up at the dark front windows.

The house wasn't as prepossessing as the old lady's Bel Air and Newport houses, but it was well kept and far larger than any of the others he'd passed on the street so far. It was all glass and concrete and hard angles, as if someone had dropped a Frank Lloyd Wright down among all the town's shingle siding and weathervanes. With all the high windows, and the third floor's wrap-around balcony, it would have a breathtaking view of the harbor. From the outside, though, the place was a bit of an eyesore.

A quartet of gleeful kids rushed behind Keegan on the sidewalk, all of them ten or eleven—a clown, two hoboes, and a vampire. They ran through the open gate of the house next door. With its dark windows and chained front gate, no trick-or-treater would give number 13 a second look. Keegan moved on.

Farther up the street, he crossed over to Vista Del Mar and headed up the hill. It was a steep slog, and Keegan felt inclined to curse the cabbie. But, when he got to the top, the restaurant was indeed where he'd been told he would find it. The taxi driver was right: it catered exclusively to locals. There wasn't even a sign out front to advertise its presence to anyone who didn't already know it was there. The two small tables set up on a brick-lined front garden—"bistro style", Danny Church might have said—was the only thing that set it apart from the other modest houses he'd passed coming up the hill.

Inside, the front room had a few oak tables, and there was a small, cozy bar tucked away in a back room. No fuss, no frills, no tourists with their Instamatic cameras—this place would suit Keegan fine.

He pulled a stool up to the bar and studied the menu chalked on a blackboard behind the row of beer taps. When the barkeep came his way, he ordered a cold turkey sandwich and a beer. He opened his paperback novel and pressed it down on the bar top. The light wasn't ideal, but he started to read.

"How's the hotel?" a man's voice asked him, when he paused to turn the page.

Keegan looked over to find the cabbie addressing him from a stool at the other end of the bar. He still wore the bright Hawaiian shirt, but his captain's hat lay, capsized, in front of him on the bar. That was probably why Keegan hadn't recognized him when he'd first come in.

"If the nap I just took is any indication," Keegan said, "it'll suit me just fine."

The cabbie picked up his glass and moved a few stools closer to Keegan. "Was Lisa working behind the desk today?" he asked.

"She was indeed," Keegan said.

"I used to have a huge thing for the kid's mother back in high school," the cab driver said. "In another life, that little sweetheart might have been my daughter."

Keegan sensed there was a story behind that comment, but he doubted it would be very interesting. He nodded, took a sip from his beer, and looked back down at his novel.

"So, what brings you to our fair island on Halloween of all days?" the taxi driver pressed on.

Keegan looked over at the cabbie and then closed the book and set it aside. It wasn't like he was immersed in it; in the two weeks he'd been reading it, he'd made only a small dent. There was no godly reason to be unfriendly. "I'm here on business," he said. "Just hunting up a few ghosts, I guess." He'd never spoken truer words.

The bartender came out from the back with a thick sandwich and a pile of potato chips on a blue plate. He came down along the bar towards them.

"What are you drinking?" Keegan asked the cabbie. "Let

me buy you the next one." Roland Dion would be paying the tab, after all; he could afford to be generous.

"The same, Tommy," the cabbie told the barkeep and then turned back to Keegan. "Well, if it's ghosts you want, you've come to the right place."

"How's that?" Keegan tried one of the potato chips. It made him want another.

"This island is chock-full of them," the cabbie said. "More dead people walking these streets than living ones, if you ask me. Tommy here"—he jabbed a thumb at the bartender—"will back me up on this."

The bartender poured a fresh shot of Old Grand-Dad into the cabbie's glass. "I've seen a few ghosts," he confirmed.

The cabbie picked up his bourbon and moved another stool closer to Keegan. There was just one empty seat between them now. He rubbed the burnished wooden bar top with one palm, like he was dusting off one of his better stories. "You ever hear of Bloody Mike's Cave?" he said. He turned to the bartender. "Tommy, you must have heard this one."

Tommy nodded gamely, as if he had in fact heard this one, but it was a good story; he'd be happy to listen to it again. "You tell it better than anyone," he told the cab driver, with classic bartender deference.

As the cabbie launched into the story, Tommy poured a second glass of Old Grand-Dad and slid it in front of Keegan.

Keegan couldn't help but smile. A round on the house with a ghost story chaser. He already felt like a local. He took a bite of his turkey sandwich, and it turned out to be delicious. For the moment, at least, all was right with the world.

KEEGAN WASN'T DRUNK, exactly, when he headed back out into the night, leaving the small lighted restaurant behind him. He wasn't reeling or disoriented—at least he didn't think he was—but he was glad he wouldn't be driving, and he was happy to know that his hotel room was a straight shot down the hill and then over a street or two. He'd find it okay, even if he took a wrong turn.

Two beers with dinner had always been his rule of thumb, and it was a rule he'd intended to stick to tonight, especially after the ferry ride beers. But when he'd finished his sandwich at the bar and was getting ready to settle up, the cabbie, not wanting to lose his audience, stood him another shot of bourbon and included the bartender in the round. That, of course, meant Keegan was on the hook for the round after that. The three of them talked and laughed and swapped scary yarns. Each time some new local washed in through the doors, the cabbie—loved by one and all, it seemed—pulled them into his flow, and a new round of ghost stories started up.

Keegan had the presence of mind to make sure the receipt wasn't itemized when he finally settled up. He could pass it on to Roland Dion's office without having to explain why there were so many drinks on it. And, as a tab, it wasn't too steep. Duke's prices were bargain basement. The total on the receipt wouldn't raise an eyebrow. It probably cost less than dinner for one at a seafood joint down on the waterfront, where they made their money gouging tourists.

Keegan was a good four or five blocks down the hill when he realized he wasn't carrying his copy of *The Grapes of Wrath*. He'd left it on the bar top, among all the emptied glasses. He stopped and turned and looked behind him up the steep incline. It was late, and he was tired. It was too much bother for a two-dollar paperback, he decided. He turned back around and continued down the hill.

The streets were empty now. The island's children had long abandoned their trick-or-treating on this school night. It was too dark to see his wristwatch, but it had to be after eleven o'clock—maybe closer to midnight. The houses on either side of the street were dark, and there weren't enough streetlamps along the sidewalk to keep the night at bay. He'd never been on the island except in the summer, and now he saw that Avalon was the kind of tourist town that started locking up early after Labor Day. When the stream of tourists dried up, the nightlife did as well.

And it wasn't just the usual darkness of night; he saw now that a dense mist had rolled in from the ocean in the hours he'd spent in the bar. This high on the hill, the fogbank was spread out below him like a grounded cloud. The roadway ahead faded into white, as if the whole world were dissolving away. He kept walking, winding down the empty street, until he melded into the gauzy pall of mist. Soon the fog was all around him, and the few porchlights he passed were wreathed in damp white halos.

One of the stories the cabbie had told was of a young, waiflike Indian girl sometimes seen wandering the Avalon streets on foggy nights. She'd appear to hapless passersby, confused and distraught, gaping around herself in the mist at the changes made to her island in the centuries since she'd died. As a yarn, it was thin as brume—more a hazy legend than a proper ghost story. But as the fog closed in around him, the thought of that young girl gave Keegan a chill. He chuckled out loud and shook his head. All it would take was some straggling trick-or-treater to emerge from the mist, a feather in her hair, and Keegan would be laid out dead of a heart attack.

It was the bourbon, he knew. In his better moments, he wasn't a jumpy man. But he was tipsy tonight and he had a lot on his mind besides. What with Madame Lena and his cottage ghost and Kipper Lusk's damn curse, his imagination was getting away from him these days. Old Grand-Dad and old wives' tales made for a potent cocktail. The cold scrutiny of reason didn't stand a chance. At least he'd have a good laugh at himself tomorrow. In the morning, he'd stir up a cup of weak instant coffee by the light of the hotel window, and he'd wince at the memory of the ridiculous eeriness he felt in his bones in this moment.

There was a faint yellow rectangle up ahead, on the far side of the street. A single lit window, set back in the darkness, on the otherwise lightless road. He saw it but thought nothing of it. It wasn't yet midnight; even in Avalon, he couldn't be the last person awake.

It was only when he was directly across the street, and the light from the window backlit the chained gate, that he realized he was on Tradewinds Lane. An upper window was lit in number 13. With a sense of foreboding, he stepped into the street and crossed. The front gate was still chained shut, but there was definitely a light in an upper window. He was sure it hadn't been lit when he'd passed this way before.

He took the gate in his hands and shook it, but it was unbudging. He pressed his face to the damp wrought-iron bars and looked up at the window. From where he stood, it was just a gauzy rectangle up there on the third floor. He could see the ceiling and a short span of crown molding, and a large, unlit pendant lamp. Then he saw a shadow move, and a face came into view.

He let go of the gate and stepped back, like he'd been hit by a bolt of electricity. He looked again to be sure what he'd seen: the narrow shoulders, the widow's peak, the hollowed cheeks. The face was gone before his foggy mind could put a name to it: Ida Fletcher. The light went out. In the new darkness, the mist off the ocean congealed around him, the silence of the street intensified. The house at number 13 was again as empty and lifeless as it had when he'd first set eyes on it.

More dead people than living, the cabbie had promised him. And Tommy the bartender had borne the assertion out.

Keegan took a few numb steps along the sidewalk and then picked up his pace like something might come after him. He fairly jogged back to the Beachcomber, his footfalls echoing along the empty streets. He rushed up the front steps, brushed through the dark lobby, and climbed the stairs to his room. With the light on, and the door latched behind him, he willed his heart to slow down.

CHAPTER FIFTEEN

THE NEXT MORNING, he felt like a fool when he stood outside the chained front gate of number 13 Tradewinds Lane on a bright, brisk morning, in the new month of November. The fog had burned off before he even woke up. Avalon now lay in the shadowless light of a high, hazy marine layer.

Nothing about the big, blockish house in front of him seemed the least bit sinister now. In his embarrassment, he glanced around, as if worried someone might be watching. A woman passed by on the opposite sidewalk pushing a baby in a stroller. Down at the bottom of the hill, a small group of tourists waited on the corner for the light to change. But what would they even see if they looked in his direction? Just an ordinary-looking man—one who perhaps needed a shave— in front of an ordinary building. The things that made him exceptional were all in his head.

He still had a bit of a headache from last night's bourbon, but Old Grand-Dad's other effects—the jumpiness, the racing heart, the rampant fancies—had fled him. He was sober now and sensible, if a bit hungover. And the big house in front of him, the one he had come here to search for any traces of Danny Church's crime, was just so much concrete, glass, and girder.

He looked up at the high window where he'd imagined Ida Fletcher's ghostly face. It was blank and blind as a daytime drive-in screen. The lack of eeriness was almost comical. Kipper Lusk could have his curse. Madame Lena could keep her tarot cards. The cabbie at Duke's could trot out his ghostly yarns. Henceforth, Keegan would be the rational, levelheaded one.

The key to the padlock was on Keegan's ring, and the front door deadbolt turned with the second key he tried. He pushed open the door to find a long entry hallway. Before he stepped inside, he reached for the hallway light switch. It worked. A row of wall lamps illuminated a plain white corridor that led to an open living area. Nothing hung on the entryway walls, though a row of brass fittings suggested that pictures once had. What had happened in old Ida Fletcher's mind that she'd sworn off graven images? The family portrait banished. The houses scrubbed of every photograph. No one she left behind would likely ever know what she'd been thinking. At least her fevered soul was now at rest.

Unless, of course, it was haunting Keegan.

He passed through to a broad high-ceilinged room. The furniture in it was hard-edged and modern. Here, again, the expansive walls were vacant. Another lifeless, empty house devoid of any hint of who might have once lived there. He took a deep breath of air, but it confided no tobacco scent. He went through the downstairs first—a living room, a dining room, and kitchen. His footsteps echoed in the big, empty spaces. He had to keep reminding himself that he was looking for the will, though he was searching places that would never hide it—pillowcases, ashtrays, backyard shrubs. What would Danny Church have done here, if he had fled to the house after killing his aunt? Would he have destroyed evidence here? Hidden something? Patched up a wound that Frank the Boxer had managed to inflict before he went overboard?

Keegan checked both fireplaces and the backyard barbecue for any signs the kid had used them to burn up bloody clothes.

He ransacked trash cans for cigarette butts. He put his face deep into sinks to look for blood and hair. All he needed was a French shirt button among the ash in the grate or a whiskey glass left out on a counter that could be dusted for prints. For once, the kid seemed to have picked up after himself.

He climbed a broad, minimalistic staircase that protruded from the wall. It was just a rising flight of open, vertiginous steps and a bannister. It made him feel, as he climbed, as though he were defying some fundamental law of physics. On the upper floors, he entered room after empty room, scrutinizing them for any signs of disturbance.

If it had just been the will he was looking for, the search would have been easy; nothing hung on the walls that would conceal a safe. The kitchen cupboards and desk drawers were all empty. There weren't too many other places where you might slip a document for safekeeping. What slowed him down was that he had no idea what else he was looking for. What miniscule clues might the nephew have left here if he had stayed the night? What might he have missed when he made his getaway back to the mainland?

On the third floor, Keegan found a bare room that looked as if it served as an office. There was a desk and a file cabinet. In the corner was a bookcase with a few boxes on the shelves and one lone row of books. The cabinet drawers were empty. He tried the desk next, pulling every oak drawer all the way out, to make sure nothing was behind them. There were only a few ballpoint refills, an old-fashioned paper knife, and a box of Swingline staples. The final drawer was locked. He tried every small key on the old lady's key ring, but none would turn. No matter. The lock was more decoration than hindrance. He used the blade of the paper knife to shove the latch back, and it gave easily. When he pulled open the drawer, it was empty.

He went to the big front window and looked out on the descending sweep of roofs and the distant crescent of blue ocean. Yachts dotted the water in curved lines. A big ocean liner loomed like a backdrop behind them. He could see the ferry terminal at the bay's south end.

He'd soon pack up his duffel and catch a ride back to the mainland empty-handed. He looked down at the front gate. He'd left the chain dangling and the latch open. It occurred to him that this must be the window through which he thought he'd seen Ida Fletcher's ghost.

He turned and looked behind him at the room. There was nothing here that might have cast a shadow on the window, that might have created the illusion he saw. It made no sense. What in this room was worthy of being haunted?

He went over to the bookcase. The only thing he hadn't searched. The boxes on the shelves held mostly stationery— thank you cards, rolls of postage stamps, a box of lavender paper with Ida Fletcher's name printed along the top. He looked at the single shelf of books, and one title caught his eye.

There it was: *The Grapes of Wrath*. It was a clothbound copy, still in its dust jacket. He smiled and pulled it off the shelf. The cover showed a blue-washed landscape, an old truck, a few downtrodden people. The book looked unread, almost new. He'd have something to read on the noon ferry back to San Pedro, after all.

He was about to push the other books together—a small gesture to cover up his theft—but something had fallen behind the row of books. He reached into the gap and pulled it free. It was a black-and-white photograph in a silver frame. It must have toppled from an upper shelf and slipped down behind.

The photo had been taken here on the island. Ida Fletcher, much younger, sat in a wooden beach chair, fully dressed and wrapped in a blanket. Her face was fuller, the widow's peak jet black. In front of her was a lanky-looking boy. In her younger days, the old lady was nearly pretty—in a lean and angular kind of way.

With all the empty walls of her houses—and the missing family portrait—this might be the only image she left behind her. Keegan slipped the back off the frame and took out the photo. *October 1950*, someone had written on the back in fountain pen.

Keegan looked at the photo again, angling it to catch the light from the window. The kid who stood in front of Ida Fletcher looked about ten. His skinny chest was pale, and he posed awkwardly, with one shoulder higher than the other. He wore baggy swimming trunks and held a plastic beach spade at his side. Fletcher's hand was on his shoulder. Both bore the threadbare smiles of people being asked to pose too long. Keegan stared at the kid's young face a few seconds and then grinned.

It was Danny Church as a young boy, and he looked ludicrous—a gangly kid with a bad haircut and saggy trunks. Keegan's heart warmed to see the old lady's nephew, here stripped of his countless layers of affectation. It was humanizing. Keegan felt something like affection for Danny Church as he had once been: a gawky, graceless kid who perhaps still lurked somewhere beneath the grown man's Italian suits and his Persol shades.

He slipped the photo between the pages of his new novel— it would be worth keeping, an accidental portrait of a killer and his victim. He tucked the book under his arm.

NORA SEEMED TO sense him outside Mrs. Dodd's door even before he pressed the doorbell. He heard her whine, her nails clawing the weather strip, the jingle of her collar as she shook with excitement.

As soon as the door cracked open, the dog rocketed out onto the porch like a quarter horse from the gate. She jumped up on his legs and then tugged at the hem of his trousers with her teeth.

Mrs. Dodd stood in the open doorway in a housedress, holding the dog's leash looped in her hand.

"I hope she wasn't any trouble," Keegan said.

"Not in the least," Mrs. Dodd assured him.

Nora ran back inside, sprinted in a circle on the hallway tiles, and bolted outside to him again, jumping up on his leg.

"I think she missed you," Mrs. Dodd said. She handed him the leash. "Anything happen over on Avalon?"

"Not a thing," he said. "No sign of the nephew. Didn't even stumble across the will." He knew better than to tell Mrs. Dodd about the ghost he thought he'd seen. She'd be off and running with all her talk about premonitions and poltergeists. He bent and grabbed the squirming dog's collar and clipped on the leash. When he straightened up, he glanced over his shoulder at the house across the driveway.

"Go on over," she told him. "You'll be fine. From what I hear, you made good. She told me you've got another date."

"Dinner," he said. "Tomorrow night."

"If I were you, I'd show up this time."

"Thanks for the tip," Keegan said. "And thanks for looking after this one."

"If I can't have my grandson here, I want that dog."

When Keegan crossed the gap between the two houses, the dog seemed to know where they were headed. She more or less pulled him across the strip of lawn, past the hedge, and up Helen's porch steps.

Helen answered the door dressed in a slate skirt and white blouse—again, her teaching clothes, he guessed.

"Just wanted to make sure we're still on for tomorrow night," he said.

Helen smiled slyly. "Seems like I'm the one who should be checking with you."

Keegan nodded and looked down at the ground. "I promise it won't happen again," he told her.

Nora had been tugging on her leash since Helen had opened the door, and now she tried to hop up over the lintel into the house. Keegan had to yank her back by the leash. "This is my dog, Nora."

Helen looked down at the dog, smiling. "Oh, Nora and I are acquainted," she said. She bent down and let the dog sniff the back of her hand. "Aren't we, Nora?" She straightened up again and smiled at Keegan. "We went for a nice walk through the neighborhood last night, looking at all the trick-or-treaters. I think I won her over."

SATURDAY MORNING, KEEGAN waited at the kitchen table, drinking coffee and trying to read his stolen Steinbeck novel. It was a Saturday, and he knew he shouldn't call the Lieutenant too early, especially at home. He finished a chapter of the book and checked his watch again. It was nearly eleven. Even if Lou Moore slept in, he couldn't complain about a phone call this late in the morning. Keegan marked his place with Ida Fletcher's old photo and dialed the phone.

"Sorry to call you on the weekend," Keegan said when Moore came on the phone. "I'm just wondering if you've dug up anything new on Danny Church."

"About that," Moore said. "Looks like we're hitting dead ends. I'm still waiting to hear from the Coast Guard about the wreckage, but I don't think it's going to give us anything." He sounded tentative—like there was more he wanted to say— but then his tone brightened: "You know, I called your office yesterday. Nobody picked up."

"Yeah," Keegan said. "I took a trip over to Catalina, to look at the old lady's house. We closed up for a couple of days."

"Find anything?"

Keegan thought of the dead woman's pale face in the window and the damp chill of the fog. It sent a shiver through him. "Not a thing," he said.

"Well, I hate to say it, Jimmy, but we might just be stuck," the Lieutenant said. "Unless something comes along, there isn't anything I can do. It's been a few weeks. Things are just going to get colder."

Keegan didn't like where this seemed to be heading. "So, what are you saying?"

"I'm saying we might have to just chalk up an *L* for this one and walk away," he said. "We don't have anything on the kid. Just a bunch of hints and coincidences. Nothing we could use in court."

"Really?" Keegan said. "You're just going to let it go?"

Moore was silent a few long seconds. "Maybe it's time to move on," he finally said.

It was too much for Keegan to stomach. The thought of that smug, oily nephew taking possession of everything Ida Fletcher owned made him queasy. The old lady was going to haunt him forever, if he let the kid go. "You had to be in the room," Keegan said. "You should have seen the old lady's face when she heard the nephew was in town. He's behind all this, Lou. We can't let him get away with it."

"Listen, Jimmy," Moore said. "You can't let these things get under your skin." His voice had taken on a gentle, coaxing tone, like he was trying to soothe a barking dog. *Hush now. There's nothing there. See? The chair is empty.*

Keegan felt sick.

"Here's the thing it took me years to learn once I made detective," the Lieutenant went on. "Sometimes the mystery just doesn't get solved. It's hard to swallow, but sometimes you never find out what happened. Sometimes you just have to live with that."

FOR THEIR DINNER date, Helen picked a place called Brogino's out in Eagle Rock. Keegan had to look it up in the phone book. It was on York Boulevard, just east of Forest Lawn, a neighborhood Keegan didn't know well.

Out of an abundance of caution, he left the house before seven and got to the restaurant a half-hour early. He looked for Helen's red Plymouth in the parking lot and was happy to see he had beaten her there. It would give him a chance to be waiting at their table with a glass of wine for her when she came in through the door. He parked the car—there was no valet, he was glad to see—and strode up to the entrance with plenty of time to spare. He could do this. He could at least make a good third impression.

Brogino's wasn't at all what Keegan had been expecting; he was the only one in the dining room wearing a jacket and tie. Middle-aged couples sat at tables here and there. What looked to be a Boy Scout troupe sat at one long table, with all their accompanying adults at a pair of tables nearby.

All the tables were draped with plastic checkered tablecloths. Some Rat Pack crooner played through the sound system. A few of the tables needed bussing, and the chairs were pushed out every which way. It wasn't even eight o'clock yet, but—judging by the general disarray—the dinner rush had already ended.

There was no one in the entryway to seat Keegan, so he went up to the counter. A girl in a denim apron—she had braces on her teeth and couldn't have been out of her teens—told him to just seat himself anywhere. She'd be right with him. He asked her for two menus, but she just nodded behind her at the big chalkboard up on the wall. This place was about as far from Jackson's on Wilshire as you were likely to get.

Keegan looked around at the available seating. He chose a table in the corner, as far away from the Scout troupe as it was possible to be. He sat down facing the door. A red jar-candle flickered on the plastic tablecloth, next to a tin shaker of parmesan.

The girl from behind the counter came by, and Keegan ordered a glass of sauterne for Helen. He'd seen a bottle of it on her kitchen counter and hoped it might be her favorite—though maybe she only drank wine at home, to get through grading essays.

Five minutes later, the glass of wine stood warming on the other side of the table, the sides glistening with condensation. Keegan glanced at his watch. It was still ten minutes before eight. He wanted to order himself a beer, but he didn't know how that would look. A glass of wine waiting for Helen would come across as thoughtful, he hoped. A big glass of Schlitz in front of him might just look uncouth. The truth was, fifteen minutes was time enough to do a lot of overthinking. Why had Helen chosen *this* place for their first real date? Was it some kind of statement? Was she telling him they'd just be friends? Did he look like a fool, wearing a tie in a place that had Little League team photos on the wall?

He shouldn't have ordered the wine, he decided. It might come across as presumptuous, overtly masculine. He looked around for the serving girl, to ask her to take it away—but she was over in the kitchen doorway now, chatting with one of the cooks.

The problem with trying to outthink an English teacher, Keegan knew, was that he was guaranteed to miss the point—at least that's what his grades at USC had always suggested. Maybe that's why he'd gone into crime reporting after college. In the world of murder and mayhem, people ended up guilty or not; there was little necessity for subtleties or shades of meaning.

When Keegan looked up again, Helen was coming in through the doorway. She looked around for him as the door swung shut behind her. She wore a pair of gray slacks and a blue blouse with a darker-blue cardigan. As an outfit, it struck Keegan as neat, but not showy. She had dressed well but wasn't trying to impress. A smile lit her face when she saw him sitting there.

That smile relaxed Keegan a little. He stood and watched her make her way through the mostly empty tables. She pulled out the chair across from him and sat down.

"Cheap, good food," Helen said, draping the strap of her purse over the post of her chair. It was as if she knew exactly what Keegan had been wondering—a Madame Lena parlor trick. "It's simple, and it's relaxed," she went on. "And I'm not going to run into any of my students' families and get the rumor mill started."

Keegan nodded. It was a good point: this was definitely not a place the Saint Matthew's crowd would ever deign to enter.

"What's this?" Helen asked, as if she'd just now noticed the glass of wine.

"Sauterne?" Keegan said. It came out sounding like a question. "I saw some in your kitchen," he said. "Maybe it was a stupid idea."

She shook her head at him. "Not stupid," she said. She raised the glass to her lips and took a sip.

Helen wasn't wearing lipstick, Keegan noticed—and he scolded himself for wondering what that might mean. "Apparently, they don't have menus," Keegan said, so he would have something to say.

Helen smiled. "I know," she said. "I come here a lot after work for takeout. Some nights I just don't want to cook for one."

Keegan nodded. He squinted over his shoulder at the chalkboard behind the counter and then looked back at Helen. "What do you recommend?"

Helen shook her head, still smiling. "I recommend you read the chalkboard and draw your own conclusions," she said. "I'm off work tonight. I don't want any responsibilities."

When the girl in the denim apron came by, Keegan ordered the chicken with mushrooms because he thought he could probably manage that without making a mess of his good Botany tie. Helen ordered some kind of ravioli. She'd taken another sip of wine while Keegan talked to the server, so he felt safe in ordering a beer.

"So, did you get all your grading done?" Keegan said, when the waitress was out of earshot.

Helen shook her head with exaggerated sorrow. "It never ends," she told him. "I will be adding commas, deleting words, and jotting pithy marginalia every night for the foreseeable future." She adjusted the silverware in front of her. "So, how was your trip to Catalina?"

Keegan looked across the table at her. He liked the

229

openness of her expression and the bright good humor in her eyes. "Don't tell Mrs. Dodd," he said, "but I think I might have seen a ghost." Until that moment, he hadn't planned on telling the story to anyone—but for some reason, it felt like something he could offer Helen tonight, a small token gift to atone for past sins.

Helen raised her eyebrows and tilted her head closer. "Are we speaking metaphorically?"

It was, of course, a very English-teacher question, and it made Keegan smile. He shook his head. "Neither metaphor nor simile nor symbol," he said. "I thought I saw an actual, literal ghost. It threw me for the proverbial loop."

"Well, this is a story I want to hear," Helen said. She took another sip of wine and then leaned in and folded her hands atop the checkered tablecloth.

"It was Halloween night, and it was very foggy," Keegan said, and, in the interest of full disclosure, "I might have had a few whiskeys."

Helen was nodding and smiling, which Keegan took to be a good sign.

"And I saw the face of a dead woman through a window."

"How do you know it was a dead woman?"

"It was someone I used to know," he said.

Helen sat back in her chair and looked at him, suddenly more serious. "Not the young woman who…" She didn't finish the sentence, but, after their late-night talk at her house, she didn't need to. She was talking about Eve.

Keegan shook his head. "No," he said. "Nothing like that. It was the old lady who hired me a few weeks ago."

"The one who drowned?" Keegan was a little surprised she'd heard about Ida Fletcher, and she seemed to read that fact on his face. "We *do* sometimes talk about things other than you," she said teasingly.

"Yes, the woman who drowned," Keegan said. "I was out on the street, and I thought I saw her face through the window of her house."

230

"And what makes you think you didn't?" she said. "See a ghost, I mean."

"Don't tell me a woman with a masters from Stanford believes such things."

"'There are more things in heaven and earth…'" she said, but she had a playful look on her face.

"Shakespeare notwithstanding," Keegan said, "why would the old lady be haunting *me*? I only met her a couple of times."

"Oh, I don't know," Helen said. She seemed to be enjoying herself. "In novels, isn't it always some kind of unfinished earthly business? Exposing the truth? Avenging someone's death? You, sir, need to think of what she wants from you. There is some kind of unfinished business to be taken care of."

Maybe it's time to move on, the Lieutenant had told him on the phone. But maybe Keegan wasn't built that way. There *was* unfinished business in this whole ungodly mess, and right now, he was the only thing standing between Danny Church and the blood money he was about to inherit.

He was about to say as much, but the server arrived at the table with a bottle of Schlitz and an empty glass. "And how's the wine?" he said instead, while he poured the beer.

THEY STAYED AT the table until they were the last ones in the place, and then they paid, and Keegan walked her out to her car.

"Can I see you again next weekend?" he asked her.

She unlocked the driver's side door. "That could easily be arranged," she said. She pulled the door open and sat down in the seat.

"What would you like to do?" Keegan asked through the open door.

"Mrs. Dodd said that I should ask to see your place," she said. "Apparently, it has quite a view." She pulled the door closed and rolled down the window. "She also said you shouldn't get any ideas if I asked to come over."

Keegan nodded and held up one hand in a Boy Scout pledge. "I promise I will get no ideas."

ON MONDAY AFTERNOON, Mrs. Dodd put the phone call through to Keegan's inner office. It was Roland Dion on the line.

"We filed the petition this morning," he told Keegan. "And I've already got informal confirmation that it will sail through. We just need to wait for all the rubber stamps. Once she's declared dead, we execute the will and see what happens in court."

"I haven't made much headway," Keegan admitted. "No will, and Lillian Cole seems to have vanished into thin air." It was just the latest in a string of failures that started with that first visit to the Chateau Marmont. No wonder Ida Fletcher was haunting him. Perhaps it was time for him to look for a new line of work.

"Well, from what I understand, there weren't many changes to the document, anyway," Dion said. "Whichever will the courts honor, it won't make much difference to anyone."

Anyone but Zinnia, Keegan thought. And the elusory Lillian Cole. And, of course, Madame Lena. "So, the nephew gets the money one way or the other," Keegan said, resignedly. "The rich just get richer."

"I suppose so," Dion said. "I was just about to give him a call."

Despite what the Lieutenant had said, he wasn't ready to let things slide yet. Not with Ida Fletcher's unfinished business. "Would it be okay if *I* told the nephew the news?" Keegan said. "I was going to run out there today anyway to give him the keys." He was making it all up on the fly. "It would mean a lot to me," he told Dion. "We've gotten to be friends."

The lie left a sour taste in his mouth.

BEFORE HE LEFT the office, he took the black-and-white photo of Danny Church and his aunt out of the Steinbeck novel. He slipped it into the inner pocket of his jacket.

CHAPTER SIXTEEN

KEEGAN DIDN'T CALL ahead. If he was going to have it out with the nephew, he didn't want the kid to see it coming. He pulled through the big open gate on Monticello Drive and was pleased to see the red Jaguar parked on the cobblestones in front of the big house.

Keegan coasted quietly up the drive. He pulled in behind Church's car and parked a few feet from its rear bumper. Before he went up to the door, he went around to the front of the red car and pressed his palm to the hood. It was cold. A couple of sycamore leaves were plastered at the base of the windshield. It had been sitting here a while.

Keegan went up the broad front steps and rang the doorbell three times without an answer. He glanced at his watch. It was after four in the afternoon, but for all he knew, the kid was still in bed. He might have closed down the yacht club's bar last night, drinking Bruno's unsurpassed whiskey sours until 1:00 a.m. Then who knew? He might have followed that up with a few strenuous hours aboard Milton Burritt's boat, aboard Milton Burritt's wife. The profligate lifestyle could be exhausting, Keegan imagined. He rang the doorbell again and beat on the burnished wood with the side of his fist. There was still no response. So much for his element of surprise.

Keegan had brought Ida Fletcher's key ring with him. That was, after all, the ostensible purpose of this trip, the reason he'd given Roland Dion. He'd planned on handing the ring over to the nephew—but not before he'd had his say. Though it didn't feel quite kosher, he still had a key to this very door. He could let himself in one last time, and it wouldn't technically be trespassing. Ida Fletcher might be on the bottom of the ocean, but, until she was officially declared dead, she was still Keegan's employer. And this was still her house. Keegan found the correct key and slipped it into the deadbolt lock.

He let himself into the broad tiled entryway and pushed the door shut behind him. He called out a half-hearted "Hello," and felt the echo of his voice bounce back at him. He went along the hall and into the billiard room. Empty glasses dotted the tables and bar top. A leatherbound book lay on the ground next to a sofa. A crystal ashtray overflowed with cigarette butts. Cocktail by cocktail, cigarette by cigarette, Danny Church was taking the place over.

Keegan looked at the high ceilings, the cavernous fireplace, the French doors, and the formal garden beyond. It was all so extravagant, riches almost beyond imagining—and in a few days, it would all belong to Danny Church. And there was little Keegan could do to stop it. There was no way that he could see to resolve poor Ida Fletcher's unfinished business. Nick Harris's catchphrase had got it all wrong: crime sometimes *did* pay. Sometimes it paid quite handsomely.

A beige wire trailed along the floor, past the billiard table and out the French doors—which, Keegan now noticed, were open just a crack. Keegan went to the glass and looked out.

Church was outside, dozing by the swimming pool. He lay shirtless on a lounge chair in the sun. The small table next to him held a newspaper, a glass of something, and the black telephone at the end of the long extension cord. The wire, Keegan now saw, snaked across the concrete, skirting the pool's edge.

Keegan pulled the door open. "I let myself in," he called out. His voice made the nephew jump, which pleased Keegan a little. "I hope that's okay. I still have the keys."

Church sat up groggily and shaded his eyes with one hand. "James!" he said, scrambling to affect a jaunty good humor. "What brings you to my doorstep on this lovely day?"

"It's your aunt's doorstep," Keegan corrected. "At least for a while longer." He pulled the door shut on the extension cord and trudged across the concrete walkway.

The nephew sat up on his chair. His hair was a little mussed, and he stretched his arms above his head. He must have been sleeping in the tepid November sunlight.

"I've got some news," Keegan said.

The nephew sat up straighter, suddenly roused. He nodded eagerly. "Good news, it is devoutly to be wished."

"I suppose that depends on your perspective," Keegan said. "*You'll* consider it good. I'm not sure what Aunt Ida would have thought."

"Well, splendid," Church said. "I suppose." He swung his bare feet down to the ground and rubbed his hands together. "Let's have it."

Keegan stopped walking. He was about ten yards from the kid but didn't want to be any closer. He looked around the bright landscape. The once well-kept garden had already gone a bit rangy from neglect. The hedges were growing shaggy and the rosebushes needed pruning. It was nothing a new gardener couldn't set straight in a few weeks' time. Keegan stood at the pool's edge and watched the water's shimmer on the nephew's face.

Church must have already guessed what Keegan was here to tell him. After all, this had been his plan all along, hadn't it? But the irredeemable wrongness of the situation was impossible to ignore. It was one thing that Keegan had failed to protect his client's interests; that had happened before; it was just part of the job. But it was another thing entirely to see this prodigal nephew scoop up all his client's worldly belongings.

"Maybe we could talk inside," Keegan said. "The sun's giving me a headache." He didn't wait for Church to answer. He walked back to the French door, pulled it open again, and paused in the gap. "And maybe you could put on a shirt."

"Very well," Church said, keeping his voice chipper. He picked a blue polo shirt off the concrete next to his lounge chair and pulled it on over his head. He picked up the phone and came in Keegan's direction, trailing the long phone line behind him. Keegan held the door open for him and waited while the long extension cord followed him inside.

Church set the phone on the green felt of the billiard table, and Keegan kicked the remaining extension cord in through the French door before he pulled it shut. When he looked up, Church was already behind the bar filling a couple of crystal tumblers with ice.

"Nothing for me," Keegan said. He hadn't had a whiskey since the night he saw Ida Fletcher's ghost. His Old Grand-Dad hangover still haunted him as well, he supposed.

"Very well," Church said again. He poured himself a generous three fingers of something, neat, and came out from behind the bar swirling it around in the glass. "And what glad tidings do you bear, James?" He sprawled on a love seat on the far side of the billiard table. He managed, with wide-flung limbs, to entirely occupy the space designed for two. "I await your dispatch with bated breath."

Keegan held up the ring of Ida Fletcher's keys and then tossed them on the billiard table between them, next to the black phone. "I came to give you these," he said. "It won't be official for a week or two, but the petition has been filed. Your aunt will soon be legally deceased. I won't be needing them. I no longer have a client."

The kid's face registered no surprise. His scheme was unfolding just as planned. The old lady's paranoia might have been frequently misplaced, but it was rooted in fact.

The nephew took a sip from his glass and swirled it some more. "What if I wanted to keep you on retainer, James?" Church said. "You know, for old time's sake. I think we make a splendid team. You've been very helpful since I got back in town."

Keegan watched Church sip his drink. The idea of being beholden to a killer filled him with a hangover-like revulsion. "So, how did you manage it, Danny?" Keegan said. "How did you kill her?"

Even Keegan was surprised he'd finally said the words out loud. The drink in Church's hand stopped swirling. The question hung between them in the startled air, like someone had struck a gong.

The shock that spread over his face looked almost genuine. It was a good act. "I'm sorry?" the kid said. Keegan had to hand it to him. He knew what he was doing.

"The old dear," Keegan said, keeping his voice even and as clear, despite the fire he felt inside him. "How, exactly, did you kill her?"

Church flailed his limbs a bit to sit up straighter in the love seat. His lips moved, but they seemed unable to produce any sound.

"Because I think you used Burritt's boat," Keegan said. "I bet he has no idea what you're doing aboard the *Recess* with his wife."

Church's face flushed, so Keegan knew he'd hit home. It felt good to see the kid pressed back against the love seat, pinned down by the ugly truth. "Yeah, I know about you and Mrs. Burritt," Keegan said. "But Milton Burritt isn't my client, so I don't give a damn whether you screw him over." Keegan came around the billiard table. There was nothing between the two men now. "I see the big picture, Danny," he said. "I just need a little help with the details."

The kid looked at the phone on the billiard table, as if he wanted to call for help. But it was right there in Keegan's easy reach. Besides, who would the kid call? Who was left to come to his rescue?

Keegan leaned back against the billiard table and folded his arms across his chest. "I figure you followed them out of the breakwater," he said. "You tailed along behind them a while, and when you were far enough offshore, you flagged them down somehow. Maybe you sent up some kind of distress signal. I don't know how these things work."

Church just stared back at him now, blinking, wordless.

"I figure you had to take care of Frank first. That guy knew how to use his fists. No offense, but a pretty boy like you wouldn't stand a chance if the fight was fair. You must have hit him from behind—with an oar or a gaff hook, maybe—and dumped him over the side. That would all fit what the coroner found." He fixed Church with his eyes. "You know I saw old Frank's body after they pulled it out of the ocean. It wasn't pretty what you did to him."

Church pressed his hands down on the love seat on either side of him, like he was trying to keep upright.

"What was it like, Danny?" Keegan went on. "What did your aunt say when she saw what you were up to? Did you hit her as well? Or did you just sink the boat out from under her, knowing she was too frail to stay above water long?"

The kid's eyes pinballed around the room, but there was no real avenue of escape.

"I don't expect you to tell me," Keegan said. "I just want you to know that one person sees through your phony schoolboy charm. One person knows you for the deadly bastard you are."

That was it. Keegan realized, suddenly, that he'd run out of words. He'd said everything he needed to say. The business still felt unfinished, but it would have to be enough. Maybe the Lieutenant was right: sometimes the mystery doesn't get solved; sometimes you just have to live with it. He shook his head and turned to leave—but then he stopped and turned back.

Keegan pulled the photo he'd found in the house on Tradewinds Lane from the inner pocket of his jacket. He looked it over: just a middle-aged woman and a gawky young boy caught forever in the snap of a shutter. It had been a sunny day, on a sandy beach. Keegan could read no deviltry in it, no portent of what was to come. He was no Madame Lena. "Here's a little keepsake," Keegan said. He flicked the photograph, spinning, onto the seat cushion next to Church. It landed face up. "Just something to remember the old dear by."

The nephew looked down at the photo, uncomprehending. He picked it up and tilted it to the light. He looked at Keegan. "I don't understand," he said. "You found her?"

It wasn't at all the response Keegan expected, and the reaction caught him flat-footed. Something felt dreadfully wrong. He stood looking at the nephew.

"Where was she?" Church asked. He looked genuinely flummoxed.

"Where was who?"

"Old Lillian," Church said. He shook the photo in the air between them. "Lillian Cole. Where did you find her?" He fixed Keegan with a look that was somehow both beseeching and accusatory. "I have no idea what's going on here, James," he said. "But I must say I'm not happy with what you're implying. I thought you and I were friends."

BACK ON SIXTH Street, Keegan rode the elevator up, still sorting things out in his head. It had been a dizzying drive back from the house on Monticello. All the facts of the case, as he reviewed them in his head—the missing family portrait, the reclusive hotel bungalow, all the sudden fallings out—fell back into place in an entirely new angle of light.

He found Mrs. Dodd waiting with the dog, ready to go for the evening. At first, she seemed annoyed with him that she'd had to wait past five o'clock. The dog, on the other hand, was happy to see him—entirely forgiving that he'd disappeared for so long. She ran in a circle around him, wagging her stubby tail, like she wanted him to chase her.

"I took her out ten minutes ago," Mrs. Dodd told him. She pulled on the cardigan she'd draped over the back of her chair and pulled her purse from the file drawer in her desk. "So, are we free and clear of Ida Fletcher and her nephew now?" she asked as she headed for the door. "Can we deposit the money and let everything get back to normal around here?"

Keegan shook his head. He was still processing the implications of what Danny Church had told him. "I'm afraid it might have just gotten messier."

Mrs. Dodd paused with her hand on the doorknob. "*Messier?*" she said. "How is that even possible?" She turned back to face him, looking concerned now. "Can it keep until tomorrow, or do you need me to stay?"

Keegan shook his head. "It'll keep," he said. "I've got a phone call to make. I'll explain it all in the morning. Maybe it'll all make sense to me by then."

"You sure?" she said, still holding the knob. "Wendell can open a can of tomato soup for once. He won't starve if you need me to work late."

"Go on home," he said. "I just need to figure a few things out."

When she was gone, Keegan went into his inner office and turned on the light. The dog trotted after him. He sat down at his desk and picked up the phone. The dog nudged past his feet and curled up in the darkness under the desk. Keegan dialed the Lieutenant's office downtown. It wasn't too long after five o'clock. There was a good chance he could still catch the man at his desk.

"What now, Jimmy?" Moore said. He sounded tired after a long day's work, but his voice brimmed with good humor. "What new circumstantial evidence have you dug up? You're like a dog with a bone."

"I need a favor," Keegan said, cutting through the small talk.

"Now, why doesn't that come as a shock to me?"

240

"It's bad, Lou," Keegan said. "I think I royally screwed up."

"Also not a shock," the Lieutenant quipped, but then his voice grew more earnest. "What is it you need, Jimmy? I was just about to go home."

"Is there a way you could get me a couple driver's license photos?"

"I suppose that can be done," Moore said. "But I'm going to need a reason."

"I'm afraid it's a long story," Keegan said. "You might want to lean back and put your feet up. Get comfortable, Lou. This is going to take a while to explain."

The Lieutenant sighed into the phone, but at least he didn't hang up.

THE TWO PHOTOS were ready the next afternoon.

Keegan swung by the LAPD offices on Third and climbed the stairs to the Lieutenant's floor. At one time, when he was a crime reporter, the cop house had been his daily beat. He'd known which detective sat at every desk, for all three shifts. He knew which clerk to hit up for off-the-record information, which floor had the best coffee on the burner.

These days he was a stranger here. The few aging detectives he still recognized from the old days were gray-haired now, their faces puffy with age. They'd become desk jockeys and clock watchers, every last one. They were Donovans in training.

At the top of the third-floor stairwell, Keegan stepped into the big open detective bureau. The white-shirted jacks in residence were all coatless, their leather shoulder holsters on display. The room was a cacophony of ringing phones and clacking typewriters and voices shouting to be heard.

The Lieutenant's office was a straight shot from the stairwell, so Moore always saw Keegan coming, threading his way among all those desks. He seemed to make a point of being busy with something when Keegan rapped on the open doorjamb, like he was putting on a show. He'd wave Keegan into a chair and make him wait. It was all part of his schtick. Today his frosted glass door was wide open. He was behind the desk, his chair angled to the window. The phone was braced between his shoulder and ear, and he was listening without talking. The Lieutenant nodded, gestured at a chair.

Keegan sat.

After a few seconds, the Lieutenant said a curt goodbye into the phone, then swiveled around and hung it up. He took a file folder from the top of his desk and opened it. He turned a pair of blurry eight-by-ten photographs and set them face up on his desk, where Keegan could see them. He tapped the one on Keegan's left. "Ida Fletcher," he said. He tapped the other. "Lillian Cole."

Keegan leaned forward and stared down at the photographs. Both were a bit unfocused—like someone had enlarged the negatives too much—but there was no mistaking it. He looked at the woman who was Ida Fletcher and knew he'd never set eyes on her in his life.

The woman he'd met at the Chateau Marmont, posing as her own employer, was in the other photograph—the elusive Lillian Cole. There was no mistaking the widow's peak, the gaunt high cheekbones, the deep-set cunning eyes. Keegan flipped both photos over to read the DMV info pasted on the back. He nodded and turned them face up again. "Yep," he said. "They got me. Hook, line, sinker, and fishing rod."

Moore leaned back in his chair. "Looks like you've actually solved a crime this time, Jimmy," he said. "Just not the one you were aiming at. Where do we go from here?"

Keegan looked down at the two women in the photographs. There were a few details left to figure out. "Hold off a little while, Lou," Keegan said. "Let me make sure I understand exactly what's going on before we tip our hand." He reached for the photos then stopped. "Okay if I take these?"

"Be my guest," the Lieutenant said. He slipped the two

photos into the manila folder and slid them across the desk to Keegan. He smiled slyly. "Just try to get it right this time."

"I'M SORRY," ROLAND Dion's ginger receptionist told him. "He's very busy."

"He'll want to see me."

"Do you have an appointment, Mr....?"

"Keegan," he told her. "Jim Keegan. No appointment, but he knows who I am, and it's urgent."

Keegan could have called Dion on the phone and told him the news—but there was a chance the lawyer might be in on the scam. He wanted to see the man's reaction.

"It's just that Mr. Dion is all booked up today," the receptionist said. "Is there a chance you could call back first thing next week?"

Keegan shook his head. Sure, she wasn't Klaus the concierge, but he was tired of being kept at bay. "No chance," he said, the irritation showing in his voice. "He's going to want to see me. You'll just have to trust me on that."

The receptionist eyed him coolly. "Have a seat, then, Mr. Keegan," she said. "I'll see if he can clear a few minutes." She picked up a phone and spoke quietly into it, head bent down, not looking at Keegan as she did so.

Keegan went over and took his usual seat next to the big plate-glass window. It was a hazy, gray day outside. The pier's Ferris wheel looked like a tarnished nickel in the distance. Catalina wasn't visible on the murky horizon. He tapped the manila envelope on his thighs as he waited.

It took a few minutes, but the inner office door cracked open, and Roland Dion peeked out, his head comically close to the ground. He shot Keegan an irritable glance. "Yes, yes," he said. "I understand you need to see me?"

Keegan stood. "I do indeed," he said. He held up the manila envelope—his Exhibit A. "This'll only take a minute," he told the lawyer, "but I think it's something you'll want to discuss in private."

Dion's face took on a worried look. He nodded and pushed open the door and then led Keegan down the busy hallway. They squeezed past an exceedingly well-dressed man and woman who were deep in conversation. Keegan caught a whiff of musky cologne as he slipped by and couldn't guess which of the two might be wearing it.

Back in Dion's office, the big oak door sealed off most of the noise. Keegan sat down in the same leather chair he'd taken last time. Roland Dion slipped behind his absurdly large desk and up onto whatever booster seat he had back there.

"What's this about?" the lawyer wanted to know. He was doing his best to sound stern, but Keegan could tell he was more anxious than angry.

Keegan leaned the manila folder against the desk's edge. "I think I found Lillian Cole," he told the lawyer.

Dion paused and nodded. He seemed to have expected something more. "Well, that's good news, certainly," he said. "But a simple phone call would have—"

Keegan shook his head, cutting him off. "I'll need you to look at a couple of photographs."

The lawyer showed a flicker of annoyance and glanced at his watch. He seemed about to make an objection but then checked his anger and folded his petite hands on the desktop. "And what are these photographs?"

Keegan pulled the first one from his folder and set it on the desk, facing Dion. "Have you ever met this woman?" he asked.

The lawyer glanced down at the photo and then looked up at Keegan. The irritation was rising into his face again. "As I believe I've told you," he said, "I never met Lillian Cole." He glanced at the photo again. "So, no." He pushed the photo back in Keegan's direction with his small fingers.

Keegan set down the other photo on top of the first. "How about this woman?"

The lawyer looked at the photo. He took his time with it. "Well, it's not a very flattering likeness, but that is our late client, Mrs. Fletcher." He looked up at Keegan. His patience was wearing thin. "What is this about, Jim?"

It was enough to convince Keegan the man wasn't in on the racket. "I'm afraid we've both been had, counselor," Keegan told him. He reached out and tapped the top photo. "Turns out *that's* the elusive Lillian Cole we've been trying to find." He slid the photos so they were side by side. He pressed a finger down on the first one. "This, in fact, is Ida Fletcher. The woman we both thought we were working for. Neither of us ever met the old dear. I'll bet Donovan never met her, either." It seemed so obvious now. How had they all missed it? "She was out of the picture long before any of us showed up on the scene."

The lawyer looked down at the two photos, frowning, like he was trying to pinpoint where the problem lay. "But Michael Donovan brought me out—"

Keegan nodded. "Yes," he said, "you and I both let our guards down because we knew Donovan, and he was the one who introduced us." He thought of the cigars and whiskey at the Ambassador Hotel. Donovan had been so pleased with himself. *She's old and paranoid and richer than Jesus.* The poor sap had thought *he* was the one taking *the old lady* for a ride. "All they had to do was fool old Donovan," Keegan said, "and the two of us would be sitting ducks."

The lawyer kept frowning down at the photos. "Fraud?" he said, his voice almost breathless. The truth seemed to be sinking in.

"I don't think Donovan was in on their game," Keegan went on, "but I wager he was handpicked because he'd be an easy first mark, and he could bring the rest of us along. Donovan wasn't going to bother to dig down and discover anything those three didn't want him to find. That kind of hard work was never his style."

"Oh my," Dion said. His boyish face had gone pale. "What

will happen when this gets out? I've got my professional reputation to protect."

Keegan couldn't help but laugh; the man was definitely a lawyer. "You and me both," he said. "I'm guessing that Ida Fletcher was dead long before you and I and old Donovan were brought into the picture," he said. He thought of Madame Lena and her neon sign in the front window. "The last date anyone saw the old lady alive was way back on Valentine's Day, when she last visited her psychic. After that, she broke off all contact with everyone she knew, including the old family lawyer. Or that's what we were all supposed to think." Keegan tried to work out the dates in his mind. "She would have already been dead before Donovan came along, so we can narrow down the date to a few weeks."

The phone on Dion's desk rang quietly, but he ignored it. He just kept staring down at the two photos.

"They fooled us all," Keegan said. "They got the will changed in their favor. They were smart about it. I'll give them that. They didn't get greedy. They just went after the fortune teller's share." He remembered the buzz that went about the room when he told them Danny Church was in town. How could he have so miscalculated what it meant? "But then the nephew showed up," he told the lawyer. "He wanted to see his aunt, and that screwed up their little plan."

"Who else do you think was involved?"

"Lillian Cole and Zinnia and poor old Frank—who no doubt got killed for his troubles," Keegan said. "But who can blame them? They'd have been left high and dry when the old lady died. A hundred thousand dollars would have meant the world to them."

CHAPTER SEVENTEEN

As a crime reporter, Keegan had been on the blind side of the interrogation room mirror more times than he could count—he'd seen countless felons broken down under those harsh fluorescent lights on the other side of the scuffed glass.

Nothing much had changed over the years, he saw now. It was still a dark, cheerless, spartan room, with nothing but a few steel folding chairs and the pervading stench of despair.

The door opened, and the Lieutenant entered the dark room holding two cardboard cups of coffee. He kicked the door to the hallway shut behind him and handed one of the cups to Keegan. He pulled a folding chair up beside Keegan's and sat down in it. "Feels like old times, Jimmy," he said, adjusting his tall, lean body to the small chair. "Ever miss your reporter days?"

"Not really," Keegan said. "I was never good with a boss."

On the other side of the two-way mirror, a woman entered the empty interrogation room holding a stack of manila folders against her chest. She was plump and silver-haired, a plausible librarian. The woman detective sat down on the side of the steel table farthest from the door and tapped the folders straight on the tabletop. She laid them down flat and then folded her hands on top of them, next to the mounted reel-to-reel tape recorder.

It was an old cop-house trick, Keegan knew. A stack of folders a couple of inches high suggested a pile of evidence amassed against you—an open-and-shut case there was no real point in denying. Anyone led in through the door in handcuffs would see them right away and assume the worst. But Keegan knew they were papers dug out of the nearest file cabinet—a two-inch stack of old shift schedules and out-of-date APBs posing as evidence. At this point, the only real goods the LAPD could possibly have against Zinnia was a couple of DMV headshots. Keegan took a sip of bad coffee and tried to get comfortable on the cold, hard chair.

The interrogation room door eventually opened, and two burly uniformed cops came in. Zinnia was so small, so downtrodden, that at first, Keegan didn't even notice her there between the two hulking men. She wore a rumpled, shapeless housedress and held a blue handkerchief in one hand.

They sat her down in a steel chair and took the handcuffs off her wrists. The cops both left the room, closing the door behind them. The detective twisted a knob on the tape recorder and the big reels started turning. She spoke into the machine in a clear and even tone.

Zinnia sat in the chair, stooped forward, wilting with grief and shame. Her eyes were red, her hair disheveled. The few weeks since Keegan had first met her had brought her nothing but havoc. She was a hollowed, withered version of the woman he'd first seen reading a Michener novel in the Chateau Marmont kitchenette.

Keegan's instinct was to look away, but the Lieutenant was right there beside him, so he checked the impulse. He sat forward and watched as the questioning got underway.

Zinnia was no match for the detective, and, after a few opening questions, the whole story began to emerge. It had all begun, according to Zinnia, with Ida Fletcher's death.

"I found her in bed," she said. "We were staying in the

Newport house, and I brought up her morning tea. I set the tray on the edge of the bed and pulled open the curtains, like I did every morning." Zinnia held the crumpled blue handkerchief with one hand and worried the collar of her blouse with the other. "When I turned back to her, I could see in the light that something was wrong. I touched her hand. It was cold. She'd passed away in her sleep. There was nothing anyone could do." Zinnia stopped talking. She squeezed the wadded handkerchief with her fist.

"And then what happened?" The detective's voice was gentle and sure, unwavering and warm. Keegan could see why the Lieutenant had put her in charge of the case. Not a whiff of threat came off her.

"I came down and told the others," Zinnia said.

The detective opened the top file. "For the record, that would be Lillian Frances Cole and Frank Luca Romano?"

Zinnia nodded.

"You'll have to say it out loud," the detective said. "For the tape."

"Yes," Zinnia said, her voice small and pliant. "Lillian Cole." She seemed to be staring down at her lap as she said the words. "And *Frank*." Her voice caught on the dead man's name, and Keegan felt a pang of pity for her.

"And what did the three of you talk about?"

"Well, we'd all just lost our jobs," Zinnia went on. "I mean, there was nothing set up for us. No provisions." She looked up at the detective pleadingly and then looked down again. "Just like that, we'd be out on the street. We just sat around that kitchen table a long time, not speaking."

A flicker of impatience crossed the detective's face, but Zinnia wasn't looking, and it was quickly swept away. She was a professional. "But eventually you came up with a plan, correct?" she asked.

Zinnia nodded. "It was Lillian's idea," she said. "But Frank thought it would work. Mrs. Fletcher had become more and more reclusive over the years. No one would have to know she had died unless we told them."

Little by little, thread by thread, the detective teased Zinnia's story loose. Frank had wrapped the old lady's body in a shower curtain. He'd taken it offshore in the sailboat and sunk it with some rope and a few cinder blocks. Lillian had then taken Ida Fletcher's place, riding behind the tinted windows of the limousine and renting a cloistered bungalow at the Chateau Marmont. They'd found Donovan and strung him along a few weeks, playing up the old lady's famous paranoia. Madame Lena was cheating her. She didn't trust that lawyer of hers. Could Donovan help her make a new will? The poor sap never had a clue. They'd planned to string him along a while, until suspicion died down, and then they'd fake the old lady's death.

"But then Danny showed up," Zinnia said. "He threw everything into chaos. We had to rush everything."

"And what was the plan you came up with?"

Zinnia shook her head disconsolately and began wringing the handkerchief again. "Lillian would go into hiding," Zinnia said. "She'd lie low. Frank would take the boat out. I'd tell everyone the two of them were sailing to Avalon. He'd fake an accident. Sink the boat, and swim to shore. He'd make a big play out of almost drowning. Call the Coast Guard. Make sure it all looked real." She started sobbing then. "Only, he never made it back to shore. Oh God, what were we all thinking?"

"And where is Lillian Cole now?"

"I don't know," Zinnia said. "She thought it safer if none of us knew."

Keegan turned to the Lieutenant, feeling every inch the fool. "I don't know where she is now," he said, feeling the heat creep up his face, "but a couple of days ago I saw her on Catalina. I think she saw me too, so she's probably long gone."

"*What*?" Moore said.

His voice was loud enough that Zinnia, startled, looked at the two-way mirror.

The Lieutenant cursed under his breath. "That seems like something you should have mentioned before now, Jimmy," he said, keeping his voice lower.

Keegan sighed. "I know," Keegan said. "It's a long story, Lou. And I don't come out of it looking very bright. But she was there in the Avalon house."

The Lieutenant was staring at Keegan now, but on the other side of the glass, Zinnia started speaking again, so they both turned their attention back to her.

"I didn't want to go along," she was saying. "But Frank thought the money would let us go away somewhere. Get a place of our own. That's all we ever really wanted."

"SHE SHOULD BE okay," the Lieutenant told Keegan when the cops came back in the room to cuff Zinnia again. He seemed to have picked up on Keegan's sympathy for the woman and wanted to reassure him. "No one was murdered here," he said. "Fraud is all we're talking about—and Lillian Cole seems to be the brains behind the whole thing. This one here can turn state's evidence."

He was right, of course, Zinnia wouldn't likely go to prison, but that wasn't the worst fate she could have faced. She'd always have to live with the fact that she'd gone along with a foolhardy scheme that ended up killing the man she loved. No one in this whole unholy mess was getting away scot-free.

Except, of course, Danny Church.

CHAPTER EIGHTEEN

KEEGAN BOUGHT THE best bottle of sauterne he could find—it cost six dollars at the Farmers' Market wine shop—and had it chilling in the Frigidaire. She arrived, right on time, with Italian takeout—a piping-hot lasagna for two, and tiramisu for dessert.

She paused a moment, when she first came in through the door, to take in the cottage's small living room. She turned a slow circle, holding the takeout bag in front of her. The place was still crowded with his late mother's old furniture and décor. It might have been an Edwardian sitting room. Helen took in the wooden rack of souvenir spoons, the shelves of Delft figurines on their lace doilies, the bookcase of Zane Gray westerns.

Her lips quirked into that crooked smile he was starting to enjoy so much. "You've really made the place your own," she said.

They ate at the kitchen table and Keegan trotted out all the details of the Ida Fletcher case—highlighting his own foolish mistakes, rather than trying to explain them away. It felt good to talk this way with her. He sometimes took himself too seriously.

For her part, Helen listened and laughed and peppered him

with questions. At a few points in the story, she reached across and pressed her hand down on his arm.

After dinner and dessert, she poured them both another glass of wine, and they took them out to the back garden to look at all the lights. Nora couldn't stop showing off, laying sticks at Helen's feet and barking up at her.

They stood a while in silence, looking down at the innumerable pinprick lights of the city spread out below. Someday he'd tell her the story about the dark Ormsby estate directly below them on the hillside. It would be good to get Eve's story off his chest, but that would happen in good time. Keegan watched Helen take in the city lights. He liked the way they softly lit her face. He felt good tonight. Being in her company was somehow effortless.

"What I don't understand," she said, "is why the lawyer's boat was in Avalon Harbor." She was still thinking about Lillian Cole, Zinnia, and Frank the Boxer. "Did you ever figure that out?"

Keegan nodded. The Lieutenant dug up the answer the day after Zinnia's confession. "Turns out Milton Burritt had a weekend of riding with some of his cronies," he told her. "The four of them met on the island." He took a sip of the wine. It was both sweet and tart on his tongue. "His alibi is ironclad. They racked up a five-hundred-dollar tab at a restaurant that has a world-class wine list. It was a real boys' weekend."

She nodded, looked down at the lights again, and then looked back at him. "And what about the nephew? Where was he when it all happened?"

Keegan tried to think of the most tasteful way to put his assumption into words. "He was probably with Burritt's wife somewhere, enjoying his own boys' weekend while the husband was away."

That seemed to make sense to her. She sipped her wine and looked him over. "I don't think you come off looking quite so badly as you think in this story," she said. "Everything you did was perfectly understandable. You weren't as foolish as you seem to think."

"Me?" he said. "The guy who thought he'd seen a ghost? How stupid can a guy get?"

She smiled coyly and looked down into her wine. "I wouldn't be so quick to dismiss it all, you know," she told him. "Your story still has a dash of the otherworldly in it." Keegan liked her playful tone.

"Don't you start talking about ghosts and broken mirrors," he told her. "I get quite enough of that from some other people I know."

Helen swirled the wine in her glass. "Well, think of this," she said. "Stop and consider everything the fortune teller said to you when you met her."

He thought back to that night on Nella Vista Drive. "That I'd go on a trip over the sea," he said. "That Ida Fletcher was dead and on the bottom of the ocean." The truth of what Helen was saying began to settle on him.

Helen nodded, smiling, watching his reaction. "And that *she*—the *psychic*—would end up in the will, when all was said and done."

Keegan thought of Madame Lena's incensed parlor, where she'd stared down at her tarot cards and seemed to divine in them, even his history with Eve. Now, on this hilltop with Helen, he felt the same chill come over him that he had felt that night.

"I'd say that's some impressive evidence," Helen told him. "Maybe next time you should listen to Mrs. Dodd."

ACKNOWLEDGMENTS

A heartfelt thanks to all those who read and responded to drafts of this story along the way: Margo Duncan and Kaysi Butler, Paige Dinneny, Santa-Victoria Perez, Heather Buchanan, Ryan Buchanan, Melody Versoza, and all the Legend Pressers, especially Lauren, Lucy, and Melanie.